AN EX-SLAVE CATCHER'S NARRATIVE

L.ALLEN FARMER

EMMI

Edgewater, NJ

Copy Editor – Claudia Mason
Cover Art – Jay Durrah

Publisher's Note: This is a work of fiction. Names, characters, places, and incidents are a product of the author's imagination. Locales and public names are sometimes used for atmospheric purposes. Any resemblance to actual people, living or dead, or to businesses, companies, events, institutions, or locales is completely coincidental.

Ordering Information:
Quantity sales. Special discounts are available on quantity purchases by corporations, associations, and others. For details, contact the "Special Sales Department" at the address above.

An Ex-Slave Catcher's Narrative/ L. Allen Farmer. – 2nd ed.

Dedicated to Mamie Elizabeth Melvin Farmer,
and Pearl Fennell Melvin and Kathleen 'Kathi O'Neill

One's philosophy is not best expressed in words; it is expressed in the choices one makes.

–Eleanor Roosevelt

L. ALLEN FARMER

ACKNOWLEDGEMENTS

I would like to **thank**: Mamie Elizabeth Melvin F, Pearl Fenell Melvin , Esther Fenell, Betty Campbell, Mr. Balaam F, Aurther Joe F Sr, Tilda F, Maggie (Ma Maggie) Graham, Lacy James F Sr., my big sister Pam L F, Mr. Andre L. Nash, Christine Halac, Sir Johnny-Ray Harris, Mr. Carlton Lockard, Sir Bernard' Tricky' Shawcross Nunes, Zana Martina T Thompson 'the real' QOS aka d Heisman, Ericka C. Mosheshe, Robin Jackson' Homey', Kim (Mariposa) Fogg, Sir Robert James 'Shuz23' Reynolds, Lady Karen Reynolds, Mr. Amos Mathews-esq, Mrs. Kendell Mathews, Juliette Assiento, Mr. Michael Little and NOA, Allison C. Mitchell-esq, the new Kara (Kara I. Prawl) ,Lisa Woods, Terry Sigler, Anita Prince, Dr. Shelly Jallow-EDD, Mr. Bruce Carroll, Mr. Sheldon White, Carmelita 'Lee-Lee' Thomas, Elizabeth Olmo, Kim ' Misissauga Ontario' Williams, Mr. Aaron' Dubb' Walker, Mr. Cole Front, Dr. Juan White, Mr. Therrion White, Mr. Paul Roberts, Kha White, Mrs. Irma Hawkins, Ina Hawkins, Tina Jackson, Irene Sala, Icaro Sala, Kathi Arigiropoulos-esq ,Grace Maria Arrindell, Mr. Kevin Howard, Michelle Robinson Scarborough, Kathi O'Neill-esq, Kym'QK9' Jackson, Dr. Allison P Riddle-DDS, Mr. Newton Ray (-Ray) Wilson, Joy Boddie, Lisa Weaver, Tammi Robinson- Minor CBT-Club Ibbiza/ Club H20/Club VIP's DC, Hillary Scarborough, Cousin Janice 'Ice' Davis, Cousin Nit Davis, Mr. Aaron Coleman, Mr. Michael Mullins, Mr. Tony Coleman, Maureen McNamara ,Senor Victor Mesias-Crispin, Colette Cipollini, Susan Cipollini, the entire Cipollini family, the Honorable Tani Cantil-esq, Carly Williams (from d Art Barn), Mr. James' Junior' Heard Jr., Dr. Mark Mack, Ruthanne Harriet Bray, Debbie McNally, Larry McNally, Yoga in Daily Life-Alexandria 'Del Ray' VA, John 'Jay' Hankins Jr., Marion Armin Hankins, Tommy Ting 'Ba' and Johnny and Helen and Suzie and Charles and Sharon and Peter and Eddie and Dickie of the Lim Yee Clan next door, Mr. Daddy Moore, Mr. Randy Lathe, Kornelia 'big Nellie' Langa, Kornelia 'little Nellie' Wilson, Quinn Wilson, Maggie and Conrad and Mat and Kat and Chris and (of course) Mark Thomas, Crystal Price, Stacey Simmons-esq, Sandi (Grey) Hines, Lisha A. Wheeler Goines-esq, Linda Riley, Cynthia Lester, Debbie Johnson, Angela 'Cookie' Turner, Sara Bronson, Kay Talley, Sandra Gibson, Sherri 'Queen Light-skin' Davis, Tina Baugh, Leontyne Price, Dawn Burgess, Martina Evans, Norma Dunn, the gracious Josephine Britto, Michelle Kelly Noberto, Cherise McKay, Kathryn Jackson, Jennifer Cox, Sherri Graves, Angela Ware, Linda Bolton, Sylvia and Pam, and Audrey

Clark, Linda Fung, Deoras Slaughter Cooke, Carmen Warren, Karen M. Gibbs-esq, Dianne Ross, Debbie Grey, Claudia Mason, Althea Lewis, Mr. Domingo Carriara, Mary Martin, (D one and the only-) Cindy Patke, Stevelyn Christopher, Monique Clark Brandon, Faye Clark, Mr. 'Uncle' Maurice Harris, Mr. 'Uncle' Richard 'Rick' Harris, the man Mr. Michael' a hop, skip and a jump' Marlow, Mr. Mark ' the real MJ' Joyner -esq, Cecelia 1 of 5, Lydia 2 of 5 ,Trevia 3 of 5, Rhonda 4 of 5, Paula 5 of 5,Marrisa Dimick-'the Procurer' , Teresa 'TP' Peyton, the old Kara (Kara Tamille Ingraham), Jeannie Chilton, Deirdre Williams, Pam Dodd, Dodd, Dineen Tallering, Lita Rosario-esq, Dr. Sharon 'Shane' Dodd -MD, Mr. Charles 'Chuckie' Dodd, Dr. Cassandra Tribble-MD, Dr. Abner, Lori George (of the Teaneck Five), Traci Jackson, Julie 'Jules' Chapman (of Wet Willie's), the beautiful Robin' little flower' Nash, Dr. Purple Terry Smith-MD, Taylor Monique Harris, Susan Harris, Tammi Robinson-Minor-CBT Ibizza,Mr. Derrick 'D-Fenn' Fenner, Princess Kit Kat (KF), Stephanie Berry, Debbie McNally, Larry McNally, Mr. Terry Jones, Mr. Larry Dine, Mr. Art Van Dusen, Mr. Sherman Wafer, Andrea 'Nicey' Wafer, Mr. Warren 'Bubba' Crommartie, Mr. Victor Love 'Greg's Barbershop', Mr. Thomas' Tommy's Barber shop ' Arnel, Sir Doug Christie, Mr. Mark Jones and family, Mr. and Mrs. Jones (of Ontario), Mr. Paul Jones and family, the mighty Darlene Carol Byrd, Dr. Connie Marie Bruce-DDS, Shelia Patrice Coates, Mr. Reggie Rocket Williams, Mr. Maurice 'Wally Poo-Bah' Smith, Marta Terfe, Coco Mademoiselle, Lady Emily Wessel, Shawn Woodson, Sherry Andrade , Regina Andrade, Jean Brown, Giselle' Jazzy' Andrews, Kanyce Andrews, Brenda Lopez, Ivonne Pinkett, Langston and Lancelle Pinkett , Mrs. Wadine Williams (Bruce's mom), Valerie Martin, Vicki Lynn Martin, Gina Carmichael, the musical prodigy Kim Jordan, Betty Franklin, Maria de Queenbee, Vanessa Powell-esq and Xaiver Powell, Alana Lowe, Jamillia Lin, and Safiya Lin, Mr. Richard Roundtree, Mr. Samuel Jackson, Angie Smith, Temika Proctor, Terry Christiano, Delphine Ransom Leslie Gilpatrick, Lauri Reishus, Donna James, Mr. and Mrs. Dodd (of Detroit), Mr. Offley' Buddy' King, Melvine King, Carolyn King, Azucena Halac, the Selecao, FC Barcelona, DC United, US National Team, Mr. George 'Tiger' Sears, the A-List Party Crew, Grits and Gravy Posse, Mrs. Thelma McDonald, Mr. Marvin McDonald, Adrian Pena ,Mr. Anthony Pena and family, Tanya Byrd, Mr. Ralph and Mrs. Joycelyn Scott, Brittany Smith, Sir James 'J.E' Edwards, Sir Jerome 'J.K' Kersey, Sir Detlef and Lady Mary Schrempf, Sir Bobby Bonilla, Lady Millie Bonilla, Sir Dorn Taylor, Sir Barry Bonds, Mr. Andy Van Slyke, Lauri Van Slyke, Sir Eric' the Red'

Davis, Sir Vincent 'Vince ' Coleman, Mr. John Cangeloi, Mr. Ray Miller, Mr. Jim Leyland, Mr. Thomas' Tommy' Lasorda, Sir Thomas 'Flash' Gordon, Iman Little, Effegia Mendes and family, Fatuma Abbdullah and family, Mariam Addula and family, Dominique 'Cousin Twin Nikki' Rougeau, Kim 'Olivia' Nikkins-Randle, Natalie Nikkins Gunn, Kim Hicks, Kim Drumgoole, Mr. Daniel ' Danny' Randle, Jordan Randle, Jonathan Randle, Mr. and Mrs. Joseph and Lousie Nikkins Sr., Joseph 'Joey' Nikkins Jr., Mr. Alvin Thompson, Rhea and Rachel and Reese and Zachariah Thompson ,Jade and Chad   Lockard, Val 'de Padwin' May and her family, Captain. Shawn Cooper –USMC, Darth Delaine,   My Michigan wife (Mary Barth),Denise 'Nicy' Brantley, Mr. Troy Johnson, Mr. Tony ' TV' Vaughn, Mr. Tony U. Rice, Mr. Chris Cathcart, Mr. Dorian 'Jay' Durrah, Mr. Manotti Jenkins, Mr. Howard Hamilton Jr., Mr. Paul Woods and family, Mr. Kendall Smith and family, Mr. Randy (Randy-Ran) David and family, Dr. Gary 'G' Warner-DDS, Mr. Niven French and family, Mr. Mike Coca Cola (Joseph), Mr. Brett Tate , Mr. Keith Tate, Mr. MikeBell and Mrs. Shawn Bell, Mr. Deangelo and Mrs. Angel Starnes, LaMona Monterio, Mr. Christan Harriott, Angel Harriott, Mr. Miguel DeCruz, Carla Susberry Miller, Mr. Johnny Miller, Imelda Kramer, Cindy Kramer, Melanie Wilcox, Paulette Murphy, Mildred Pennington, Mr. Artie Dukes, Mr. Dave King, Mr. Chris Pickle, Mr. Phil Dowdell -esq, Dr. Dede Catril-DDS, Mr. Catril, Mr. and Mrs. A Lewis-esq. (Of Grand Rapids), Mr. Devin and Mrs. Jyoti Bhatt, Reshma Patel, Mr. Darius 'Lolly' Daniels-USMC, Mr. Tommy Hazel, Mr. Dewayne 'DW' Williams, Big John 'BJ' from Philly Wright, Mr. Al 'Kenny Rodgers the Gambler' Gordon, Habitat for Humanity –Fredrick MD Chapter, Dr. Terry Lamb-MD, Dr. Wade A. Boykin, Dr. Alfonso L. Campbell, Dr. Jules P. Harrell, Dr. Leslie H. Hicks, Mr. Tim and Mrs. Teresa Whatley, Berri-CBT, Maria Mendes CBT from Mister Day's, Erin Dodd CBT from Mister Day's, Dianne Manian CBT from Mister Days's, Mr. Wesley Steven 'Snidely Whiplash' Melvin,   Mr. Steve Brown, Mr. Drungo Hazewood, Mr. Lester Vegara, Mr. James Vegara, Mr. Marion Jerome Woods, Virginia Woods, Lynnis Woods, Leslie Woods, 1234 Silver Ridge Way,   Betty Jackson, the (first) Joanne'the Bakery in CC Underground' Kim, Mikyum Joanne' Joey' Kim, Christine Nguyen Belmamoun (Snow White), Thu-Hong Nguyen, Aunti Christine Davis, Aunti Hazel Irby, Uncle Aaron' Rat' Melvin, Aunti Cat, Jeanette' Netty' Melvin, Jackie Melvin, Uncle Smokey Fenell, Uncle Calvin Melvin, Aunti Nancy Melvin, Uncle Thurmond Melvin, Aunti Janice Melvin, Uncle Lavonne Melvin, Aunti Juanita Melvin, Uncle Carlton Melvin, Aunti Marva Melvin, Mr. Mark John,

Mr. Donald Temple, Mr. Kevin 'Goldie' Williams, Hazel Taylor, Maria Ramos, Mr. Bobby Rosario, Mr. Hemengildo ' Pucho' Cortez, Mr. Dewey Stanyard, Mr. Paul Vessels, Janay Bridgette Mullin,' Nikki' Nicole Front, Erica Cepeda-Sanchez, Mr. Michael Cepeda- Sanchez, Mr. Jaque Simms, Mr. Sam Crowell, Mr. Jitesh Batra and family, the extremely lovely Joyce Davis, Carmela Pinkney, Mr. Rudy Spears, Michelle Mitchell, Mr. Harold 'Hoppy' Hofman Jr., Mr. and Mrs. Harold Hofman Sr., Mr. and Mrs. Allen Mitchell, Lisa Anderson-esq, the Honorable Carmella Harris-esq, Mr. Kevin Browning, Margret ' Maggie' Fischer, Monica Vaile, Mr. Steve Souverain, Amie Hessling, Simone Bomkessel, Jennifer Watkins, Mr. Luqman Sh-Hersi, Sharri Simmons, Staci Mathis, Mr. Tamas Jakob, Tisha Lindsey, Mr. William 'Bill' Susinski, Mr. Mark Pond, Ann Caton, Mr. Rich Licato, Mr. Chuck Thackson, Mr. Dwight Crawford, Mr. Tyrone Gaither, Mr. Clarence Seegars, Mr. Keith Venzke, Mr. Karl Ebert, Marsha Ann Shaw, Kerri Mills, Kristin Nickerson, Lorraine Johnson, Edith Buffalo(-Adobe Design), Mr. Chuck Hawley, Liska Brodrick, Kim Riddle, Mr. Jordan Talmor, Mr. and Mrs. Carl Wilson-esq, Mr. Abshir Abdi, Mr. Juan Evans, Madja Guzina Tesfaye, Sibila Omerovic, Georgiana ' George' Benson, Allison Moses-esq, Mr. 'Black' Ed Davis, Mr. Brian Conley, Mr. Darryl Wiggins, Carla Sapp, Mr. Ernel Grant, Mr. Howard Moses, Mr. Alvin Thompson SR., Mrs. Gloria Thompson, Ivanna Westfall, Jamie Pitsonberger, Dr. Kathy 'Kat' Radford-MD, Jerri Johnson, Mr. Terrence Langford, Wanda Greene, Wanda Jackson, Mr. Terry Hite, Yoland Spud, Sonya Greer, Sherri Edwards, Mr. Jon Laskin, Mr. John Kyle, Mr. Ted Saxurued, Tanyette Babbles, Solange da Cruz, Mr. Keith Williams, Mr. Mark Davis, Mr. Chaudlier Moore, Mr. Theo Wilson, , Courtaney 'Court' –CBT Hunan One, Mr. Alphonso and Mrs. Gloria McNeil Sr., Mr. Gabriel McNeil, Mr. Alphonso 'Pete' McNeil Jr. , Mr. Fletcher McNeil, Mr. Joe McNeil, Marcia and Charles, Taloria Baxter and family, RAP-Rodney A. Palmer and family, Susan 'Suzie off the block' Burnett-esq, Michelle Tyree, Stephanie Wilson, Angela Stewart, Sevil Altinsoy, Mr. Tony Lance McCaroll, Mr. Bruce Franklin, Mr. Jeff Treadway, Raquel Acevedo, Mr. Ed Schoeborn , Rachel Newman, Mr. Eddie Reese, Mr. Philippe LeMarie, Master Spooner, Mr. Steven Coleman, Mr. Mike 'Max'Maxwell, Mr. Darius' D' Holmes, Lisa Wilson ,Mr. Keith Washington, Rochelle Pinkett, Mr. Mike Libby, Mr. 'Mystro' Mike Herrity, Mr. 'Diamond' Jim Watson, Mr. Bruce Berndt , Mr. Tom Casalino, Mr. Asteway Merid, Mr. Tim Henley, Mr. Chuck Fischer, Mr. Thomas' the Six million dollar man' Jerosch, Mr. Jim Fallon, Mr. Phil Myers, Mr. Peter Murao, Maya Murao, Mr.

L. ALLEN FARMER

Michael Tarajos, Judy Huffman, Zdenka Bojanic, Mr. Jay Hoffman, Ivka Bojanic, Lisa 'Indallie' Snead, Darlene CBT of Sax, Mr. Franco Torres of Sax, Mr. Jason McRae, Mr. Ray(-Ray) Lee, Mr. Garrett Moore, Mr. Patrick Moore, Mr. Ricky Moore, Sharon Moore, Mr. Carroll 'KC' Chandler, Mr. Trevor 'Chip' Pitts, the Lodge, Mr. Arthell 'Chuckie' Jones Jr., Mr. Kevin Craig, Mr. Rodney 'Moon' Bell, Mr. Peter Cooke Jr., Mr. and Mrs. Rudi Acree, Mr. Bernard Darryl' D' Fountain, Mr. Jefferson' Jeff ' Friday, Mr. Darryl Hudson, Mr. Willie Roberts, Cindy Lane, Mr. John Dixon, Mr. Edward 'Ed' Henry Lane, Mrs. Mary Lane, Elizabeth Lane, Dolly Lane Jackson, Jalyn Hinton, Lisa Owens, Mr. Carl Henry, Mr. Adil Rasti, Mr. O. T. Wells-esq, Simon Baptise, Shevon Baptiste , Michelle Steadman –Ganga, Mr. George Kuhlkin, Ada M. Babino, Karen Babino, Savannah 'Savvy' Babino, Terri Gentry, Shannon Cunningham, Joymore Matsikure, Vernita N'dofer, Mr. David Collins, Mr. David Landuyt, Mrs. Landuyt, Mr. 'P'(Mike Premo), Mr. Alfred Alschultz, Joanne Kotsarelis, Archalenna Knight and family, Sally Dodson, Danielle Ricks, Mr. Marcus Price, Becky Cheung, Dianne and Nancy and Judy Hollins, Mr. and Mrs. Hollins, Angie Cheung, Lisa' Lerkey' Ennis, the Ennis family, Sue Mac (McNamara), Mrs. Mac (McNamara), Peggy Mac (McNamara), the McNamara Family, Jennifer Washington, Mr. Al Green, Mr. Clark Hanner, Uncle Trevor and Aunti Jay Selman of Crown Bakery, Mr. Victor Selman, Yuki the dog, Seven the dog, Tinky d cat, Misty the dog, Dupree the dog, King the dog, Maxwell d cat, Lori Labat, Carla Labat, Inger Susan Segre, Dori Ray, Yvette'Niney' Kinsey, Lisa Dukes, Lori 'Bake Bake' Baker, Sonjay Shields , Mr. Allen Cooley, Mr. Herbert' Herbbie' Leiva CBT, Mr. James Lawrence, Mr. Duane Sutton, Mr. Matt Morrell, Mr. Michael Rice, Mr. Mogus Kebede, Mr. Leonard Kwok, Latrece Savage-Zimmerman, Sandy Bell, Mr. Montgomery Nkosi, Mr. Carlo Fontallio, Maria ' Marvi' Domigpe, Mr. Angelo Domigpe, Cecile Dinh, Shelly Younger, Michelle Montes, Sylvia Ogunseye, Tanya Nass, Mr. Doug Nass, Mr. Mike Gilliland, Hattie Bullock, Gail Faire, Mr. Darwin Curry, Mr. Steven 'Chris' Young, the always fabulous Gina Claytor, the Claytor's, Jamaica Roxanne, the Libby's, the Augustine's, the Smith's, the Fabians, Marilyn Betts, Ed Greene, Mr. Derrick Cobbs, Mr. James Thomas, Mr. Big Jim Thomas, little Miter JW Thomas, Dawn Thomas, Mr. Jimmy Hicks, Mr. Victor Gatin, Mr. Big Don Brooks from Texas, Mr. Robert Fong, Mr. Jimmie Fong, Mr. Jeffrey Wong, Mr. Patrick Watson, Mr. Jerry Chappelle, Mr. Ronnie Walters, Mr. Johnny Ware, Mr. Kevin' KK' Ketchum, Green Lake, Mr. James 'Hiram' Johnson, Mr. Myron Harvey, Mr. Michael 'Lamb-chop'

6

Lambert, Mr. Sammy Keith, Mr. Juan Fant, Mr. Reggie Turner, Mr. Bill Cartwright, Mr. Art Richardson, Mr. Chris Richardson, Mr. Mike' 30 from 30' Mead, Mr. Ernest' the Truth' Lee, Mr. Damon' Crazyhops' Collins, Mr. James ' Big Dip' Donaldson, Mr. Keith 'Silk' Johnson and Mr. Carl Johnson, Mr. Carl Irving, Mr. Terrence Jones, Mr. Don Rodgers, Mr. Rodney Rodgers, Mr. Rovan' All World Hops' Turner, Mr. Sweet Lou Williams, Mr. Bart Bowers, Mr. Jerry Warren, Mr. Johnny 'Red' Walker, Mr. Joe Harvey, Mr. Jed Harvey, Mr. Edison Hicks, Mr. Leonard' Len' Bias, Mr. Bernard Perry, Mr. Chauncy ' Tree' Terry, Mr. Norman Nixon, Jackie and Toni and Kim Pate, Sammy Lunchmeat, Mr. Victor Gatin, Brother Rev Sherwood Charton, Leah Roe, Betty Gatin, Vickky Jefferson, Mr. Jose Labrada, Mr.' Booh' Berry Carter, Mr. Fast Black, Mr. David Carney, Mr. Victor Andrade, Mr. Henry Andrade, Denise Cherry, Mr. Joe Davis, Mr. Johnny ' Jiz' Reece of Roxbury, Odette Rodgers, Mr. Redskin Ryan Barnes, Kim Barnes, Linda Lynch, Joanne Christine 'Joey' Nash, Lil Eric Dates, Mr. and Mrs. Nash, Nicole Melvin, Celeste Murry, Robin Melvin, and Michael Melvin, Patricia, Terry and Keith Melvin, Scooter Brown and Toni, all of my cousins and fake me out cousins, all of my associates , my uncles and aunts, the Armed Forces School and Bret Harte Elementary, and California JHS and Sacramento SHS and Sac City College and Howard University Educational families, Metropolitan AME National Cathedral, Bishops Pruitt and DeVeaux, Abyssinian Baptist Church(ABC), Alfred Street Baptist Church(ASBC), Kingdom Hall South Congregation, Rev Dr. Calvin Butts of Harlem's ABC, Rev. David Durham, Rev Dr. Howard-John Wesley of ASBC, the Sacramento Children's Home, Liberty House, the Airlines Reporting Corporation (ARC), Carl's Jr. Restaurant chain, The Department of Commerce-PTO, The Library of Congress(LOC)Copyrights Division at the James Madison Building, Residential Renovators LLC, lake Merritt, lake Tahoe, lake Coeur d'Alene, lake union, Lake Washington lake Superior, lake Erie, lake Michigan, lake Ontario, Folsom lake, the American river, the Sacramento river, Puget Sound, Mr. Pulria Marshall, Donna Deluze and Mr. Andre Martin, Lil Harold McCoo, Lisa Beal, Dr. Pam Brady-DDS, Pamela ' Mother' Johnson, Debbie Beckles Screen, Mr. Philip Screen, Ingrid Beckles, the Johnson's, Nancy Finley, Mr. Paul Barbour, Sandy ' Scandi' Diggs, Lori Penn, Rev Dr. (J) Joan Johnson, Judy Howard, Sara McGrail, Mr. John McGill, Rhonda Meeks, Mr. Darrell Scott , Mr. Davy Fabi, Mity Green, the good Rev. Lisa Dunson-MDIV, Jeannine Hankinson, DJ Hashan 'Harvey' Nunes, Cousin Richard Nunes, DJ Blacklight-Fred, Mr. Eric Schlam-esq, Mr. Matthew

Seiler-esq, Eileen Quigley-esq, Dottie Hogan, Shirley Cumberland, Mr. Arch Moser, Martha Solomon, Hailey Solomon, Mr. Shitalkumar Sabne, Mr. Nigel Bailey, Page Nelson Jalette, Mr. Perry Heath, Mr. Wade Highley, Jackie Ayllon, Mr. John Traversaro, Mr. Tom Deevy, Mr. Michael 'Jamal' White, Mr. Marshall Trotter, Mr. Ramon Lara, Mr. Thomas' Bootsy' Jordan, Dauntria Reynolds, Darnice Samuels, Thomasine Williams, Corliss Slade, Crystal Russell, Jaela Grayson, Tiana Moore, Heather Judson, Jane Davenport, Dianna Maino, Deanna Anzevino, Minervia Flores, Lillian Rodriguez, Bonnie Sovalgabarro, Cheryl Proctor, Dahab Beyene, Mr. Omar Zelaya, Mr. Tekachew Tekle, Marjorie Wingate, Jennifer Ayenson, Sylvia Caldwell, Deepa Patel, Mr. Salah Mohammed, Suad Mohamed, Sherron Bello, Sara McKonnen, Amy Roane, Katrice Cross, Lisa Young, Cathy Meyer, Debbie Myhre, Mr. David Widjaja, Debbie Erickson, Mr. Darwin Regeher, Mr. Omar El-khodari, Mr. Vincent Ippolito, Kristin Nickerson, Angela Bigsby, Srilaxmi Velichala, Haritha Bhoomireddy, Yashika Jain, Delgretta Dobbs, Dana 'Dae' DeVeaux Harris and family, Lisa Crooms-esq, de Mayor Sir Kevin 'KJ' Johnson, Betty Williams, Mr. Ricky McDaniels, Jean McDaniels, Mr. Larry Ellis, Mr. Minor Bird Ellis, Juanita McKinnley, Sister Thomas, Sandra Arnold, Debbie Moore, Tish Campbell, Marilyn Lee, Paulette Colbert, Joyce Fanner, Suzette Charles, Dorthea Jackson, Michelle Blankenship, Monica Bean, Arta' Frosty' Flemons, Rhonda Dalson, Belen Banzon, Ellen Hamatani, Donna Randolph, Janice O'Neil, Shirley Tom, Rene Lanchaster, Sandra Ingrum, Paula Tranter, Shirley Ollero, Denelle Ellison, Mr. Anthony and Mrs. Lisa JemMion, Mr.'s Matso and Tatso Harris,Tanika Seaborn, Anna Marie Bishop, Mr. Chris Lohan, Debra Byrd, T. Suber, Dr. Mervat Hatem, Dr. Alvin Thornton, Dr. Ron Waters, Dr. Lacy Spate, Dr. Lillian Kelly, Dr. Jonni Greene, Dean Howard, President James E. Cheeks,Dr. Francis Cress Whelsing, Dr. Mary Francis Berry, Dr. Dorthy I Height, Mr. Nate Jones, Dr. Ron Blanchette DDS, Dr. Spencer DDS, Denise Hampton, DeeDee Dobins, Lil Reggie, Mr. Delvin Williams (of Jackson MI), Mrs. Carrie across the street and her family, Grandma Bessie, Jeanette Binion, Jennifer Thompson Hawkins, Mr. Todd Davis and family, Mr. Alan Muten, Mr. Chris Muten, Mr. Stacey McNeil, Helen McNeil, Mr. Aurther Joe F Sr. and Aurther Joe F Jr., Beatrice 'B' F, Tonya Talento and her wonderfully family, Tim and Teresa Whatley, Shirley Tom, Susan Noguchi, Principal Adolphus McGee, Coach Dave Hotel, Mr. Renfro, Mr. Craig Taylor-esq, Peggy Cooper Cafritz-esq, Mr. Ron Williams-esq ,Eileen Torres-La Reina de la Salsa, Krystal Johnson, Mr. Kevin Daniels, Mrs. Hatcher, Mr. and Mrs.

Jackson (of Madison), Mr. and Mrs. Jackson (of Toledo) Mr. Kyle Whitaker, Sondra Sinclair, Amber Speights, Dolly Turner, Indria Kuntawala, Sheliah Ball, Joan Hearns, Mr. Calvin Wilson, Cecile Wilson, Mr. Wilson Goode, Roxanne Bundy, Teresa Farrell Tankersly, Selina Allen and family, Tracey Williams, Suzanne Kraus, Mr. Adam Clayton Powell the IV, Mr. Martin Luther king the III, Rev Bernice ' Bunny' King, Mr. Wes Powell, Mr. Percy Sutton and the Apollo Theatre, Mr. and Mrs. Ross, Mr. John Ross, Pam Ross, Karyn Hines-esq, Mr. Matt Talbourt, Mr. Kurt Katsumoto, Rae Katsumoto, Mr. Bebollas, Phylicia Ayers Rashad, Debbie Ayers Allen, Mr. John F. (Jon-Jon) Kennedy Jr., En Vogue, Mr. Rafael Siddiq, Mr. Chuck Brown, Julia Hardy, Lynn Cosby, Mr. William (Bill) Cosby, Mrs. Camille Cosby, Mr. President William (Bill) Clinton, the Honorable Mr. William (Bill) Green, the Honorable Mr. Ellijuh Harris, the Honorable Willie Brown, the Honorable Ronald (Ron) Dellums, the Honorable Edmund Gerald (Jerry) Brown, Aleah Hammond-esq, Mr. Brent Bernard, Joan Grey, Mr.Barry Lemley, Mr. Brian Lemley, Lisa Johnson, the whole Jennison Family, Al, Amine and Yasser) and the Benadadda family, the Farmer; Melvin; McNeil; Davis; Irby; Fenell; Lim-Yee; Thomas; Harris; White; McNally; Nunes; Reynolds; Williams; Pate; Thomas (of Sacramento); Hankins; Thompson; Fong; Pitts; Mullins; Lathe; Ross; Hatcher; Butler; Moore; Moore; Libby; and Brown families, Trouble Funk, DTH-Dance Theater of Harlem, Zora Neal Hurston, Dorothy West, Mr. Colin Channer, Mr. Walter Mosley, Dr.Cornell West, Dr. Henry Louis 'Skip' Gates, Terri McMillian, J. California Cooper, the Watha T. Daniel Library, Keene Mill Elementary school, 3546 37th Street,216 T street NW, LeDriot Park, 1445 N Street N.W., Oak Park, South Oak Park, James McClatchy Park, 12th Avenue, Hughes Stadium, Mr. and Mrs. Steve Issac, The Dance family, the Satellite Room, Sax, Jack London Square, Ivy's Freaky Monday, Camp Nou, the Revel, the Wynn and the Encore, the Borgata and the Water Club, the Bellagio, State of the Union, Marvin's, Policy, Republic Gardens, Bentley's, VIP's, Brown's Paradise Lounge, Silks, Touch of Class (Trash), N.O.A Gallery, H2O, Zanzibar's, Xclusive, Club 88,Club Black- Bueno Aires, Club Black –Rio de Janerio, B Bar, Royal Jelly Burlesque, Yoshi's, the Garage, Savage, Taco Bell, Trader Joe's in Clarendon, Tortilla Coast on 15th and P NW, the Dinner in Adams Morgan, Coop, Wet Willie's, Café Deluxe, Sequoia's, Studio Dos Mil, Meia Pataca, Café Atlantico, Help, 11th Street Diner, Pampy's, the Pork Pitt, Circa, Red Sea, Brickskeller, Oylimpo, Casa de Campo, Avionne Ferrier, Horace and Dickie's, Cinema and Drafthouse, Mango Mike's, Ricks Café, Eastside(@the Wynn)

9

L. ALLEN FARMER

Encore Lobby Bar and Café, Parasol Up, Parasol Down, Blush, the Chinese Dragon, Fish Wings and Things, Mango's Tropical Café, Mango's (of Fort Lauderdale),Windows on the World,Rumors-AC MD, Little Social, Cha Chi, Hakkasan, Hawksmoor Guildhall, Bar Boulud, Aqua, Salt Yard, El Bitxo, Café Zurich, Atlantico Café, Hunan One, Spider Kelly's, Pazo's, Cities, the Mall of America, Fuego's, CC Factory's, the Park, Dream/Love, Mr. Mark Barnes, the Heights, Treme, Miter Day's, the Clevelander, Lost Society DC, Busboy's and Poet's, Eatonville, Mr. Andy Shallal, Fat City, Black Bottle, Van Dyke, the Old Ebbitt Grill, Grill from Ipanema, the Matador, el Gaucho, Art Barn, South Beach, Manderin Oriental, 4 Seasons, Griffins, Red Rooster, Russian Tea Room, Tabaq, the Classics, Marty's Chapter 3,King Fish Café, Bay Shore Inn, Stan's, Café Tabac, Broadway on the Beach, Sky Bar, Club Lob-bay(Lobby), Dookie Chase, 40/40 Club's, Crystal City's Sports bar, Crystal City Restaurant, Edna's Gourmet Seafood ,Clarendon Grill, Clarendon Ballroom, Liberty Tavern, Lyon Hall, Northside Social, Mad Rose, Eventide, Gala Hispanic Theatre, Caribbean Breeze, A-Town, Chi Cha Lounge, Bourbon Street, Quatro/Quatro, Takoma Station, Mr. Marshall Keyes, Music in all of the various forms that have attracted my attention: Jazz; Soul; Neo-soul; Hip Hop; Rap; New Age; R& B; Jazz Fusion; Jazz New Age; Funk; Classical; Gospel; Brazilian; Reggae; Reggaeton; Latin; House ; Rock and Roll; and Country and Western, the cities and towns of Toronto, Rio de Janerio, Barcelona, London, New Orleans, Philadelphia PA, Ocean City MD, Virginia Beach VA, Phoenix, San Diego, Los Angeles, Anchorage, Valencia, Berlin, Frankfort, Ashburn VA, Reston VA, Kaiserslautern, Sao Paulo, Minot, San Francisco, La Romania, (Money-earning) Mount Vernon NY, Sausalito CA, Madrid, Buffalo, Thunder Bay, La Romania, Miami, Miami Beach, Fort Lauderdale, Montclair NJ, Atlanta, Myrtle Beach SC, Fayetteville NC, Clearwater, Tacoma WA, Federal Way WA, Paris, Rome, Amsterdam, Ibiza Town, Kaiserslautern, Frankfort, Berlin, Bonn, Siegelbach, Munich, Minneapolis/ St. Paul, Atlantic City NJ, Seattle, Portland OR, Baltimore, Chicago, Grand Rapids,Negril, Toledo, Orlando, Halifax N.S., Newark NJ, South Orange NJ, Montclair NJ, Windsor ON, Mexico City, Cancun, Detroit, Acapulco, Madison, Pine Ridge Reservation, Oak Bluff, Boston, Sarasota FL, Sacramento (the last stop of the Pony Express), Oakland CA, Tampa ,Mobile, Cincinnati, Denver, Vancouver, Montego Bay , Richmond CA, Berkeley CA, Port of Spain, San Juan, Santo Domingo, Richmond VA, Charlottesville VA, Montreal, San Francisco, NYC, Buenos Aires, Detroit, Coeur d'Alene, Cambridge MA , Ashville NC,

An Ex-Slave Catcher's Narrative

Houston, Stamford CT, Yonkers NY, Teaneck NJ, Inglewood Cliffs NJ, Fort Lee NJ, Willingboro NJ, Camden NJ, Greenwich CT, Key West FL, Richmond VA, Lynn MA, Las Vegas, Reno, South Lake Tahoe CA, Lake Tahoe NV, Annapolis, Wrightsville Beach NC, Charlotte NC, Mercer Island, Kirkland, Bellevue, Renton, SammaMih, Snqualmie, and Washington DC. And a **very special shout out** goes to one **Avalyn J. Pitts esq.**, of Toledo Ohio, because none of this would have even been possible without her editing support.(believe that) **Avalyn**, I truly appreciate your support and love throughout   this   whole   process.   .

I would also like to say a special shout out to all of the beautiful and relaxing beaches and water related places, around the entire world (Copacabana, Ipanema, Caye Caulker, Fort Lauderdale, Negril, Isla de Saona, Clearwater, Panama City, Siesta Key, Casa de Campo, Madeira, Miami Beach, Key West, Barcelona, Caladesi Island State park, Wrightsville beach, Fort Desoto, Myrtle Beach, Cape May, Venice CA, etc.).
And a very special 'thank you' to **David Ferreira and Lauraine Edir**, (and little Miter **Lim Alexander Ferreira**) of the city by the Bay named San Francisco, who saved me from an uncertain fate in Sao Paulo Brazil. I will never ever forget about how you both befriended me and took care of me at a difficult time. You both will always be near and dear to me, because a random act of human kindness does wonders for the heart, mind and soul.

A special thanks to Kathi O'Neill, who is both my mentor and my friend, and an even greater person.

Last but not least thank you; Mr. Pablo Nunes, Tami Patke, and Mickey Patke, Michelle Cooper Kelly, and Chef Valerie Woods.

I want to thank my publisher for all of her support and love because without her all of this in its current form would not have been possible.

'We are all a reflection of those who have come before us.'

L. ALLEN FARMER

COVER ART

An original work by Jay Durrah.

Jay Durrah is a fine artist based in the Washington, DC metro area. Jay, a gifted artist trained at the Corcoran School of Art and the Montpelier Art Center. His work has been shown at galleries throughout the DC metro area.
Please visit JayDurrahsArt.com to view other works by Jay.

An Ex-Slave Catcher's Narrative

PREFACE

Okay how to explain what this odyssey has been all about? Well, I decided that I wanted to leave something behind, as a testimony to my time here on this planet. What should it be? Well to me, my time here has been marked by my choices and or decisions that have helped to shape my time here. Every single decision that I have ever made, has affected what I did, and eventually how I thought, and chose to live my life. Was I right or was I wrong, or does nothing really matter in the end of one's time here on the planet? So to defend and define this quest or journey, and path that I have been on, I decided to leave something behind, that could explain why a whole subset of American culture has been so misunderstood and at times seemingly left behind and somewhat forgotten or invisible. Because I truly believe that American society has never adequately addressed the situation of slavery, nor has it sought to assist the victims (think forty acres and a mule) of this business enterprise. Even today from a generational standpoint, many are still suffering from its heinous effects, evidenced in part by: the lack of self- esteem and or low self-esteem, high illiteracy, low educational standards, high educational dropout rates among high school students, high rates of various addictions, high pre-marital birth rates, high single parent households, impoverished urban environments, high crime and soaring murder rates among descendants of African slaves in America.

These factors all represent the lack of respect for one's self, and for human life in general. How else can you explain why certain segments of this great society have not risen up, and not flourished as a whole, despite the advancements of technology and culture? This, I believe, can only be attributed to the lingering effects of this 300 year plus institution of slavery and even though we are only 150 years past its demise, the effects are still very evident and extremely troubling if we choose to truly see them for what they really are. So how can I do my part to change the overall perception towards this particular subset of human beings? Perhaps we should all do our parts collectively and come together from all segments of this great society to fight this negative perception.

Then, also throw in the situation of the Native Americans, and, you should start to understand that they too have been affected by the very same factors that have affected the descendants of the *business enterprise*. Their situations basically mirror one another, in an alarming manner. This then, is my attempt to do my part, a start so to speak, at making a worthwhile change, which I believe inevitably begins by divine design with each and every individual to ultimately positively affect us collectively. So, we must focus on the behaviors that create these situations, and with any resultant behavior that emanates from our individual and collective choices.

This ambitious and at times draining project that has taken over seven years of my life for one reason and another, most certainly this quest has been extremely taxing yet rewarding. This then is my attempt at showing how a lifetime of choices can affect a person in so many different ways, shapes and forms. For "nothing is promised, and time waits for no one," so it is always vitally important to make the most of everything before your individual time runs out on the planet.

I also want to thank everyone in my life who has positively affected me, and please believe me when I say that " I would be nothing without your love and support, so thank you from the bottom of my heart." So with that said, I give to you An Ex-Slave Catcher's Narrative."........

An Ex-Slave Catcher's Narrative

INTRODUCTION

It's 1924 in King County, Washington, and Balaam Root Calais Vega all 88 years young is dressed in his finest suit, sitting in a rocking chair in the family's room of honor, awaiting the arrival of his youngest daughter, Paula Tammi's son, Saladin, to paint a portrait of him. As the sounds of laughter from children happily at play in the yard outside, gently bounce off the closed window, inside the house smells of greens, roasted chicken, corn, potatoes and cornbread float all about the air from the kitchen, creating an amazing aromatic sensation to the nose. As he looks out of the window surveying the scene in the yard he settles back more fully into the chair. Smoothing out his somewhat rumpled suit he breathes out loud as he mutters to himself, "I wonder just how long it will take this boy to finally show up?" He has been slow all of his life from his birth till now, thought Balaam aloud, and he acts like he believes that time always and only begins when he arrives, and not a moment sooner or later.

When he asked me to sit for a picture, because he needed to have an example of his creative abilities as a portrait artist, I was at first hesitant because my time is precious to me. But when everyone explained to me, that this was to showcase his talents as a way of getting into Wilberforce University in Ohio, I could not say no. We have family and a host of friends in Xenia, Ohio, which is only about three miles away from the University, and we also have some family across Lake Erie in Chatham, Windsor and North Buxton, all of which are in the province of Ontario in Canada.

So Wilberforce would be a good place for him, if he is good enough to be accepted that is. And, submitting this portrait is the final requirement for him to be admitted. The family as a whole, from the adults to even the littlest ones—God bless their souls—all continued to remind me of this fact every minute of every day it seemed, until I finally said yes. Balaam, then, was stuck in limbo, awaiting the arrival of a person who had no real concept of time.

Finally, after another 20 minutes or so he could see Saladin walking ever so slowly up to the front gate, carrying his easel under one arm, and gripping a well-worn leather briefcase. He strode confidently about with an air of a kind of self-importance about himself. He slowly walked through the gate and up into the yard and as the children rushed to greet him as he placed his things upon the ground and he addressed each and every one of them individually with either a hug for each boy child, or a hug and a kiss to the cheek for each girl child. Then only after each child had been addressed in this manner did, he turn his attention back to his task at hand. And with that, he rushed into the house and straight into the room where his Grandfather was awaiting.

"Howdy Pop-Pop," he says, as he comes into the room smiling, and warmly hugs the old man. He rapidly sets up his easel, unfolds a rather small folding chair and removes his paints and drawing pencils. He asks his Grandfather to rotate his chair away from facing the window so that it could now face towards him, and he quickly begins to create the picture by drawing the initial outline. After Balaam complies with the request about the chair, he smoothes himself and gently eases back into his chair.

Then as their eyes make contact, Balaam, in his usual squeaky low voice asks, "How long do you think that this is going to take because I am already tired, because I had to sit and wait for what already seems like forever?" Pop Pop, replies Saladin, in a serious sounding tone, "It will take me maybe anywhere between four to five hours for me to do this right. And you must just please sit still and relax as best as possible."

"Maybe four to five hours," replies Balaam, "so what then am I going to do to keep my mind occupied?" Balaam asks. "Well Pop Pop," Saladin patiently tells him, "you could either just shut your eyes and try to go to sleep or better yet, maybe you could start telling me about your earliest memories as a boy and come forward to the present...and don't leave anything out, please tell me everything about your life," suggests Saladin expectantly. Balaam ponders for a moment, somewhat startled by the adult sounding nature of his Grandson's request. With that, he turns his head slightly to the left and looks into the mirror that sits on the wall now facing directly across from him and the rocking chair. As his mind races back and forth, he starts to warm up his memory and it is as if his memories from a long time ago start to come alive, in the reflection of the mirror itself. Balaam begins to tell his story...

An Ex-Slave Catcher's Narrative

L. ALLEN FARMER

VOLUME ONE

PART ONE

Quaere verum/Cogito, ergo sum
Seek the truth/I think therefore I am

*Each player must accept the cards life deals him or her: but once
they are in hand, he or she alone must decide how to play the cards
in order to win the game.*

An Ex-Slave Catcher's Narrative

ONE

....

Well let's see, my first memory was that of the Vegas' main large house, that had an upstairs, and also many rooms and big halls that ran off the big kitchen area. I was allowed most times to run up and down the halls as much as I liked, because my mother was the main cook in the big house for the Vega household, but she was always making me go outside, with all of that noise and ruckus. I remember that I just used to laugh and play and run around all by myself for hours upon end, all about the property, as long as it was within eyesight of my Mother. And, it was as if I had no troubles or worries, and these were the best of happy days for me.

The Vegas' were our original owners, who had a sprawling estate and property that went as far as the eyes could see and further. It stretched in some places to almost the town of Santiago de los Caballeros, I was always told. The property was located about in the middle of the Island and was almost over a whole day's ride and a half from the capital city of Santo Domingo. The cities of San Francisco de Macoris, Santiago de los

Caballeros, and Concepcion de la Vega were all very close to the estate and, San Felipe de Puerto Plata was about a half-day's ride away on the coast. It was also where the Vegas' had 4 of their ships docked along with another ship that stayed docked at a place that was called Nagua.

There was the big main house, the two smaller first and second houses, 5 large barns and two smaller barns, a lot of livestock, fields of sugar cane and more. The Vega Estate was the main employer in the region because the Vegas' were the largest landowners in the entire area and it always seemed like there were people coming and going to the Estate. We lived closest to the town of Concepcion de la Vega, where the Vegas had a store that sold things that their vast estate produced. Concepcion de la Vega was a small town that was said to originally be on Vega property, that the Vega family sold to start the town, but it did not seem to me, to have the same importance and energy of Santo Domingo, and it was just one of those sleepy kind of places.

My next memory was when mi Abeulo and Master Vega would take me on the long annual trip each year to the great first city of the New World, Santo Domingo. Abeulo would laugh at me, because he could sense my excitement and see how just my being in that place at that exact moment in time always affected me. They would let me run up and down the Calle de la Fuerza, which was named so because of its proximity to La Torre del Homenaje, which is a part of the great Ozama Fortress, which is the oldest military building of the New World. The Alcazar de Colon, or Fortress of Colon was down the street and it was the home and palace for Don Diego Colon, who was the son of the great Admiral Cristóbal Colon and his wife Maria de Toledo. Santo Domingo just had a certain life and finger snap to it and it was the constant hub of activity, as people moved back and forth between the Old World and the New World, some coming, some going, some leaving, some arriving, people just moving about at all times of the day and night. There were always soldiers moving about with their impressive uniforms on. Then, add in all kinds of people like religious folks, merchants, laborers, gentlemen and ladies, farmers, craftsmen, nobility types, and all in between, processing a sense of self-importance as they made their way through this capital city, which was a former colony that the Spanish royalty had carved out to be the center of their New World. So, Santo Domingo would always be my very favorite place in the whole wide world, because it is the capital of República Dominicana, and so Hispaniola will always be my home, and the Island of my birth.

My next memory of note was the day that I walked into the kitchen area and asked my mother, "What does my name mean?" She immediately stopped what she was doing, wiped off her hands on a cloth towel, and sat down in a nearby chair. She gently pulled me onto her lap as she wrapped her arms around me and with her serious sounding voice, asked me, "Well Balaam, why do you ask that?". "Because I heard Abeulo say that every name has a meaning, so I was just wondering what my name meant."

She turned me around so that she could see my face and eyes and she then said, "The name 'Balaam' was chosen for you by your Abeulo, because of the prophecy that was foretold long ago by our ancestors. The prophecy said that one day there would be one that would deliver our family from its wandering in the wilderness, a so called chosen one, and that this one would be cursed by some, and revered by others. This person would also be seen by some as a sorcerer with an ability to cast spells and see future events, and that Amen-Ra would give this person the power to both bless some and curse others.

This person would also be the lord, husband, and leader of his people into his or herself, just as a king or queen does symbolically, with their subjects when they share one another's lives. So before your birth while you were still in my belly, your Abuelo while having a nighttime dream saw in a vision that you would be this person, and also that you would be a boy child, and that in the Holy Book of his masters, he would find your name. He then consulted the Good Book of the Familia Vega's and in the Book of Numbers he found the name Balaam, which meant exactly what the prophecy had foretold. "So see Balaam, you have always been destined to be a 'Balaam' she said sincerely as she looked me dead into my eyes, and then she leaned over and whispered into my ear "We are always who, we are meant to be."

My next big memory was the day that Master Vega came to tell us that he had lost us in a card game. It had all first started for him, when he lost his beloved wife Senora Maria Sophia Garcia Vega and their youngest child, little Emmanuel, along with my Father who all drowned in a boating accident on the Yaque del Norte River, as they were all coming back from visiting one of her sisters who lived in San Fernando de Monte Cristi.

This started him down a path of drinking and destruction that he could not escape, because the losses of his wife and youngest child were just too much for him to bear, and sadly, life had lost all of its meaning for him. So, for almost 6 years he had stayed drunk nearly every day and then, eventually to offset his mounting loses and debt because he had stopped caring for his vast business interests he started gambling and drinking down in Santo Domingo as a way in his mind to get back his lost business money, to clear up his ever mounting debts and to restore his lost self-respect.

But the more he lost the more he gambled, and the more he gambled, the more he lost. He then one day weeks later, found himself in a card game called poker with a couple of Blancos who were Americans, and who were either very lucky or who were secretly both in the game together for a common cause. They defeated him in one of those card games that could go either way on the very last hand.

He had committed the cardinal sin of not having enough on the table money to cover his increased wager, so it was suggested by these Americans that he bet his most coveted asset which the Americans seemingly already knew about. He had his reservations, but he bet anyway because he thought while using the mind of a drunk, that he had the winning hand. But to his horror, he lost.

So, I will never ever forget the look of shame mixed in with sadness on his face, when he had come to tell us the bad news, with tears in his eyes because of all of his prized assets, of the things that he had acquired in his life, mi Abeulo was his most coveted! For mi Abeulo was his self-professed greatest asset or commodity, the greatest hunter tracker, guide, gatherer, merchant-for-hire on the entire Island of Hispaniola. It was mi Abuelo who had brought him fame and fortune and riches, beyond his wildest dreams.

I will also never ever forget that day about five weeks later that we left for good. Everyone on the whole Estate came out to bid us farewell, all except Master Vega though who never came out of his room that day. He was drunk beyond measure, with grief piled high on top of despair. I have on many occasions since then, always wondered just whatever happened to Master Vega, and if he was ever able to straighten back out his crumbling life.

And, as we awaited the arrival of our transportation to this strange New World, we said our goodbyes to everyone who had come from both near and far to see us off. And, when the wagon finally arrived, it had bars on it that covered the back part! Mi Madre, mi Abeulo and me, along with our meager possessions were quickly herded like livestock into the back of this wagon, as some people in the crowd who came to see us off began to cry.

We then were driven in an extremely fast manner to San Felipe de Puerto Plata to an awaiting ship. As we went upon its deck we were placed in chains and taken below into the ship's cramped hold and chained to the wall next to the livestock area, as the ship began to take off on our voyage. This area which was a wired-in area, already held cargo that consisted of a goat, a bunch of chickens, and two lambs.

For the next two weeks or so, we pitched and rocked in a swaying type of manner and I was sick almost the whole time of the trip. So I only remember certain things about the trip, more like bits and pieces of it, but some things have always stuck with me. Like, I do know that we were all uncomfortable both mentally and physically, because the chains were rough on our ankles and feet and caused sores that did not heal fast or well, and were even rougher on our minds because, the Vegas had never ever required us to wear chains, not even once.

Yes, we were their property, but they treated us kind of like distant family members, out of the profound respect that everyone had for mi Abeulo. And, besides we were on an Island so unless we stole a boat during an escape attempt, just where would we be really going, chains or no chains if we even tried to escape? I remembered how you could smell all about in the air the salt from the sea. I also do vividly remember the way that everything in the hold of the ship smelled, whew, like something terrible lurked and reeked in the water, and all throughout the boat itself. Both had this musky funny smell that cut through everything, even through the goat's [crusty] stench. It smelled like what I have come to know, now in later life, is death. That was not the only place where I had smelled it on that trip either. We stopped in a place called Jamaica and it was here that they finally let us come up on the deck to stretch our legs and walk a bit, with our chains still on. And from the deck of the ship this place looked like a nice place, and okay to live in. We next stopped at some islands off the coast of the mainland called the Gullah Sea Islands, but they made us stay in the ship's hold on this stop. At each stop the crew took some things off and loaded some things on, but we were the only slaves on the whole boat, and the crew came down at times to get a look see at the prized catch. When we finally dropped anchor, we were in America at a place called Charleston, in the Carolina's and when we were brought upstairs on the deck of the ship as the air rushed upon us, we could see many other ships that were docked next to us. And, then we could see on land side, the hectic movement of people that seemed to just whirl about like wind does around a bee-hive on a windy gusty day. There were also a lot of voices all mumbled together, all of which created a loud noise filled pitch, or buzz that sounded both strange and threatening.

We were then led off the ship, with our chains still on mind you, and taken right to a place, were the noise was even louder than outside, and where one could barely hear anything, it was called the auction block, which also was the very next place that I had again noticed that smell of something terrible lurking about. And as we waited for our turn, for what seemed like hours, we witnessed firsthand just how cruel this place called the United States of America truly was, as we saw up close, how families were broken apart just to satisfy the demands of commerce and business. For there was a family of slaves, who were all in chains like everyone else of the darker hue were in this place. It looked like a father and a mother, and five children who looked like the both of them. The three boys were split up, with one going to a Blanco from a place called Baltimore, Maryland and the other two going to different owners in some place called Cobb County, Georgia. The two girls were sold to a slave trader from down in some place named Tennessee, and the husband was bought by a rather young-looking man, from some place named the "Old Dominion." The wife, with an outburst, started to cry very loud, and then a rather hard looking Blanco with a whip, stepped in her direction and started yelling something at her. I think, because my

English was not good then, "to be quiet," and he then proceeded to slap and kick and beat her down upon the dirt floor, until she had difficulty breathing. And, only then was she naturally quiet enough to suit his taste.

She was sold to a plantation owner from near Charleston, because in his words, which I found out later from mi Abeulo, "she still had the look of a good breeder," and with that without so much as a goodbye or a hug, or a anything, they were all led away and were family no more. Sadly there was nothing that any of them could do about it either, if they even wanted too, and besides they and everyone else in the room, with the exception of mi Abeulo, were all still pretty much scared and still in shock from the mother's beat down onto the floor. There was this look of terror that was on all of their faces, and this is something that I will never ever forget as long as I live. As I look back upon it, this was just a form of mind control that the slaves' owners and slave traders used, to subdue the victims of that kind of a business transaction, one which simply involved a simple business equation of "me and you equals, we both get paid."

The slave traders made their capital or money on the front end of the business transaction, off the actual sale of the commodity. The slave owners made their money or capital on the back end of the business transaction, once the commodity became a part of the slave owner's free work force which led to increased growing and harvesting, and then this created more units to sell on the free market exchange that is called, commerce. So, control of the commodity in this type of hellish business enterprise was essential on both sides of the business equation. Which if you remember is "me and you equals we both get paid." The need to break the spirit of the commodity right off the "hop, skip and a jump," off the boat was usually the rule, and never the exception. That is, if the ship's voyage itself did not do that first.

It seemed like people of a darker hue were not even seen as human beings in the auction block place. So, letting everyone see and know the dealings of what was actually to be the reality of their new lives when the boat had docked, appeared to be for some people, a normal way of life, in this place called the United Snakes of America. So when you knew that there was nothing that you could do to stop this business transaction from happening, absolutely nothing, you had to have a strong mind and a strong will to make it through the fully awake, daytime nightmarish experience which is called, the auction block.

We waited our turn, and finally when it was our turn, I'm guessing because they ushered us up to the front of the area to where the old looking man who was running the auction stood in front of a desk. A couple of Blanco's came into view from some side entrance through the crowd and walked straight to the front and then they huddled around with the old looking man who was running the auction. They kept turning around looking at us as Abeulo looked dead back at them right in their eyes, each and every time.

Then one pulled out a paper from inside his jacket and gave it to the old looking man running the auction, who read it then he laid it down on the desk, signed his name onto it with a quill that he had removed from its old and dirty inkwell that he had placed in the middle of his desk. He then blew on the paper with his breath, folded it and gave it back the other man and shook that other man's hand, smiled proudly at him and then appeared to say something to him in his ear that was just between the two of them. They then both laughed out loud and said something else to one another.

Then the two Blancos turned and said something to the guards who immediately escorted us all out through a back door that led through another doorway, which led to yet another wagon with some men on horses, who were all waiting for us, to appear. The guards then put us into the back of the wagon with our chains still on, to begin our journey to our strange and new home, as they smiled and said their goodbyes to the men in the wagon and on horseback. The ride took about almost three days to actually reach our destination, because we did a lot of stopping at this place or that place.

We immediately started to notice the differences between our old Island home, and this new place. And, what struck us first off was the thickness of the air, and how it smelled and felt on our bodies and skin. There was also this strange smell that cut through the air, at all times of day or night, that we came to later know was the smell of tobacco.

Even the animal sounds were both strange sounding and different from what we were used to hearing. And, as night fell every evening, we could hear this strange humming sound that came from some kind of bug, Abeulo said, that seemingly grew louder and louder as midnight approached. There was also an oppressive heat that was moist, that never went away, day or night.

It was always hot and the heat at certain times of the day, like when the midday sun was at its highest point in the sky was downright oppressive. It was extremely dangerous, or so it seemed to my young mind. Because it was easy for the sun to drain you of both your energy and strength and dry you out and this is why I always felt very thirsty there. The heat also kept you wet to your bones and your clothes were constantly soaked, and there did not ever seem to be any relief.

Upon finally reaching a place called Cumberland County, North Carolina, on the outskirts of a town called Fayetteville, we finally got to The Strickland Plantation. I was immediately struck by how different the landscape was with woods and trees everywhere one could see. Along with the numerous trees, there was very sandy topsoil that was soft and moist and had a sound of crunching beneath your feet, whenever you walked upon it.

The property had a nice stream that crossed through it on the southeast corner of the land, providing the owner with a constant water source for his family, the crops, his livestock and his free labor commodities. The main compound consisted of a big house, with a downstairs, and an upstairs with a lot of rooms with fancy manicured lawns all around the house, like you hear about in a place called France. There were 4 large barns along with 3 smaller barns, a medium sized place for the Plantation overseers and work hands to live in, 2 curing salt shacks and an open-air blacksmith area that had a covered roof area.

There were 3 pens and stalls for a large and growing livestock population, which also had a small private livery barn that was semi-attached to it. There was a small mill by the stream, and someone was always at the mill doing something. And, there were a series of slave quarters, that he used to house his free labor commodities, and as his free labor force grew, he just built more quarters.

There were over 200 slaves, or free labor commodities, on The Strickland Plantation, and it was one of the largest tobacco and cotton producing plantations in the whole state, and all throughout the Carolinas. This made the owner a very rich and influential man, who had business interests all over the Carolinas, and he was a man who also usually got what he wanted. He had always liked to hunt and track down wildlife game when he was younger. This was kind of like a true passion for him but as he got older, he just did not have any more time for his true passion because of his considerable business interests, "because in the business world money never sleeps," he always used to say.

He had a big property with plenty of game and wildlife running all over it and therefore, what he needed was "a damn good hunter tracker, who was dependable and who would not always come back empty handed, like, his slaves and sons and plantation hands always seemed to do. So, he needed someone different or new, who would do his job, not say much and come through and perform his job with a high success rate. So, one night when he was sitting at some social function, with some visiting foreign dignitaries and businessmen, from the Islands to the south of the United States—somewhat bored to death, by chance he eavesdropped on two gentlemen's conversation about the sad misfortune of a friend of theirs, a Señor Vega.

They remarked about his once valuable estate and properties that were almost now gone, since the loss of his wife and youngest son caused him to lose his passion for life and for business in general. But of all of his possessions, his hunter tracker merchant for hire was his true money maker. And he still owned him, for the time being but that too, seemed like it was only a matter of time that he would lose him also, at the rate he was going, by his drinking so heavily.

This tracker is just what he wanted and needed, so if he could just figure out a way to pry him from this poor drunk's grasp, he could solve his own perplexing problem. So he took his time, and after maybe three years of cultivating contacts and bribing folks, he was given information that seemed to imply that Mr. Vega's weakness was perhaps, a combination of cards and booze.

So he skillfully sent his cousin's son Newton Ray, who spoke fluent Spanish, along with a trusted partner's son whose name was Sheldon, both of whom worshipped drinking and card games like a religion, down to Santo Domingo to play him. He then staked them with 250 dollars each for the trip, along with a secret that made the two card worshippers giddy with glee and anticipation. This secret was, that he had opened up a secret bank account that contained a supply of cash that they always had at their disposal to gamble with. They would play the role of two high stakes want to be professional gamblers, who would gamble all over the Island, and end up eventually in the Capitol, which by word of mouth would entice Mr. Vega into their trap. It was a trap, which was designed to use his greed against himself.

One or the other of them must beat him and get the asset, no matter how long it took, within reason of course. Once their mission was successful, they would wire him, so he could set everything up on all ends, so, that when they landed in Charleston, he would then have them to sell the asset to him. This would be easy because after all, he had secretly owned a third of the Charleston auction block anyway, and this would be like the simple business transaction that occurred there six days a week, and 288 days each and every year.

So, everyone, except the slave population we saw in the fields, was awaiting our arrival to the Plantation. And it was as if we were on display and at a circus, as we pulled up to the main house, everyone crowded around the wagon, to see what was so important about this negra that Old Master Strickland was so determined to have as an asset.

Now, we naturally assumed that we would go right to the fields, because the sun had not even reached its high point in the daytime sky yet. But, oh no, Abeulo was far too valuable to be used in any fieldwork. And, my mother was a great cook and there was always a need in any kitchen for a great cook. So we were taken straight away, still with the chains on mind you, to our new quarters which was the small and private livery barn quickly given some food and water and then locked up just like what one would do, to secure his most valuable possessions at night, for safekeeping, even though the sun was now hanging in the middle of the day time sky.

L. ALLEN FARMER

An Ex-Slave Catcher's Narrative

PART TWO

Qui docet discit
He who teaches learns.

It is difficult to free fools from the chains they revere.

TWO

....

M y next memory was of the very next morning, after
we had arrived, which was our official day one of
our new lives in this strange new place. It was at
the crack of dawn, when mi Abeulo was unchained from us and
taken right out to show what he could do, and to everyone's
amazement, he came back well before midday with some wild
pheasants and a nice sized rabbit. Old Master Strickland was so
happy that he appeared to be down right kind of giddy. And he
was hopping around like he was going to pee on himself. He
muttered something over and over to himself about Nimrod and
Genesis chapter 10 verses 8 and 9 of the good book that spoke
of a mighty hunter before the Lord. And, he seemed as if he just
could not contain himself, for thinking about what the great

feast was going to taste like, that he was soon to have for his dinner that evening.

The whole Plantation was abuzz with the news of the newcomer's skill, and how it did not even appear to the witnesses that had accompanied him on the hunt, that he was even trying all that hard. So, because of all of this happiness and excitement, our chains were finally taken off. But we did acquire a guard, our very own guardian angel, who was there nearby outside at all times of the day and night and whose job it was, to keep his eyes on any of our movements at all times.

Maybe the next day or so after that, mi (my) Madre, was taken up to the kitchen. There, she was paired with the main cook who was an older lady, who was likened unto a complement, to assist her with anything that she may have needed help with. And actually, mi Madre was being positioned to learn the business of running the kitchen for the Strickland household.

Then about a week or so later, I was taken around the whole estate to find a suitable job for myself. And, even though my English was not good, I was given the job of being a water bearer for those unfortunate, and lost souls who were in the fields. This job really only required hand signals and keeping one's eyes glued to the head overseer's commands, to perform it. So it was easier than a lot of other jobs that I had observed.

It was to be only for about a half 'a day supposedly for six days a week, but it truly lasted for about only a week and a half. And, really it then became only five days. Because of the chance occurrence of my water bucket having cracked, and my having to look for another, which I was told it was supposedly up by the Big House. Through the fickle finger of fate, I met Old Master Strickland's youngest son, whose name was Jack.

And, even though he was about four years older than me, we still took an instant liking to one another. He was smart and very knowledgeable, and the first thing that he ever said to me was, "Hey you. Yah you, do you know anything about pirates, and have you ever heard of Blackbeard?" I just smiled back and waved at him, as you would do to someone that you had known for a long time, even though I had no idea of what he was even saying because my English was extremely limited in those early days here.

We both laughed and with that, began our friendship in an innocent kind of naïve sort of way. He was always asking his father if we could hang out and play with one another on day six of the workweek. Because he had no one in his age group, for miles and miles around, that he could even go to and visit. So he had always felt somewhat lonely, because he had no one to talk to about pirates with or to play with. And, just like his father's prayers for a hunter for his estate had been answered, so too, strangely were his youngest son's prayers also answered.

Old Master Strickland had no choice but give his favorite son what he wanted, because out of all of his children, he was the one who had shown the most promise. And, he then went right into his office that was just off the study area of the Big House. And, he drew up a paper that explained that this young "negra" was lawfully and dutifully in the company of his son, "JACK-SON," who was at all times in total control of this young "negra" commodity.

He then blew on the paper, put the paper in an envelope and told Jack to keep this on his person at all times so that if anyone stopped them, and they should always be stopped with questions, the matter would be clarified in a dignified and businesslike manner. So with that, he started taking me around with him for sure on each and every day 6, rain or shine. And, we surveyed every part of the vast estate because after all, it was his family's property and one day he may be tasked to run the family's entire business enterprise.

So, this then was seemingly just his way of getting ready to get in some practice, of being the boss, and checking everything out. More importantly, he had begun to become involved on all levels and at all times, in the running of the Plantation. So this practice required him to be everywhere at all times, all at once, so that he could stay in the know.

So, on day six, we were always up and out at the crack of dawn. Master Jack always had a lunch made which he stored in his knap sack, that he had slung over onto his back. And, he had a small metal water canteen that was always slung over his shoulder. Also, he carried along a stick-like pole to fend off any unwelcome creatures that we may have encountered on our travels.

We would show up here or there, and never in the same place twice, to just observe the business operations in action. And, Master Jack always scribbled down some kind of notes on pieces of paper. We used to walk the entire property line, to see where the property began and ended. We would also sneak onto the neighbors' property, to see how they did business, and really how they did or did not keep up their property and assets.

It was as if he was his father's secret eyes and ears as I now look back on it all, and this is why his father truly favored him the most, out of all of his sons even though he loved each of them equally. Because, Jack from a very young age, had always shown a keen interest and desire in the family business and more importantly, he had always put it first and foremost in his life of privilege.

We were always gone from sun up to almost sun down, and day six became the day of the work week that I lived and even longed for. It even made the other five half days of being the water bearer for the fieldworkers somewhat bearable. Before I knew it, one day a week had turned into two days a week, and then three days a week. And we then started going fishing and trying to track Abuelo and the men, along with the guardian angel that rode with him, to study Abeulo in action, and everything else became like a blur.

Pretty soon they had to get another water bearer, because Master Jack required my services almost every day of the week, or so he said. Some days we played games like hide-and-go-seek or tag-you-are-it, and on other days, Master Jack started to try to teach me words and then phrases in English. The first words that I learned were "Hello, goodbye, yes and no," then the first phrases were "my name is Balaam, your name is Jack," and so on. He then began talking about what a pirate was, and he kept repeating a name over and over again, which was "Blackbeard."

All the while, mi Abuelo was immediately making a name for himself, and his reputation grew with each and every passing day. Deer, boar, rabbits, possum, fish, elk, pheasant, and even a bear were just some of the things that he hunted and caught in those first few weeks. And, he was, as a result given a certain amount of independence.

So Sundays, our one day of rest, became the one day that I got to spend with mi (my) Abeulo, just him and me. And along with our constant guard, that always shadowed our every movement of course; we would go out and hunt for our own family.

Although, whatever Abuelo hunted down and caught, had to be split with Old Master Strickland. So, we always had to catch a bit more, Abeulo would say, with a twinkle in his eyes. So given that, our haul would always look impressive, because we always had to give away half, in honor of Abeulo' s rule from Old Master Strickland.

I remember that my time with my Abeulo was always precious to me, because he was the first man that I ever met and got to know on a personal basis. My father, died in the boating accident on the Yaque del Norte River that terrible day, after first saving mi Madre with me still in her belly, he went back to secure Senora Vega, who was trying to save her youngest son and sadly, all three of them drowned. A floating log, with the help of a swift river current took them all to their deaths.

His name was Septimius Severus Calais. And, he was so named because at the time of his birth, when he came out to meet the world for the very first time, he had this regal look of nobility about himself. So, they named him after the very first African soldier emperor who reigned for 18 years as Emperor of Rome.

So, I never had any father figure but Abeulo, he was like part father, part friend, part teacher, and he was someone who took his time with me and made sure that I was always okay in my mind and body. He availed himself to me, because he knew how not having a father or father figure could affect a young life. And, he was always sad that I never got the chance to meet my father, whom mi Abeulo always both liked and admired because of his style and mental substance.

For my father was Abeulo' s original first student or what we now call an apprentice, and he, therefore, was the true very first warrior of The House. So mi Abeulo always made sure that our time together was always ours, and that nothing ever got in the way of this time, either. He used this time to always ask me a lot of questions and to teach me so many things that he felt were important to my growth and development. And really, Abuelo taught me how to survive in general, like how to hunt and fish and track and how to protect myself—all of which I took with me into manhood, and still use even today.

He would say things like "How do you catch a boar?" or" how would you catch a bird from the sky"," or "how do you catch a rabbit?" Well Grandson, he'd say in Spanish, catching a boar is somewhat easy, because boars just as most animals and humans, are creatures of habit. So one must find its daily route or path and lie in wait and ambush it as it runs along its path.

While a bird must be caught on land, so it must be enticed to land and then be trapped. Birds have good eyes, while boars have bad eyesight but have a great sense of smell. So, you must understand your prey, and learn to anticipate and know what its instincts will make it do. Everything in nature has natural instincts, and everything in nature, has things that it will always do, that also includes even people. So, to answer your question of "how does one catch a rabbit?" Well, the elders always said, "to catch a rabbit, one must follow it quietly to the rabbit hole, and then quietly be patient for as long as it takes and wait to trap it when it is leaving its sanctuary. So you must have patience and fortitude, along with knowledge of your prey's instincts my grandson, and if you always remember these basic things, they will make you into a good tracker," he wisely said.

But I would always ask, how do I become a great tracker, Abeulo? His eyes would twinkle, and he would laugh and say,

"Greatness comes with age and greatness comes with time and patience. And, to be a great tracker, one has to be able to use or control all of his senses. Like, standing down wind and being able to smell the prey, or to hear the prey from a ways off, or to see it from a distance before it sees you.

All are examples of how one must use the senses of hearing, seeing and smelling, all combined with patience, age and superior instincts to make one a great tracker, and if you are willing to work at it, you could be great also. But only time will tell my grandson, if you will truly become one of the great ones. It takes work and effort to make being a hunter tracker look effortless my grandson. But, once you have your basic strategy down, you just adapt to any situation that you come across in the wild, and you will be fine. You just have to practice to improve your different skill sets and when you are ready, one day we will go hunting with you on the lead.

And with that, I practiced as much as possible and learned to use ropes, snares, fishhooks, knives, spears, the bow and a lot of arrows, traps, pikes, and everything else. So, I learned to fish, to hunt, to track, to trap and how to remove the animal skin or fur, or feathers. And eventually one day Abeulo ushered me to take the lead, and I had my first crack at leading a hunt that was all based upon my due diligence. It was looking rather bleak during morning, because if I was not spooking the prey then, I was giving away our location when we were up wind, causing the prey to always be seemingly one step ahead of us.

But after a nice lunch of honey cakes and beef jerky, all washed down with some cool water, things started to change, and I was able to find a trail. We tracked some deer hooves until we crept up to a small clearing deep into the woods, and saw a lot of dear hooves and markings, and a lot of droppings on the ground, all around that clearing. I spotted a good vantage point behind a thicket of bushes and we settled back in silence and waited for something to happen by.

After about almost an hour a nice looking medium-sized buck deer came prancing slowly into the clearing, moving directly towards us and right when it got almost on top of us, it turned slightly to the side. As I rose up and steadied my bow and readied my arrow while holding another arrow between my lips, strangely the deer sort of froze as it noticed me. I took a breath and then as I exhaled, I fired two arrows in rapid succession with both of them finding their mark, which was on the left side right above the hind leg area that curved into the deer's back. The deer tried to run, but it only got a few feet away as it crashed to the ground with a thud, like some dead weight. I will always remember the look in its eyes when we got to it, as its life slowly bled out and went away. Abeulo seemed extremely pleased and proud of my very first kill, he took my hand and rubbed it in the blood that was oozing out from its mortal wounds, and then smeared the blood all over my face.

Then, suddenly he let go with a thunderous yell that roared like thunder, on a quiet and clear day. He then stated, "Now you have pleased the ancestors my grandson, and you are now a part of a long line of trackers, whom some say are the greatest and most feared trackers in the entire world. We have hunted and tracked well over a two thousand years, from the mountains of the moon, to the plains of the Serengeti, and all in between.

We have tracked and hunted for Kings and Queens, witch doctors, nobility, rulers, religious leaders, important people, unimportant people, military leaders, soldiers of fortune, political types—and even for other tribes, who would ask our leaders to loan us out, to help them for whatever reason—be that political or social.

Because of this, we have always been seen as mercenaries or hunters for hire, and even though we have always been a peaceful people who used our abilities to first survive, and then to maintain. And it was when we learned to conqueror the animals in nature that we then became what we are today. We have through our traditions, hunted and tracked everything from lions, tigers, rhinos, water buffaloes, hippopotamuses, giraffes, elks, zebras, and gazelles. And, there is nothing in nature that cannot be hunted down and tracked by us— especially not man.

You, my grandson, have continued this line of our ancestors, and if the saying "The ancestor is the womb," is true then you are now what we have always been, said Abuelo. With that, we brought home the kill, and Old Master Strickland first off, got the best parts, then we took what we wanted, and I took what was left down to the slave quarters. From that day onward there was nothing beyond my grasp, and I thrived on hunting things that I had never caught before, especially the elusive animals, which improved my skills, and aim. I reckon that I hunted and trapped some of everything even skunks, porcupines, bees, snakes, ground hogs, hawks, and so on, just to say that I had done that before. But, little did I realize just how this unique skill set would come back to haunt me in the years to come.

My next memory was that of the day when Master Jack got his very own first horse. Time had really been moving right along, even though it seemed like it was moving slow, and Master Jack and I both were taller and stronger. Master Jack told me that he had been asking his father for well over a year, just when he could get his own horse, because he had been taking riding lessons for over two years. So his Father told him that when he turned thirteen, he would see about getting him one.

When he woke up in the morning on the day he turned thirteen, a pretty chestnut brown colored horse was standing in front of the Big House tied up to a hitching pole. It had a shiny new saddle with a reddish colored blanket, just waiting for Master Jack to arrive and take possession. Master Jack was over the moon with delight, and he immediately came and got me for a ride.

Master Jack made me hop up onto the horse's back, and away we went. The next few months were loads of fun and filled with excitement, because the horse made us able to travel even further out, on our travels and observation visits. We went any and everywhere, and I was able to see the surrounding countryside, which had this hauntingly beautiful look and feel about it, and there seemed to be an endless supply of game all around us.

So we started using the horse to aid us with our own hunting trips, because there seemed to be better game away from The Plantation. One day, Master Jack and myself were out before dawn, doing our usual hunting, when as fate would have it, trouble struck. It was kind of cold, and I really did not want to even go with him, but he talked me into it, with his usual brand of excitement, as he talked and emphatically moved his hands.

I said that I would only go with him, if he did not talk about his usual favorite subject, who is known to the world as, 'Blackbeard the Pirate.' He just laughed, and said, "Now Balaam, you know that you find all of this pirate talk, highly interesting, and likened unto a good mystery novel. But what you do not realize my friend, is that these men were extremely successful businessmen and the seas and oceans of the world were the marketplaces, upon which they conducted their brand of commerce." As I thought to myself "Oh really?" With that, he started talking hard, while focusing in my general direction, as if he just knew that I cared for the knowledge and wisdom of his words about his studies concerning pirate history, and how pirates even had a period of time that was called 'The Golden Age of Piracy.'

We found a trail of something, around mid-morning and I hopped down off the back of the horse to see what the trail showed, and it appeared to be something rather large, because of the deep hoof impressions in the dirt. I then started on foot to follow the trail as Master Jack slowly rode behind me, and after about a half mile as we rounded a bend, something was stirring in a bunch of bushes. Master Jack quickly grabbed his un-holstered rifle, as I picked up a rock and threw it in the direction of the bushes.

With a squeal, out came running a large male Boar, and Master Jack instantly shot at it, but he only had wounded it and he then holstered his rifle and galloped ahead, to follow it and to finish it off. He was right behind it, but in his haste, he was not looking at the terrain, and his horse stepped into a hole. And as his horse fell, it tumbled atop of Master Jack, trapping him under the fallen horse, and breaking his leg.

The wounded boar whirled around, and immediately smashed in into the stomach of the downed horse, with its razor-sharp tusks. As the horse cried out in pain from the goring it was receiving, it's blood and flesh splashed everywhere, and all upon Master Jack and into his eyes, which served to only further disorient him. I could hear the sounds of the commotion, and it sounded like a great battle was erupting.

I dropped everything that I was carrying, except my bow and arrows and set out running hard, fast and steady, towards the sounds of the apparent agony. As I got to a clearing, I could see that the horse had had it, and was finished. The boar was now turning its attention towards Master Jack, who was still trapped beneath the dead horse.

He was screaming and scared and clawing at the moist red soil beneath his fingers. And with the horse's blood all over him he could not see and seemed drunk. As the boar started its murderous run toward Master Jack, I knew that I only had at one shot. And, if I missed, Master Jack could possibly die.

I dropped down to one knee, drew back the bow, and silently aimed my longest arrow at the hard charging boar. I drew a quick breath, and as I exhaled, I let it release and watched the arrow's flight. It struck the target true and hard, knocking it off stride, and into some nearby undergrowth.

As I got up and ran to Master Jack, I noticed that he still appeared to be in a drunken state, but he calmed down, once he heard my voice. He was a bloody mess, covered all in his favorite horse's blood and sheared flesh—but he was alive—with a leg that was broken in two places. The next thing that I noticed was that his rifle was still in the holster, underneath him and he had not even tried to locate it, he was just dumbfound and scared.

The horse's blood had gone into his eyes, taking his vision away from him. And, like Abuelo always used to say, "Men do strange things or act funny, when death is looking at them in the face." I pulled Master Jack from underneath the dead horse and tried to calm him down a bit more, because he was in quite a bit of pain.

I then fashioned a quick splint of sticks for his leg from pieces of the saddle blanket, so that his leg would remain still. And then I went over to check out the boar, because a twice-wounded animal is extra dangerous. The boar was dead, and the arrow had found its mark, lodging itself in one ear, the arrow point barely sticking out of the other one.

And the boar had died in the way that it had lived, on the run, being a boar. So I remember asking myself, "What if I had missed, or better yet, what if I had not even come?" as I looked at its dead carcass. And I began to pull it toward where Master Jack was positioned. Then, I fashioned a litter of branches and what was left of the saddle blanket, into a splint and then pulled Master Jack and the dead hog both up onto it—and began to slowly drag them back toward home.

Master Jack was quiet for a long time, but when he finally spoke, he said, "Balaam no matter what, I will repay you for your heroic deed and act of kindness. For any other servant or slave would have left me to die, or left me for dead, but not you. You have always been different, and you will see that I will always be in your debt, because I owe you my life."

With that, he passed out, in obvious pain. And, I continued to drag them inch-by-inch, foot-by-foot. Nighttime came and we were still a long way from home, so I found us some shelter and started a fire and tended to Master Jack. I gave him a piece of beef jerky and a drink of water and pulled him close to me so that we together could conserve body warmth.

In the morning a search party found us and put us into a wagon for the return trip home. When we got home, Master

Jack described over and over in great detail, how my actions had saved his life. Mi Abuelo and Old Master Strickland were both amazed at the accuracy of the shot, and how big the boar truly was. My arrow shot, was well over ninety feet—they both estimated, and considering the urgency of the situation, everyone marveled at how cool and calm I had remained, during the whole time.

All of Master Jack's family repeatedly thanked me over and over again to no end. And, as the word began to spread around the Plantation of my feat, and folks began to gather, they all seemed to marvel at my skill and accuracy. And I heard everything, from one man saying "Dat boy has got Injun in him" to another man asking me, "Was I scared to take the shot?" I looked first at mi Abeulo, and then turned to the man and said, "Nope, not really, because I did not have time to think or to even be scared. So, I just aimed and shot true—because being a hunter tracker is in my bloodline."

That right then, was the very first time that I ever saw mi Abeulo' s teeth, as he smiled with both pride and satisfaction. After saving Master Jack's life, things changed for me in many ways, and Old Master Strickland even insisted, that I was no longer required to go into the fields at all. And my time became all of Abeulo' s, when and if Master Jack did not require my assistance for anything.

I could go with him every day if I liked, to assist him in his hunting and then in about five or six months, when Master Jack's leg had mended up properly, we became even more inseparable. Master Jack seemed downright possessive of me, and during all of those months of being bedridden, he decided right then to change my life, in all ways. His father had always not had a favorable opinion of us "negra," and he always felt as though we were unable and unwilling to learn, but to Master Jack, I was the exception to the rule.

So I would be his great experiment, to ultimately show his father that I was different and how truly wrong he was for thinking that we negra "were all alike," and more importantly that we "were not fellow human beings." He then would secretly teach me everything that he knew and everything that he had been taught in school. He would give me the power to change my own life through an education of sorts. And ultimately, one day I could and would be able to change my own destiny.

So, that began my formal educational process, and he set everything up. One of the line shacks in the woods became our secret schoolhouse. He was the teacher and I was the pupil, and he made sure that two or three days each and every week for years upon years, at least until I turned about nineteen, if my old memory serves me right, I was in our classroom. No matter if he was away at school or not. And, if Master Jack was at home for whatever the time frame, he always made sure that he gave me an educational lesson.

I first learned how to formally read and then write, and then mathematics, and science, and history. Then finally, he taught me Latin, because it was the basis of all of the languages of Europe. I read all of the books that he had used at all levels of his schooling, from elementary school through his college books.

He attended William and Mary College, which is the second-oldest institution of higher learning in the Unites States, founded in 1693. And it is located in the Old Dominion, in the town of Williamsburg. William and Mary College has educated three US Presidents, and 16 of the original signers of the

Declaration of Independence, besides a host of other important people who helped to develop the young nation.

Master Jack did quite well there, and he got a double degree in History and English. His books then turned into law school-books, when he went to the University of North Carolina school of Law, at Chapel Hill to secure his law degree.

He also requested that I read the Classics, and study about the Enlightenment figures which included Shakespeare, Montesquieu, Marquis de Condorcet, John Locke, Rousseau, Emile du Chatelet, Alexander Dumas, Edmund Burke, and the great Francois-Marie Arouet, who the entire world knows as Voltaire. All of these works and ideas influenced important thinkers of both the French and American Revolutions. And, out of all of them, I really liked Voltaire the most, I think, because of his amazingly liberated mind and, really for his "forward in time" way of thinking. He has this one powerful quote that will stick with me, for the rest of my time here, while living this life. And it says, 'Life is thickly sown with thorns, and I know no other remedy than to pass quickly through them. The longer we dwell on our misfortunes, the greater is their power to harm us.'

Master Jack also requested that I study a French fellow named, Alexis de Tocqueville because of his book, *Democracy in America*, which was published in two volumes, 1835 and 1840 respectively. In them, he explores the effects of rising equality of social conditions on the individual, and the state in western societies. Another book that he had me to read was his most prized possession he used to always say, it was called *A General Historie of the Robberies and Murders of the Most Notorious Pyrates*, by Charles Johnson, which was first published in 1724 in Britain. This was a book about pirates, which seemed strange to me.

And, I could tell that he still was just as obsessed as he was from when he was a young boy, but it still made for good reading.

I also was required to learn how to play the game of chess, which has some of the same elements of life itself that are crucial parts of the game. Things like being able to have quick thinking and an ability to strategize moves that are to come and plotting two or three moves down the line, based upon what your opponent would, or could do.

Chess then would ultimately help me to understand and view life through the learning of the game itself. Because chess is a simple yet complex game with all of its many facets and dynamics that involve all of the different possible moves that occur with the object being to outthink your opponent. So, in as much, Master Jack was downright pleased with my educational progression.

Because, he said that I had a thirst for reading, once I had learned how to read that is. And, just about everything that he had formally learned in school, he taught to me or eventually taught to me. And secretly unbeknownst to him, I then, in turn, taught it to our family members.

Think of it as passing on the learning. So this then, is the real reason why our family holds a special value on obtaining an education, because, education has changed all of our lives. Okay, then about the time that I turned ten, mi Abeulo took me aside one evening before bedtime, and told me in front of mi Madre, that it was time for me to take the next step and begin my formal warrior training. Warrior training...I thought, what is warrior training? He then explained that my learning routine would be to first build up my endurance and stamina, and strength.

I would then learn how to deal with the cold and the heat, and all other elements. After I had mastered the first phase by the passing of a test or a type of challenge, I would then learn how to use all of the types of known weaponry with the first lesson being, to learn how to fight up close using the art of stabbing with a small blade or bushido—with one, or both hands as a basis or foundation. Then I would learn the use of the long blade or bushido with one or both hands, and then, the use of a bow and short and long arrows, which he felt that I had already somewhat mastered, because of my life saving shot that had saved young Master Jack.

I would then learn how to properly throw things, like spears and stars and then finally, how to effectively shoot guns and rifles. After the weapons stage was mastered, by the passing of a test or challenge, I would then be introduced to the use of my hands and feet, and teeth as weapons.

This weaponry stage had its own individual seven levels or techniques that had to be learned, and then mastered in something called a training circle, by the passing of its own test or challenge. This "circle," as he called it, would be critical in the learning of these seven levels. Then and only then, after time had passed, would I have earned the right to become a warrior or a razor, which is an implement or tool of war, he said.

So, the very next morning, we went out before daybreak and after easily giving our guardian angel the slip, we went to a secret place that Abuelo had found, where we could begin my training in total privacy. The first thing that we did when we arrived was to sit down cross-legged and concentrate by looking into each other's eyes. And, Abeulo started to tell me about one of the oldest fabled cultures of written European record, a place called Sparta, which was one of the very first of the Greek warrior city state cultures to gain prominence.

Some of these Spartans, like the great warrior King Leonidas, were even said to supposedly be direct descendants of the powerful half human and half god warrior called Hercules. When all Spartan children were first born, they are inspected right then and there from out of the womb. And, if they were deemed not fit and healthy enough to be allowed to live, they were immediately discarded.

As early as two years old, Spartan male children were introduced to the fires of combat, and were expected to fight back, and learn to respond to any and all threats. These Spartan male children, mi Abeulo said, were taken from their families, as early as 7 years old for the ritual of Agoge with its three stages, and plunged into a world of violence and combat, and then turned into true warriors, that were in service for Spartan society. They had a saying as they went into war which was 'With this or upon this,' which meant to either, come back carrying your shield, or come back upon it.

They were taught to fight and scratch and claw, and that 'every day was a good day to die,' and that there was no greater glory for a Spartan Warrior to achieve in his lifetime, than to die on the field of battle, while in the service of Sparta. They were actually trained to never surrender and to never retreat on the battlefield, and to never show mercy to any enemy.

After they had received the maximum training lessons at the paides or first stage, and had passed its series of tests, they were turned out butt naked. Each one, alone with nothing on his person, no matter the elements, be that super-hot or freezing cold, even a steady downpour of rain, or dangerous gusty winds, or blinding snow. And then, he was told, that he must survive in the wilds of nature at all costs. And, if he were able to make it back, then he would prove himself worthy to be called a true Spartan.

They were bred to be warriors first, and to deal with pain. And, they trained all of their lives for that heroic moment, when they would be called into service for Spartan society. They were truly the world's first professional soldiers, and some say that they were the finest soldiers that the world has ever known. These Spartan warriors' training principles would then be our guide, in terms of his overall training of me.

We would then add in, what he had learned in the lands of mi Abuela, to complete the seven levels of samurai warrior training. And to really add precision, relentlessness, and fierceness from the lands of mi Abeula, to enhance the battlefield style that he wished for me to acquire. Because, his mission, for the sake of our Family's survival in this strange land, was to create a living weapon—that had no peer or match. One who was our family's guardian and ultimate earthly protector.

So with that, mi Abeulo made me get up and start running back and forth, for hours upon end. All that I did the first few months was nothing but run, and run with and without, the use of my arms—with my hands behind my back, holding a stick. I ran so much that many a night, after training was over, all I could do was barely get to where we lived and pass out asleep as soon as I got there.

He had me run everywhere, all of the time. And, then low and behold, he had the nerve enough to start running with me. And, I remember that at first, I always had a hard time, just keeping up with him. He even used to tie a rope around my waist, and then tie the other end around his. And when we ran, I had to learn to be light on my feet, so that his running style would not pull me off my own stride. He had a really smooth stride and he never appeared to ever get tired, and his energy level seemed bottomless and really endless. It was as if he ran with the determination of a horse, and he also taught me how to run in a similar manner.

Finally, after I had—it seemed to me—run forever, he told me about a word called 'Agon,' which was a word from the Greek language and translated, it meant "for the pain to overcome." Abeulo, as I look back on it, was only making me ready to deal with any situation and he trained me hard each and every training day. So that by learning to push myself, I could learn to deal with and overcome pain, and thereby overcome any obstacle.

So he would just say 'Agon' to me, over and over. And, just when I felt as if I wanted to give up, he would shout 'Agon,' which always made me grit my teeth and try just a little bit harder. Finally, after at first strictly just running, he then started to add other things that he required me to do.

He had all of these tests that he devised to make me stronger, like taking a rope and tying one end around my waist and then taking the other end and throwing it over a tree branch. Then he'd take the free end of the rope and require that I crawl or run to a line, that he had scratched out in the ground in front of me. He would constantly pull hard on his end, which made the rope snatch me backwards, and I could not stop striving, until I had reached the line mark set ahead of me.

This would always make my legs burn like fire and hurt. He always told me to push myself, 'Agon, think of your task, and work through and or around the pain and, concentrate Balaam,

'Agon,' 'Agon,' he would always say. So I was trained to see pain as just a state of mind, or being, and something that I had to learn to accept and then deal with, because it is a fact of life on the battlefield.

My mind was a key to my salvation, so a strong body was nothing, if the mind itself was weak. So Abeulo did all of these things to make the body and mind hurt, and then repeat the torture until I almost felt like passing out. So from standing in freezing cold water, to standing in heat straight from Hades—to standing in hail the size of walnuts, and everything in between, I was forced to endure it all.

Until one day, pain or really the thought of pain, became small or insignificant to my mind. I learned how to not think about it and how to block it out, and not let it stop me from [handling] my task or duty. I was also trained to breathe effectively, and learn to concentrate upon just taking air in, and releasing it out properly from my lungs in sequence. I was then trained to use the breath to do a series of exercises that were pronounced "ujjayi," or something like this. Because Abeulo' s pronunciation, of Abuela's native language was sometimes hard to pronounce, in the tongue of los Blancos.

These exercises made me concentrate on the prana which is the energy or life force that governs everything that we do in this lifetime. In reality, this was a real key to helping me become more centered within myself, and this helped my overall balance. These exercises also were designed to increase my overall flexibility and made me more agile.

More importantly, they also were designed to make me concentrate on controlling my breathing, because in the heat of any battle, the heart rate always increases. And, improper breathing could lead to a loss of focus, and of one's desire. So I was taught how to ration my breaths, and to make sure that I stayed relaxed, so that my heart would not beat all wild and out of control, which could lead to my downfall on the field of battle.

I was also taught how to hurdle and jump over objects like big rocks or tree branches that were stacked up onto one another, and how to climb up and onto and over things. Then I was taught to live and forage off of the land and how to survive, and how to evade in the wilds. He also taught me how to swim and how to float.

He taught me how to evade in water by using a reed, which was simply a certain kind of hollow stick to breathe through, while lying motionless on the river or lake bottom. He always spoke of words that would become ingrained into my very fiber and being, and these were: "duty, respect, and honor, improvise, adapt and overcome." These words, which were really the pillars of my foundation, he said, were vital to my survival. And, they would at some point come in handy, so I must learn their meaning and how they related to whatever was my task at hand.

Abuelo, also taught me to use the Sanskrit mantra of 'Om Mani Padme Hum,' along with my breath, as a way to cool down and end my training for that day. I would first take many deep breaths, and then begin saying the mantra out loud or silently to myself, over and over again, until which at some point, everything becomes soothing, as my racing thoughts slowly faded to black. The use of this mantra is supposed to somehow invoke powerful blessings of something called Chenrezig, which is the Tibetan embodiment of compassion. So this was perfect way to relax and let my body, spirit and mind all rest by, speaking the true sound of truth (the mantra), as I passed into the black and dark void, that is called sleep.

Abeulo would constantly make me practice over and over, and he never accepted anything less and if he thought that I was not fully focused on my task that was in front of me, he would make me stop and begin running until he thought that I was finally paying attention to it. His job as he saw it, was to get me to a place where I could work out with him, in other words he was training me to come up to his level. I one day asked him, "Mi Abeulo, why must I constantly practice over and over?"

He pondered my question and looked deeply into my eyes, and said, "I am training you to become a warrior, or really a razor which is a tool of war, Balaam. Because, don't think for one minute that you are always going to be a slave!" For you are destined for far greater things my young apprentice and remember that the things that I am showing you, are only things that will aid you in your journey that you are now on. Your path is predestined Balaam, and Jeremiah chapter 29 verse 11 of the Good Book is my rule, in this case for success, so I must do my part to ensure our family's survival.

So from that day moving forward, I never again asked about my excessive training regime, and just did whatever I was asked or told because, Abeluo was always very serious and, he had this look of determination and of something sinister about himself. And, he never smiled and to some he was downright scary. And looking back, he actually to me, looked very much like a First American, with his buckskin pants and moccasin shoes that shod his feet.

He had a bow and a quill of arrows always slung low over his shoulders, with his blowgun hanging from his quill of arrows.

He had a very large buck knife, with small bladed sword and a smaller knife that he could throw from some amazing distances and angles, all of which were attached at his waist. He also had some metal in a star or 5-point design. And, he could throw the "stars," as he called them, rapidly and on target, as he kind of just flicked his wrist from the side.

His hair was closely cropped on the sides, but the rest flowed down his back, like a horse's mane. But most times he kept it in one long braid that went down his back almost to his waist. His eyes were piercing and strong, and he looked like one tough Hombre, and not one to ever, ever mess with. He was the one person on the entire Plantation, who was both feared and respected at all times, by everyone, even the Blancos, and you could tell this because when he walked, people moved out of his way.

And, when Abeluo opened up his word hole, they listened because it was as if they knew something that we did not, which was that, it was always very important to understand what he was saying at all times. He truly was a man of very few words, and when he did talk, he always choose them extremely carefully. He would also quote different proverbs and sayings that he had learned and believed in when he was a little boy, like " If you look in only one direction, your neck will become stiff" or " true to God who made me."

He could speak many languages, at least seven or maybe it was eight. And, he had a very unique belief system, that was based upon his belief in two things, one—'The Tree of Life' and all of its many forms, that are seen in all of the world's religious beliefs and two The Ethic of Reciprocity.' Mi Abeluo believed

'The Tree of Life' to be the common thread or symbol in nearly every culture in the world.

And more importantly that, in the different religions of these cultures, that the tree symbolizes both resurrection and renewal. And, that it is both masculine and feminine. And, that it also bears fruits and seeds, which contain the essence of the tree and its source of constant regeneration. So, because this tree is constant in all world religions, it therefore is the link between them all, and therefore to a similar belief system, with a commonly shared but unknown deity.

So he believed in the unknown and original One True God of all the gods, whom he said was originally named Amen-ra, who is the Egyptian sun god. And, because of his supreme belief in The Tree of Life, he felt that we were really just, in reality praying to the same God. Even though we think that our gods differ from one another because of our different reasons and concerns, and cultures and or languages. So because of this self-professed conviction of his, he was therefore able to connect with any and all religions of the known world, and probably those in the unknown parts of the world, too.

He talked about 'The Ethic of Reciprocity,' being an ethical code that is also known as 'The Golden Rule,' that basically states that, "one should treat others as one would like others to treat oneself, or one should not treat others in ways that one would not like to be treated." Simply it just means that each person has the right to just treatment, and a reciprocal responsibility to ensure this same treatment for others. It can be found in all of the world's cultures, and it is present in certain forms in the philosophies of many of the oldest world cultures, and hence the world's religions.

From Ancient Egypt to China and the great Confucius, to even the Code of Hammurabi, this framework appears in many different civilizations, but possesses the same or similar sayings, that are all basically saying the same thing. All of which, coincidently has come down through humankind, all throughout man's known history on the planet. From 'An eye for an eye and a tooth for a tooth' or ' Do to the doer to cause that he do' to Isocrates who said' Do not do to others what would anger you if done to you by others,' to Plato's Socrates who said, 'One should never do wrong in return, nor mistreat any man, no matter how one has been mistreated by him' or the great Confucius who said, ' Do not do to others that which we do not want them to do to us.'

So mi Abeulo was able to say and think of this rule in many different ways, and he was always saying it over and over again, just in different ways, which always seemed intelligent and insightful. He would say, 'Blessed is he who preferreth his brother before himself' or 'Do unto others as you would have them do unto you' or 'Putting oneself in the place of another, one should not kill nor cause another to kill.' Or 'One should never do that to another which one regards as injurious to one's own self...' Or he would say, 'Never impose on others what you would not choose for yourself' or 'And as ye would that men should do to you, do ye also to them likewise," or 'Hurt no one so that no one may hurt you" and 'Love your neighbor as yourself,' which all sounded to me like 'Love your fellow as yourself.'

He also liked to say, 'I am a stranger to no one, and no one is a stranger to me, indeed I am a friend to all.' And, 'Those who show their affection to such as came to them for refuge and entertain no desire in their hearts for things given to the latter but give them preference over themselves.' One day he even took me aside and showed me in the Good Book itself, in the Book of Genesis Chapter 21, verses 23 and 24 where it was written down, and thus it was an important concept to both respect and live by. This is how he lived his life and how he believed that we as people should truly treat one another.

He also believed that life was like a circle, where everything in that circle was connected to one another on different levels. So what one can see is affected by what one can't see, and vice versa. So that is why life to him had to be respected, and was precious at all times because, the interconnection between everyone and everything was clear and very evident, if you just looked hard enough.

He also was not here to be anyone's friend, and he never needed anyone to ever like him either. Mi Abuelo just wanted you to respect him, his family and his work ethic. He just wanted and demanded to be left alone, and his sole motivation was to train me to be the best that there ever was, because that is how he was trained himself.

That is why every detail went into my training, every movement, every motion, was drilled over and over again into my very being. He was making me into what he already was, and to be honest, he did even a better job than he had hoped for, because in the end I became much more than just a hunter tracker or guide, but the first complete and true warrior for The House of Calais Vega. With his training, he carefully sculpted me like a clay maker does to a fine vase or dish.

Now while all of this training was going on, I began to notice this very pretty girl, who appeared to be about my age, and for a long time I did not even know her name. So on good day, which was Sunday picnic day, I finally got a chance by sheer luck to both see her up close and also to learn her name, which was Mamie Elizabeth. And I only learned that, because I heard someone shouting it out loudly. I would never even have had the nerve to go up to her and ask her, because I felt as if I would simply melt in her presence.

She was bronze in color and had this really sweet way that her mouth looked when she smiled or looked happy. Her eyes were hazel, and her hair was like corn silk, and her skin was buttery smooth. I was in love with her, I reckon from that moment, and my next problem was how to 'court her,' but not *seem* like I was courting her. Because she had a lot of suitors, and admirers and men of all ages always marveled at her beauty and grace, and she had a lot of attention from everyone within the slave community, from the field hands to the house servants, and all in between. But her Daddy, Henry Allen, who was nobody's fool, was well aware of what men saw when they looked at her, so he was really quick to interfere with anyone's plans of capturing and conquering his much beloved and only daughter.

She worked in the big house, as a servant to Old Master Strickland's children. And, so this made her able and ready to deal with anything that came in her direction, especially when it came to her fellow slaves. Her father was the main blacksmith, and thus he had certain freedoms that were also given to her. And they were always going into Fayetteville, to get the things that he needed to perform his daily duties. I did not even know that she even knew who I was, until one day we had a chance encounter at the big barn, where her daddy was working on something that particular day.

Master Jack's new horse had thrown a shoe, and I was told to walk it over to the big barn and get it re-shoed, so that we could go out and hunt that afternoon. As I walked the horse, a fine-looking grey bay to the barn, my heart fluttered like a newborn bird's wings, as I wondered if she would be somewhere around the barn. Her daddy had his back to me as I entered the barn, but as soon as he heard me approaching, he turned around and smiled and said, "Come in young man, and you are the near famous Balaam, are you not? Please sit here and rest your feet," as he took the horse, and he had this smile on his face.

And, as he stepped back, out stepped the lovely Mamie! Okay, so I still had not uttered a word yet, since entering into the barn, and now I really had lost all words. Mamie was also smiling, like folks do when it is time to eat on the good day or like on Christmas morning. She then said, "Balaam you sure have gotten taller, and you are becoming quite a man these days." So she knew my name, but "becoming quite a man," so what did she mean by that I wondered?

"How are your Ma and Grandfather?" she asked next. She then asked, "Can you even talk? Kitty Cat got your tongue? Do you even talk at all, and maybe all that being up in the woods all of the time, hunting and fishing done took your voice?" She then turned to her father and said, "Poppa, what is wrong with him, is he deaf or something?"

"Hush child with all of that foolishness," said Henry Allen, not even looking around at us, "he is just a serious young man, from very serious people is all, and please don't judge him by his lack of talk and such. For I have watched him grow up, and he is quite capable of talking if he needs to." I just stood there and smiled at Mamie. And finally I said, "Pleased to meet you

Mamie Elizabeth. And my folks are fine. And, no the woods have not taken my voice, I was just caught off guard by your kindness is all, so I just needed a moment to re-gather my thoughts."

I stood there watching her reaction to my simple explanation, and then she just laughed out loud, which caused me to laugh. And pretty soon, we were acting as if we had known each other for all of our lives. Her daddy finished shoeing the horse, and so I said my goodbyes to the both of them. And as I was leaving out, she suddenly reached out and ever so slightly touched my arm at the elbow and said in a smooth tone that, "It was ever so nice to finally get a chance to meet you Balaam, the hero of the Strickland Plantation," as her eyes twinkled with satisfaction, and delight.

So with that, we became like an item, and it was only her, that I constantly thought about over and over in my mind. I could hardly wait until I got a chance to see her the next time, whenever that was, and she always seemed so happy just to see me. Her sweetness has always made me ask a simple question, "I always wonder does the fish know that it has swallowed the hook when it eats the bait," because I had swallowed her hook, and it sure felt both good and right.

I will then always remember the first time that she kissed me on the cheek. I thought that my knees would buckle, and I felt flush and kind of hot about the face. So from that very first day in the barn until now, I have always loved my beloved Mamie, because she saved me from a lonely fate.

And, she gave me the strength to learn to love another human being. She accepted me and my many moods, and she always had this way of making me feel like a whole person and that only I mattered at all times, in her universe. She also always made me feel like a person that had value and a certain importance in her life, and she has always had this way of just holding me and when she did, it seemed like everything in my world was okay and right.

The next thing that sticks out in my mind is how, when I was eleven, my Mother pulled me aside one day and told me in her serious sounding voice, that she had something mighty important to tell me. She took me in front of the barn and started to talk but she stopped. Because, up until that time, it had only been just her and me and she seemed really nervous.

"My darling Balaam," she started off with, "now you know that you will always be my 'Baby, and my Little Man' don't you?" I nodded and said, "Yes Madre," feeling somewhat scared, like she was about to tell me that she was about to leave or something. She went on, "But I am," she stammered, " I is..." she then gulped hard and then said loudly, "You are getting a new Daddy. His name is Rufus, and he is a good man, and we are going to get properly hitched, and I want you to know that no matter what you will always come first in my life. I need you to understand, and not feel put-off by all of this, because we will both love you."

And with that she yelled, "Rufus come here please." Rufus stepped from around the barn smiling like he had just found some real money on the ground, and he grabbed a hold of my Madre's hand, and looked me dead in my eyes, to gauge my reaction to the news. So that is why he was always coming around, I thought. Almost at the same time, I thought, hum why does he not even have a last name, everybody has a last name.

I finally asked, "So what does Abeulo think? Well he has already given us his blessing, he answered, and Abeulo said that only if you agreed, would he agree. I looked at him up and down, and then back at my Madre, and they both had this look of uncertainty, while I took my time and pondered for a few moments. Now, Rufus was the head yard hand whose job it was at all times to maintain and keep the grounds on the entire property well-groomed strictly for appearances sake, because as Old Master Strickland use to say, "The first impression, is always a lasting impression."

He was tall, over six feet for sure, and he was strong as an ox, and a tireless worker. He had first noticed mi Madre on our first day on The Strickland Plantation, and he had openly courted her ever since. He had a reputation as a vicious fighter, and he tended to drink heavily whenever he could acquire a taste of the shine liquor.

But he was very gentle with mi Madre though, mostly because he was scared of mi Abuelo, who had let him know right off that his family was off limits for any kind of foolishness, and that he had no problem gutting him like you would do to any hog, if he ever forgot his place. So after being properly warned, Rufus, had just bided his time, and slowly worked his way into mi Madre's life, mind and heart. I gathered my thoughts and said, that I guess it was okay with me, as long as he respected mi Madre at all times. Because trust me, if he did not, it would not only be Abuelo that would be looking for him.

They both looked a bit stunned by my comments, and Rufus nervously kind of half laughed it off, but they had both gotten what they had wanted, so they hugged and smiled and with that, they went to Old Master Strickland to get his consent. They were hitched in less than six months, and mi Madre moved out of the barn and into the slave quarters to begin her new married life.

And, in less than four years, my little brother Robert and then my little sister Sophia, and my other little brother James, were all born in a row. Now Rufus already had three other nearly grown children, all boys, from the first woman in his life. They were never married, and their union was just to have some fun let's say. And, one day after not being able to take being a slave any longer, she tried to escape and was never ever seen again. Although some folks said that she had met her maker as her fate for running away, and that the overseers had kept it hushed up, as to not to arouse any suspicions about her murder.

So our family became bigger and bigger, with now ten mouths in total to feed, because Rufus' three eldest sons considered my Madre their new Madre. Because, she was really the only mother that they had ever known, who acted like a mother that cares for her children, so they always came to her for every meal that they ate. I stayed up in the barn with Abeulo, and out of their way, because eight mouths to feed was hard, let alone another one or two with my and Abuelo's presence. So I did not get a chance to see them very much, with my training and helping Master Jack out and all, but it was always fun when we did see one another, for I have always loved my two younger brothers and sister all very much.

Rufus' three sons, John, Mark and Paul, were all field hands, and were all somewhat quiet people, but with Rufus as their father they seemed destined for trouble, because trouble was born inside of them. Because secretly, Rufus, as it turned out was always a lot of trouble, and had a bad reputation because after he had, had a taste, he liked to fight. He had broken one man's nose, and another man's arm, in drunken fits and the more he tasted, the more he became unmanageable, and he eventually lost his desire to work.

Now fighting fellow slaves was okay in certain respects because it kept everyone, in the slave community divided. But when the grounds started to look raggedy, Old Master Strickland felt that he needed some discipline. So, he ordered that he be flogged with twenty lashes, and then locked away in one of the salt shacks, for thirty days—to teach him a business lesson.

But when the thirty days were over, Rufus came out a changed man who was determined to run away that very day, without his family. He told no one in the family of his plan, and after a welcome back meal of greens, pan bread, and honey, he quietly disappeared into the night taking only a blanket and some water with him. It was about midmorning of the next day, when people finally had realized that he was gone. And although he had almost a half days head start, it was hot that day and he was lazy and thirsty, so finding him with the dogs was easy. When the Blanco overseers caught up to him, he resisted, fought back, and was actually winning on all accounts, until they got tired of fighting a human ox and just finally shot him to death.

Around midday of the next day, the overseers returned with his body that was all bruised and beaten up and thrown over the side of a horse. His neck had rope burns on it, his body looked as if it had been dragged along the ground, and his face was barely recognizable. Mi Madre screamed in horror and mi Abuelo had to restrain her from trying to approach his body.

She was never, ever the same again because, every man that she had ever loved had died on her, leaving her husbandless and all alone, with hungry mouths to feed. We were all made to watch, as they strung his lifeless body up on a tree branch by the slave quarters for all to see what happens when you ran away and then tried to resist.

All of us boys especially Rufus's three older sons, were all angry and hurt. And I truly believe that it was being forced, to watch our dead daddy, swinging from that tree that terrible day, which is the reason that those three, all changed for the worse. And sadly, that they all ended up in the situations that they eventually did. Fate has a way of repeating itself, and Abeulo was right, that, "if you don't learn from your mistakes, or from the mistakes of others, you are doomed to repeat them."

The life of a slave up until 1822 was a tough but livable, an existence based upon the pillars of capitalism and free labor. Working six days a week, and seven during all harvest times, the slave was up before first light and in the fields at least until dusk. Field slaves had no life except for the fields, and it was a constant strain on the body and then the mind. Then after 1822, the laws changed even more, and slavery became an even more hellish ordeal, which resulted in a lot of slaves simply both wearing out and burning out from the strain.

My new older brothers had a hard life, especially after their daddy died, and they all were never the same. John, who everyone called "Good Ole John Boy" being the oldest, was affected the most by seeing his father's death and naturally he became the most rebellious of the trio. He simply would not work any longer. And, he really did not care for the great institution of slavery.

So, no matter what they did to him, be that physical beatings, or floggings with either the lash or the whip, he resisted by lacking the willpower and energy to work in the fields. It was as if his daddy's dying had sapped his strength. And, he had this anger all built up inside of him that would not go away—like a raging storm. He had become like a powder keg that was ready to explode. He then started sneaking off, in the night and getting into fights and, taking on the general disposition of his late daddy.

He got into a fight one day in the field with another worker, and he severely hurt the young man, over a joke about how he looked, because he was still hung over from the night before— that was filled with drinking. And, "Good Ole John Boy," was flogged thirty lashes with the whip, for damaging another commodity. Upon his recovery he was caught for stealing and with that, Old Master Strickland right then had had his fill with his behavior.

And, he decided to send him to another plantation, down in a place called Louisiana that was bordered by a swamp. John was suddenly taken away one day in chains, to a new life of constant hardships and despair. No one even had a chance to say "Goodbye" to him, and with that, mi Madre had lost another loved one, but at least he still was alive—or so we always thought. We never ever knew what became of our "Good Ole John Boy," because communication between plantations was strictly prohibited and forbidden.

For slaves were always kept in the dark, so to speak, as to the goings on at other plantations and we dared not ask about him either. For the slave life in itself was tough, and as a slave you were not even allowed to gather in groups larger than four at a time. Slaves were also never permitted to use their native languages, and they could not even openly sing songs from their old tribes.

Slaves also could not believe in their old gods, and the breaking of any of the rules was punishable by maiming and or death. And many a slave had body parts that were chopped off as a consequence for breaking a rule or law. The slave owners needed complete control and openly acting out was dealt with quickly and harshly. So, John, after another flogging that was sixty lashes this time, was dealt right away to another life right before our eyes. This was also a serious and ruthless warning, to anyone else who wanted to follow in his hardheaded footsteps.

The next thing that I remember is that after years of courting, when we both turned seventeen, I finally got up the courage and asked Mamie's Poppa for her hand in marriage. I really did not know what to expect, and really had no clue as to how her parents felt about us getting hitched, but her poppa was very pleased. And when he gave us his blessing, Mamie leapt up into my arms with unbridled joy, and she actually started to cry tears of happiness.

About eight months later, we had a small, quiet and simple ceremony in the main garden area of the big house, in front of mi Madre, and my sister and brothers, along with Master Jack, mi Abeulo, and Mamie's parents. Master Jack read from the Good Book and conducted the service, and when he was finished Mamie's daddy and mi Abuelo both held the broomstick. As I looked at Mamie, my knees got really weak, because she looked absolutely beautiful.

She had an old and somewhat faded crème colored satin dress on, that the Strickland's had provided, and her hair and skin both glistened and sparkled. The womenfolk had put some nice flowers in her hair, I think lilies and she smelled like a wonderful cross between flowers and sweet honey. Her smile was so pretty, and she looked incredibly happy, as I just watched the expressions on her face.

As I scooped her up in my arms, I marveled at how light that she felt, up in my arms and I was struck with a deep sense of responsibility that comes with having a wife. I, or excuse me, we then hopped over the broomstick, and our lives together were now one. We went to the barn to be alone for our wedding night and it was fixed up really nice. There were candles everywhere, already burning, which gave the whole place a very reassuring look. Someone, whom I found out later, was Abeulo, had put flower petals everywhere—all around a small bed, on the bed, and even leading into the barn.

On the table was an already prepared meal of johnny cakes with honey and blackberries, some boiled-in-water taters, fresh string beans and a jug of lemon water. As we sat down and ate very slowly, and silently smiling at one another, I realized just how much I truly loved her, as the candlelight reflected off of her beautiful face. She was my woman, and I was her man, and as she smiled, and smiled, I knew that our union was right. Within ten months, our first child, a girl was born—whom we named Carmelita Ceceilia. She had her mother's looks, with long straight beautiful black hair and she had mi Madre's eyes.

The whole birthing process was hard on Mamie, and she was really weak and tired, so I took "Lita" from her arms and sat there just holding her, until Mamie finally went to sleep. I then took my little girl outside to meet the moonlight and nighttime air for her very first time, to meet the ancestors for the very first time. And I held her up to the starlit sky, and as I held her aloft, I started to chant.

"In the tradition of my elders, and our ancestors, I offer up to you, my first-born child, and please bless this newborn girl child, and keep her safe. Because if the ancestors are in the womb then she is, what we have always been. She is a link to the past, and a key to our family's future. So, please help me to stay strong, so that I might keep her and her mother safe. And thank you so very much for giving to us, such a healthy and pretty little child, as she will make a fine addition to our family." At that exact moment in time, I was then even more determined to make a good life for her and Mamie or die trying. Because looking at that little baby in swaddling clothes, who was so helpless, yet alive here for barely less than a day, and who was part of me and Mamie—all made my heart melt, like a flame does to a candle. What type of life would my little girl have in slavery, I wondered?

How could I improve or change her lot in this life, so that she could live the life of a freed person? What must I do to change her life? As I pondered these questions over and over in my mind, I looked above to the heavens at the stars, and I strangely started to realize that my life with Mamie would never ever be the same again. Because, we now had an added responsibility, that was simply bigger than the both of us.

Little Lita or "CC or Leelee," as her sisters always called her, was a happy baby and she never cried, unless she was hungry or wet. And, she used to smile a lot in her early years of life. She had this bubbly kind of laugh, and her eyes could focus on something from an early age, as if she was studying or observing whatever she was looking at, with a keen interest and so you could just tell that she was smart as a whip.

Then before you know it came her sister Christine Lydia who we called "Chris or C, Lydia or CL or Tine." And then, in time came Kimberly Treva who we call "Kit,"or KT, and then the twins first Hazel Rhonda, and then two minutes later, Paula Tammi who we call "H and P" for short, because at first it was just hard to tell the two of them apart. The twins have always called each other twin, or my twin, and even to this day; this is how they address one another. And they only respond to one another, and no one else in this manner, as if they and only they alone, have the privilege to use this special name, that is strictly between the two of them.

Then as time kept moving, we were finally blessed with a gift of a son, whom we named L' Ouverture, after the great Haitian General, Toussaint L' Ouverture, who came into our family last but not least, bringing up the rear. The girls were extremely excited to have a little brother. And he became like a living baby doll that the girls could dote on and play with, and love to no end.

PART THREE

L. ALLEN FARMER

Diabolus fecit, ut id facerum
The Devil made me do it

We cannot wish for that we know not.

THREE

....

M
y next memory was of mi Abeulo, and how on the night before each New Year, he would make us go to the nearest body of water and he would set adrift a small wooden boat. He said that this was done with a prayer and offering to Iemanja, who is [the Brazilian Sea Goddess] an Alkebu-lan Sea Goddess who watched over her worshippers. She was the protector of everyone who has ever traveled on the seas and has been watching over folks from the beginning of time, some say. She also had protected him in all of his sea voyages so that is why he continued to pay homage to her for the rest of his natural life.

So afterwards on each and every New Year, no matter where I was, I too would carve out my own little boat and with a tree branch or limb, I would set it afloat in any water. It is strange the way that this yearly ritual affected me, and how grateful I was to just see another year. I wondered how this was being repeated all throughout the world, and if this act ever brought anyone a certain amount of comfort, in other's minds like it did for me, and mi Abuelo. I always felt after everything that had happened in a year that this ritual was seemingly a way in which the past year's troubles were washed away, like a hard summer rainstorm does the heat.

But this event had an even more somber effect upon Abeulo, because it was his way of paying homage to the past. And also, it was as if he was paying a secret tribute to some figure in his past, which I found out much later, was to mi Abeula. Mi Abeulo never talked about her but on a certain date each and every year, March 19th, which I found out was always on her birthday, he would seeming close up into himself and shut everybody out and disappear until the next day.

I remember that I secretly followed him once, or so I thought, and watched him as he lit a fire to a small toy boat that he had carved out of some wood. And, he pushed it out towards deeper waters, and then watched as it was taken out further away from the shoreline by the rhythm of the water's waves. He slumped down cross legged, on the shore and watched in a lonely manner, as it burned up into nothingness and became no more.

Only after it was totally gone, did he acknowledge my presence, and sort of become himself again. I looked him in his tear-filled eyes, and asked him what was wrong, and was there anything that I could do to cheer him up or to ease his pain. He got up and put his arm around me and we walked back to the fire that he had built next to some logs, and as we sat on the logs, he began to tell me about her story.

(Abuela's story)

Mi Abeula was from a land that was far, far over the sea on the other side of the world. And, it was during Abuelo's time that he spent in that foreign land where they first met, eventually fell in love, and had mi Madre—and that was that. But the real story was much deeper and complex.

Mi Abeula, was from a nation that valued both respect, and honor above everything else. And, for the two of them to initially meet, and then fall in love is even more remarkable. Abeulo was given the task of protecting his master Senor Vega's youngest brother, who was involved in various sea trading activities.

His ship was on a trading mission when it was blown off course in a storm, towards a group of islands that were known as "off limits" to all traders and seafaring merchants, because of the warrior and feudalistic behaviors of its inhabitants. For most visitors were rounded up and never seen again and were presumed dead or were killed.

The young Master Vega's prized boat was nearly destroyed in the storm, which made seeking landfall imperative—with no other option. The bow and the mast had both cracked under the constant weight of the wind and water, and the entire crew was lucky to even be alive. The landing party upon setting foot onto this foreign soil was immediately noticed as strangers, and almost within a hour of being on land, they were attacked in a series of running battles or skirmishes that only seemed to get worse.

They were finally captured after a final protracted and heated battle that saw everyone except Abuelo, either wounded and or killed. These angry warriors were almost crazy in their approach or eagerness to join the battle. And, even in the face of death, they displayed an honor in battle not ever seen by any Blanco. They attacked and attacked, and even Abuelo himself was amazed at how they just kept coming and coming until the landing party had run out of ammunition.

It was during the final assault on their position that the bravery of Abuelo caught the eyes and minds of the warriors, as he defended his severely wounded young master, until he was forcefully overcome, as they overran their position. They were all about to be dispatched to the next life, when another group of warriors, who were opposed to the initial group, swooped in and saved the day by rescuing them because they had secretly been watching the battle the whole time, and they too, were impressed with Abuelo's bravery, and skill with a knife and sword.

They took them quite a ways away, into the mountains to their compound, where they lived in houses that had funny shaped roofs. They took what was left of the landing party into a large house and their womenfolk were called to help tend to the wounded, and one of these women turned out to be mi Abeula. She was pretty, very pretty with soft round eyes, and smooth and firm hands, and she seemed very unsure of herself in the beginning because she would not look at him in his eyes. She soothed his wounds with some kind of salve, and she tenderly wrapped his bandages in such a manner, that he did not even know when she was done.

Their rescuers were from a rival clan, and to them these odd-looking strangers seemed valuable. Abeulo was then taken before the leader of the clan, and although he could not understand what they were saying, he had the impression that strangely, they respected him. Strangely he was the only one of the landing party that was allowed to walk about freely in the village, even though he did have a constant guard, who watched his every movement.

And, everywhere he went, everyone would run or walk up to him and touch his skin and smile. One day he came across a group of men and boys practicing three distinct Iaido fighting styles that involved using swords. He was invited to join the group, and thus began his daily routine of turning himself into a finely tuned weapon.

He was an extremely fast learner, and within five weeks he had mastered all of the three distinct fighting styles, and all seven principles of the warrior's creed, much to the surprise of his captors. He then learned all eighteen arts of fighting styles mastered by the greatest of these warriors. He was already really good with a knife, so learning to wield a sword or to use a long lance was easy for him. His rescuers were then even more amazed, at his ability a few weeks later, to "best" the champions of the clan, even the Bokuden of the clan, and with how this stranger could duel with the masters—with a certain style and uncommon grace.

He was then taught how to build a sword, which is a two-week process, and during this process he was told of the legendary and greatest sword maker of them all, who was named Masamune. He was then held in even more esteem, when months later another rival clan, attacked the village compound just before the morning sun arose. And, just when everything seemed to be turning for the worse, Abeulo jumped into the fray, and turned the battle back to the side of his rescuers.

He also saved the life of the wife of the leader of the clan, by diving in front of her and taking an arrow in his shoulder that was meant for her. All the while, he was still battling the assassins with a stunning display of sword wielding, that even the attackers were amazed by. And, he single-handedly routed the attackers and saved the day.

So, for his act of bravery, he was then inducted into the clan. And, he was given the symbol of the clan, which was etched onto his back with ink, which was that of a mythical creature that some of the elders of the village said, had roamed the land over 20,000 years ago and which that breathed fire and brimstone. Once he was a part of the clan, Abeula was then free to openly associate with him, and show her true feelings for him.

He said that he knew that he was eternally hooked on her, like a fish on a fishing line, when one day she told him that "she really liked him, and she hoped that they would always, and forever be friends. For yesterday is but a dream, and tomorrow is only a vision. But today's friendship makes every yesterday a dream of happiness, and every tomorrow is a vision of hope."

In time they fell deeply in love with one another, and they were eventually married in front of the entire clan, in an old-fashioned ritual. And, their happiness only grew daily with one another. They would take long walks always holding hands with one another. And, they both enjoyed the beauty of natural settings, and valley's that were green and fertile with numerous beautiful flowers in the summers and were snow-filled in the winter months.

Everybody seemed pleased at this union. And, mi Abeulo, was becoming an indispensable and highly valued member of the clan. But he knew that this would all change one day soon. Because, he was bound by his duty to his young Master and, also, to the crew of their ship, and also bound to them all returning to their home.

Abeulo had secretly been in contact with his young master, who was still being held as a prisoner, as well as was the ship's executive officer, who had never come ashore. And, he had also arranged for tools and supplies to be sent to repair the crippled ship and had been in touch with the rest of the landing crew, who were still alive and were prisoners. Also, he had helped to hatch a plan for them to escape.

Besides, time was flying and over seventy-one months had passed since they had first arrived in this strangely wonderful and beautiful land, and it was time for them all to get back to their lives. But what was he going to really do either go back or stay? This troubled him greatly because he felt a peace within himself that he had never ever known or even felt before, and the thought of leaving made him restless and hurting within his mind.

Abeulo' s status was growing each and every day, and now he was given the primary job of guarding the leader, as a part of his private security detail, as the leader moved about from place to place visiting their clan's various locations. Abeulo was also given jobs to perform, like to raid certain places or to dispatch certain individuals, to collect tributes and to bring justice and order in disputes. He was then, one day, instructed to attend a ceremony where to his own surprise he was made into something called a samurai. And he was told, that to be one of these, that he could never, ever dishonor the clan. And, more importantly he was to never get out of the clan, for the rest of his natural life.

He was then taken into a side room that was filled with other samurai, where he was introduced to the Destiny Sword. This fabled sword was one of only three that were ever made by one of the oldest civilizations on the planet. And, this particular one was stolen from a place that was across the sea, but only less than 16 days there and back, from where they were by ship.

It was made in an ancient bushido sword making process that was forgotten or lost, from over 600 years ago. And, some say that this sword itself was considerably much older than that, like easily well over a thousand years, some have even implied. It was extremely sharp, and what made it different from the other two Destiny Swords, was that this one was made from a flaming and glowing rock that came crashing down from the heavens, on the exact night that a certain prophecy had foretold would mark it's coming.

This rock, when it cooled down was so hard, that it took over 60 years just to cut a single blade or bushido from it. Then it took many, many more years to create this fabled sword. And, hundreds of people were involved in the entirety of the sword crafting process.

It had been used in many battles and wars, and many battles and wars had been fought over it. And, a specter of death clung over it the way that fog, hovers over the ground on a cold foggy night. The sword now would be the spoil of the next greatly anticipated battle that all of the four sects of the clan, who were involved in the stealing of it would participate in—in order to dispatch their mutual enemy. Whatever sect distinguished itself in battle would then claim the sword, and from there have an undisputed leadership role in all clan matters.

The sword would be the prize, and every sect of the clan seemed taken with the gleam of the blade. And, with how regal and impressive it looked with its extremely beautiful gold-trimmed green jade hilt and matching white jade handle. There were skulls that were skillfully carved all over and around the handle, and it was said that each skull meant or stood for something.

A gold-filled inscription was carved or really etched onto the handle that symbolized the saying 'Only Faith with Honor and Truth is the Way,' and this only added to the mystique and mystery of the sword because the making of any sword is a religious experience, to cure each sword makers mind, body and soul. They all left the gathering feeling determined to become the owners of the sword, and everyone immediately started gathering their forces and preparing for the upcoming battle.

The battle would take place on a high flat plain that faced the sea, and almost 1500 warriors would be involved. On the day of the struggle, the opposing forces gathered on the high plain facing one another with all of their colorful suits of armor on, and with battle flags flying high in the light breeze. When the horns would blow, it was their signal to commence, and the opponents slowly started marching towards one another and into what seemed like an imminent onslaught.

When they got about 500 feet from one another, they all politely bowed towards one another. And with that, they then attacked each other with a savage fury—the likes of which no outsider, like Abuelo had ever seen before. They smashed into one another again and again, and it was Abeulo who had distinguished himself and his sect.

And at battles' end, Abeulo was the hero because he had fought side by side with his leader as they cut a path directly towards the rival clans' leaders. He was the one who sensed a weakness in the enemy's flank position and led the charge of the elite guards to attack that exposed area, even when his horse was cut down from beneath him in a hail of murderous arrows. He still continued to attack on foot as he wielded his bushido like no other, and he was the one who actually made the opposing head leader surrender, or face death.

When the rival clan blew its horn, which signaled an end to the hostilities afflicted against their side, he finally looked around and what he saw was shocking and appalling to even him. Because, the battlefield scene looked like a wholesale slaughter of men and horses, all littered about the plain with well over 800 men dead or dying. Everything had blood on it, nothing was spared, and the grass was in some places looked like a sea of blood and death with dead bodies floating within it.

When the battle was over, the elders of his clan presented the sword to his leader, who then became the undisputed leader and master of the entire Yamato clan. He just groveled in his newfound fortune, as everyone bowed to him, as he passed by— and he just smiled with satisfaction at his triumph and luck. When they finally got back to their village, Abeula was the first one to run up to Abeulo, and she held him tighter than ever before, because many great warriors had died to suit this blood lust.

All of these warriors had died good deaths, but something was different about this battle. Because, it was about a sword, and not about the many lives that were lost to obtain it. This was not about any honor or duty it was about a relic from the past, that was haunting the present and the future.

Abeulo was the key to all of the leader's growing fortunes, and the leader at the celebration dinner had openly stated as much. And, that now he would never, ever release Abuelo and let him go—he was kind of half laughing, but still serious.

He also realized that young Master Vega was the key to keeping Abeulo both obedient and loyal to his clan and cause. So, now these funny looking strangers would never be permitted to leave, ever, no matter what happened. He needed to keep his power consolidated within his grasp, and Abeulo was therefore, his most important and valued treasure, after the sword that is, and he was determined never ever to lose either.

But after the battle, Abeulo had made up his mind, and once he told Abeula of his troubles, she convinced him that they must leave together. Because, what kind of place did they live in, where the master only craved absolute and total power? She then stated that this would be no kind of place to raise a child, and their child needed to be raised up in a peaceful place.

"Their child," he stated, "they were having a child? Why did she not tell him? When did she find out? How long had she known?" He was so excited and happy that he blotted the business of leaving out of his mind, as he concentrated solely upon his smiling wife and her needs. Nine months came and went, and my mother, who was given the name KireiShinju (which translated into English meant ("Lovely Pearl"), who was mostly called Shinju (which meant "Pearl" in English), was born.

And, Abeulo was even more determined to set his young master and the surviving members of the landing party free, so that they could all leave together, and go back home. The boat had been secretly repaired in stages and it was almost ready to face the rigor of the open sea again and besides, there was only a limited timeframe left to sail, before they would be stuck there until the seasonal tides changed, which would then allow them to leave.

So time was of the essence, and Abuelo's plan to help them all escape was a solid one. It just had one flaw and that was, his new master had either felt incensed that something was going on or, he was watching his newfound young apprentice's every move like a hawk. So on that eventful day almost two months later, even though he was extremely careful, his new master's spies were everywhere and one of them saw him aiding and leading the escape of the surviving members of the landing party to a long boat.

And, as he carefully attempted to sneak back into their dwelling to get my Abuela and my sleeping mother, and then slip back outside, much to their total surprise, his master with the destiny sword in his hand and his security detail were standing right there, waiting for them. They were surrounded, and Abeulo's swords were taken from him. Then they were escorted by lance and sword point into a large oval shaped room.

The leader, who was extremely upset, denounced his leaving and told him that he would lose his good luck. But Abeulo, who was holding mi Madre, still was determined to go, and he looked at the leader and said, "Can we be permitted to take our leave, PLEASE!" "Please," laughed the leader, "Please you say?" The security detail even laughed at his words, and with that the leader un-shelved the destiny sword, and coldly in a low voice said that he would kill Midori, and then the baby if he wanted to leave. That would be the price of his freedom, and he should make up his mind as to what he wanted.

Abeulo and Abeula, hugged each other, but the guards separated them, on a look from the leader and they pushed Abeula towards the angry leader. He then all of a sudden pulled out a small bushido and without so much as a thought and in one action, savagely stabbed her in the small of her back, as she cried out in enormous pain. And he then left the sword impaled in her back.

Next, he then used the destiny sword to behead her, as everyone gasped out in both horror and surprise. Abeulo, as well as everyone else in the room, was stunned and shocked by his actions. And then he made his fatal mistake, he picked up her head, holding it by her hair, as it swung in air, he then turned to Abuelo, and said, "Your daughter Shinju will be next."

Abeulo right then at that very moment in time, changed into the Abuelo that I have known all of my life, the focused, the iron-willed, hard as a hammer and anvil person that no one trusts or wants to ever take their eyes off of. He broke free of the men who were trying to hold him, and in one swift move. He then smoothly placed my still sleeping Madre on the ground, and with tears running down his face, he turned to face his attackers.

He wielded and pivoted left and he somehow got the sword from his nearest attacker, and he then became the messenger of death, as he killed everyone who got in his way—as he made his way towards the leader who was his master. Some of these men were his friends, and close companions that he had come to know and respect since his time in this strange and foreign land. But it did not matter, as nothing mattered anymore.

He was not even thinking—he was just dispatching these men, with ruthless precision and skill. When he finally got to the leader, he dodged his foe's awkward swinging attempt, and he caught the leader off guard with a flying knee to the chest.

And, he then knocked the destiny sword out of his hand. And, once Abeulo got a firm grip on the jade handle, it was like he was empowered to do the sword's sinister bidding.

For this sword had tasted a lot of blood, and in its lifetime up until then, it was responsible for hundreds if not thousands of deaths. It had a gleam to it and when you swung it, it actually had a hum to it, as if it was trying to talk. And, Abeulo swung the blade like no other and he blocked out his new leader's screams that begged for forgiveness.

And then he killed the murderous leader, whose hands were upright in the air, pleading like a scared old woman. With a single powerful blow, Abuelo wielded the destiny sword, which split his head at the side on the top of the crown all the way down to the neck. This left both sides of the wound hanging, as his brain leaked—and slipped out onto the ground, and into a pool beside his lifeless body, looking just like a jellyfish out of water.

He then turned his attention to the remaining people, and at least some of them tried to fight back and show some courage. But it did not matter, for he killed everyone and everything, even the dogs that had approached him. And in the end, he was covered in all of his victim's blood.

He then went back to the room and picked up my mother who was now awake, and tip toed over to where Midori's body and head lie. He wrapped them all up in a large sheet and placed them in the back of a wagon. And he gathered up my mother and their things, which now also included the destiny sword, and he drove to where the awaiting longboat was—and they sailed to meet the ship that would take them back to their world.

Upon reaching the ship he was hailed as a great, great warrior, with a young child to boot, and he received great praise for being the hero who had saved the day. But he did not feel like a hero, because he had just killed over 60 people with an ease that seemed uncanny. And, if my mother had not been around, he probably would have tried to stay behind in this strange land, to kill off the entire Yamoto clan.

Once on board the ship, Abeulo constructed a small log raft, which when finished, was pulled behind the main ship by a rope that was attached to it's stern. On the small raft were my Abuela's remains all still wrapped up together, in the sheet along with most of her possessions and, this was like a floating funeral pyre.

He then shot a flaming arrow into the pyre that eventually totally engulfed the raft into flames, just as was done for all warriors, at the time of their deaths. He wept like a baby and prayed solemnly for her safe passage into the next realm of life. And, he swore to take care of their daughter, no matter what.

He stood there holding their daughter as he looked back at the almost totally burnt up funeral pyre and the land in the distance, as tears streamed down his face. And, this is the reason why, for the rest of his life on the day that marks her birth, or first coming to this realm, he always looked east and prayed to whom he believed was the god of all gods Amen-ra to bless her memory. This is also why he lights the fire over water, because he will never ever let her memory die out and be no more. For he is now like a sea horse that has lost its mate, and he was adrift in the waters of time forever, all alone.

My next memory is of the night that Old Master Strickland died. They say that his heart just gave out and he died, in his office that was off the study. It was after dinner while having a cigar, doing some paperwork and sitting in his favorite chair. He had six children and by the time that he had died, he had amassed a whole lot of property.

He was Irish, and originally came from this place called Ireland, and the story he always liked to tell, was that he and his brothers were all barefoot and penniless, wearing rags for clothes, when they first arrived to this Nation. Imagine that! His brothers and him had all worked day and night, in New York City, until they had enough money saved up, so that they could go down south and become business and gentlemen. They settled into slavery, because slavery was free labor for their cotton and lumber and distillery businesses.

The three brothers had decided early on, that though they did not like the idea of human slaves, but for them to be prosperous in their new country, they had to keep in step with the times. So owning slaves was a must in the type of businesses that they were committed to pursuing, and to ultimately expand their businesses, they needed to increase their free labor force. They started off slow, and expanded, their interests with careful planning and caution.

They originally had wanted to go to Louisiana to grow rice, but a maternal cousin had told them of his good fortune in the Carolina's and how with hard work they too, could be rewarded with a good life. So the Carolina's became their new home and the land that they had first acquired had grown and grown, until one day they had enough of it to divide it equally into three fairly large portions.

They had initially sought out timber, but quickly they found out that cotton could also be a moneymaker, because America was still young and growing. For, cotton related by-products were in high demand in America, and also worldwide. Especially, in a nation called England, so the worldwide cotton boom created the slave labor or free labor boom in the southern states. All of which went hand in hand.

Saltwater Negra's with the help of the lash or whip could be willed or whipped to work, and although producing cotton was a tough job, and was extremely tough on one's hands and knees. Slaves were slaves, so why did it matter about them anyways when it came to money or capital. The brothers felt that they were not inhumane people and they even liked certain Negra, but when other plantation owners were around or present, they strangely were quiet, or silent.

When the brothers were alone together in each other's company, however, they expressed thoughts that they were not alone in their dilemma. Because, even the presidents of these United States of America—from George Washington on down, had owned slaves. And some still spoke out against the evils of slavery, but they were immigrants, so they naturally had to be quiet.

They would just amass as much as they could, and if their overseers or work hands acted too inhumane or cruel with the commodities, then they would lightly admonish them, but keep the status quo intact. For three Irish men were not going to change a whole system of bondage, so why should they get truly involved in the question of slavery? They worked hard for everything that they owned or acquired, and things were not ever going to change, or so they honestly thought.

Master Strickland had at the time of his death, a large fine house, a small original house that he had first built, six large barns and 3 smaller ones, 2 medium sized houses for the over-seers and work hands to live in, 4 curing shacks, over 350 slaves or commodities, and over 1000 acres of land in his name in various parts of Carolinas.   He was the part owner of a lumber factory that he co-owned with his brothers near town, he had a thriving cotton business with many English merchants as his customers, had a mill, and he had a couple of boats that were docked in Willington, and Charleston.

He also was a silent partner and co-owner of both of the Charleston and Savannah slave auction blocks. He had a very profitable tobacco business that was grown on his plantation, which was shipped to various places in Europe to make fine cigars. He also had a liquor company that made a lot of money distilling sugar into fine spirits.

He was worth some say well over three quarters of a million dollars, at time of his death, and of course Jack, his golden child, was the main beneficiary of his will. He gave his other children small tracts of valuable land and money, but Jack was given the day-to-day responsibility of running the family enterprises, so all of the businesses were put into his name.

Master Jack who was in his second year of his start up law practice, which he and his law school classmate had begun in Raleigh, the state capital, after they had graduated from Chapel Hill. He immediately had had to come home, with some sadness. Because he knew that things for him would never be the same ever again once he took over the reins of the Strickland family's business enterprises.

Because life for him had just gotten much tougher and more complex and besides it is never easy for the head that wears the crown especially when it comes to business and finance. Old

Master Strickland had done right by his heirs, and had prospered in a foreign land, but he ultimately was perceived to be a bad man by the slaves. Because he had a deaf ears and blind eyes when it came to slaves, and as long as Negra's stayed in their places, he would never react or seem the least bit affected.

But if it messed with his bottom line, which was his money, in any way, then he had a problem that only the whip seemed to fix or solve. That is why that night as the news of his passing started to filter and spread about the plantation, the entire slave population in the slave quarters started to dance and even sing songs, and rejoice, just like it was a holiday or something like that.

The next memory was of the very next day after Old Master Strickland had died, because that was the day when Abuelo first had found El Diablo. El Diablo was our family dog and was all wolf, but we always said that he was a dog. Because, dogs are in the same family as the wolf, even though we all knew really what he was, so that people would not be scared.

His mother was killed in a fight protecting him, and the pup was left whining over her dead body. Abeulo had watched the whole thing unfold, and only when everything was over, he ventured down from his position, and took the pup with him. I will always remember when he got home that night, because he said that he had a surprise for everyone, and from out of his burlap bag he pulled a wolf puppy. We were all a bit shocked, and taken aback, but the pup was cute and lovingly, and he seemed so alone and helpless.

We kept him in the barn, and it was our family's little secret, that we all shared and treasured. We all had a hand in training him. But Abeulo and me conducted more of his actual training.

He was very obedient, and mindful, and he was strangely almost like a person. Because, when you spoke to him, he responded back, and he was smart and remembered everything.

He followed instructions to a tee, and when you told him something, after some practice, he would do it. He also was a fast learner and he seemed to love being taught new things. If you told him to lie down and to be quiet, he would do it and, it was as if he was asleep but, his head would be up. And, he would just watch and wait in silence for me to give him the signal, which was a birdcall that he had learned from Abeulo, before he moved. He was also extremely very kind and loving when it came to all of our family members, but he was ruthless to all others.

He was always quick to bite other people and fight any other animal that crossed him in the wrong way. He was always the absolute master of all of the beasts on the entire plantation. Anyone who made the mistake of challenging his superiority was immediately dealt with, in a harsh and sometimes cruel manner. As he got older, whenever he appeared, everyone and everything would get a bit nervous and scared. Because, they knew that he had this reputation for roaming at night, and sleeping in the day, and showing his teeth and snarling at anyone who was not in our family. And when messing around with him, you could very well get bitten.

He was not ever to be trusted, in no one else's but our eyes, and he knew that everyone was scared of him, so he used this to his advantage. Like, by simply showing his teeth to get the desired effect, which was simply at all times, to be left alone. He was certainly given the right name by Abeulo, which was always funny to us because it described him to a tee, for as we all knew, his name translated into Standard English means "the devil."

I used to always like those lazy Saturdays and Sundays when I would take El Diablo out to our secret places. And, we would frolic and roll around in the grass and enjoy roughhouse playing all about. This, I truly believe, is what developed our close bond with one another, which would be invaluable to me, in the turbulent years to come.

El Diablo was much more than just the family dog, and in reality, he was more like a silent friend and protector. And if it was not for El Diablo, I do not even know if I would be here this very day. At the same time all of this was happening, Master Jack's transition to head of the family business was smooth and effortless.

And, he had planned all of his life for this eventual occurrence to one day happen, so he was ready when the time came. Everything seemed fine on the surface, and he kept things mostly the same, day-to-day on The Plantation and in the rest of the businesses. But underneath he was far different than his daddy, and like mi Abeulo had said, "All Blanco's are not bad, so never think all—think, "some," but never all."

But in reality, he had a problem, because he had come to know and respect certain Negra, and he realized that all Negra were not shiftless, lazy or bad. His whole perspective had been changed some said, by me having saved his life that day, but he had a real dilemma. He had hung out amongst Negra, and he even had been known to carouse about with Negra women, and some mean- spirited people had even said, that he even preferred Negra women to his own kind.

He was gentle and kind, and he was even known to be a bit harsh to the Blanco hands or workers who displayed cruel treatment of Negra in his presence, but his hands were truly tied. When his daddy had died, people came from all around, inquiring about his marital status, to see if he was available and eligible and if he was seeking a wife, and things like that. He was a single and suddenly rich young man, with a great education and good looks.

He shortly became engaged, and after a whirlwind courtship he married, a society girl from an equally rich family from the Charleston area of the Carolinas. Even though, it was for show and to appease his mother. He did love his wife, but she could never ever truly understand him. And, on the surface, yes, his skin color on the outside was Blanco, but on the inside, he was always loyal to the plight of Negra's. And, he would never forsake the Negra's that he loved and cared for because, to him it would not feel right.

He moved all of us—my own entire family, which was Abeulo, and Mamie and the kids, to private quarters, which was away from any prying eyes and ears. And, he also removed Abeulo's guardian angel watchman. We still went out, but there was no set day, like "day six" anymore, so my life became much easier and more relaxed.

He respected and valued my opinion, and he always asked me to accompany him on his longer trips, using horses so that we could talk and exchange ideas. He shocked me one day on one of these rides, because he encouraged me to make sure that Mamie and my younger brothers and sister also be taught to read and write. Because, he said, it was important, for one day in the future, "change was going to come." And what we then knew as slavery was going to eventually end. All of this would be our little secret of course. And he was serious about all of this, and he not joking or playing a cruel trick.

Winter came in this strange land both fast and quick, and it always was a shock to my system, because it was like the warmth just would up and run away. The cool breeze would first come over the tops of the mountains and hills and leave its cold breath on everything in its wake—a sobering reminder of things yet to come. Then the leaves would all turn from green to brown and fall off the branches and eventually blow all away.

And with that, the animals would become scariest when the winter snow or cold would hit. And, everything would stand still, frozen in time until the warmth came back to renew the lands. This time of extended cold was to most slaves, the hardest part of the year because nothing outside survived. And, this is also when the masters fed them the least, to keep their energy levels low, to avoid against runaways and insurrections.

Most slaves often found themselves huddled up around a fire, wrapped up in whatever, which was mostly rags from head to toes, fighting the strange cold, for their very lives. The misery and despair all around really seemed heavier during these periods. But it was also when most slaves decided to make their breaks and try to find better lives.

Because everyone, even the slave owners themselves, did not want to go outside—they just accepted these winter breakouts as losses, and reckoned that if the cold did not kill them, and they were able to somehow survive, then some loses, were just loses. "Chalk it up and just purchase another commodity in the springtime, work 'em nearly to death and when the next winter cycle hits, count up your dollars and get ready for the next years' planting and harvest time," was the consensus.

Now, slaves tried to escape in the summertime also, and most slave masters were always on guard year-round for any such idea, but the winter breakout routines were becoming regular and starting to increase in frequency. So, something had to be done to stop all of this, and Master Jack was summoned to Raleigh for some kind of big meeting at Isaac Hunter's Tavern, among the 91 slave owners in the whole state who owned over 100 slaves. And, he was gone for days.

When he finally came back, he seemed quite grim as if something ghastly had occurred, for he was quieter than usual, and kept to himself. Days later, one morning he summoned me for our usual morning hunt, but instead of us riding horses, he was in a wagon. And, he instructed me to leave my hunting tools behind, and just climb into the wagon with him.

Humph? No hunting weapons, I thought, something big must be going on. We started out and only until we were alone, and quite a ways from the big house, did he explain his "dilemma," as he put it. One slave owner who lived up near Raleigh had hired an accountant, which is a person whose job it is to keep the books and track profit figures for a whole year for the businesses. This person had noticed a trend that was quite alarming, which was that slaves were escaping now more in the winter, than they had ever done so before.

This coupled with the rest of the year, meant that these losses were now mounting up year-round. And, if you looked at the losses statewide for us slave owners, who owned over one hundred slaves, then it appeared that slave owners as a group in North Carolina were soft and losing control of their capital and commodities. If this trend continued, then North Carolina would appear to be weak in Washington.

And, as the Governor's office had so eloquently stated, "there would be no weak links in the Southern voting block," because a weak North Carolina affects all Southern states. So all Southern governors were aware of needing to give off the right appearance, and losing slaves was the wrong appearance at this particular point in time. So there was now a statewide mandate from the newly elected Democratic Governor, Thomas Bragg, to tighten the grip, to make the appearance of slavery profitable in all phases of the enterprise.

And, if everyone did not comply, they would then be subject to a brand-new type of tax. This tax would be directed primarily, and truly, at the ninety-one slave owners statewide, who could not control their commodities. Because, who really had money to lose? And, slaves were money.

Thus, who had extra money each and every year to replace lost or runaway capital? So, an auditor was being dispatched from the Governor's office to survey all of the plantations statewide. And, those plantations that consistently lost slaves would now be subject to a head tax to help offset lost revenues of state taxes. No one was exempt, from the smallest to the largest owners, and as owners of chattel, all slave owners statewide, were now being held responsible for the upkeep and control of their beasts of burden. Because, one could not have them just lurking about the county side. "The whole thing stinks," Master Jack, sighed. And, what was about to happen was beyond his control.

Thus, the larger slave owners in our region of the state had come up with a plan to work around this tax. This was to create a special team or teams of slave catchers comprised of white men from every plantation, to bring back these runaways, dead or hopefully alive. So that when the auditor did come, their numbers would be correct.

Because, the new law did not say "alive" heads, just heads, and even if they had to put dead bodies in beds with blankets covering them, they would escape this silly new tax. His dilemma was that his white work force was comprised of older men who had been loyal to his father, but who were now not able bodied enough for such goings on year-round. Besides he needed them to stay put, to help him run the day-to-day business operations, as they had for his late father.

All of his other business interests where taking up a lot of his time. And, he needed someone from his plantation who could not only participate in these hunts, but one who would seek also to at least try to bring most of them back alive. So, what he really needed was someone who not only knew what he was doing, but who also knew and understood the seriousness of the situation.

Other plantation owners in different parts of the state were even hiring special slave bounty hunters, but these men were usually ruthless and cold-blooded killers, who were in it strictly for the money and the game of it all. They loved the hunt and the taste of blood and death was always around them. Just like the sharks that followed the slave ships during the great crossing over voyage, known as the 'Middle Passage.'

There is no human kindness associated with these kinds of men. So to Master Jack's, the hiring these kinds of men to be representative of his plantation was something that he did not want to do if he could help it, that is. There just were not any able-bodied men in town to hire and he was in a pinch.

Because, the auditor would soon be dispatched, and he knew that he had suffered numerous breakouts already. He was involved in many joint ventures, so he had spread himself quite thin, money wise and he just did not have the money for this new tax right now—maybe, in six months, but not right now.

He would just have to foreclose on some of his new business ventures, he reckoned. But he was really not willing to do so because, the potential short and long-term profits would—or should be immense if he could stay the course. "There must be a solution out there somewhere," he said, as he pondered a while, and the cold air brushed the skin on our faces and front sides.

He then pulled out a small flask from under his coat took a brief swallow and pondered a bit more. He looked so very sad and solemn as he slipped the flask back under his coat and made the horse come to a stop, as we rounded the crest of a small hill. When we looked back at the valley we could see in the distance, a lone bird leaving a leafless tree, and flying skyward.

And, he gathered his thoughts and took a deep breath and then said, "Balaam, now I know that you are wondering what this all has to do with you," he said, "and why we are not hunting today, but being very honest, I need you." I guess that I must have looked at him very strangely or appeared to be shocked, because he reached out and put his hand on my shoulder, like you do in a manner to reassure a person.

You are the only one that I truly trust. And, I need someone that understands what my interests are and who will act accordingly, as my personal representative for the Strickland

Plantation. You have always had this ability to help me think, and help me to clear my mind, and therefore you are perfect and the right choice for such a delicate situation, he said as he looked straight into my eyes. "Master Jack, I stammered, have you forgotten two things?

That, one—I too, am a slave? And, two, do you also realize the dangerous situation that you are putting not only me, but also my whole family in?" Yes, I certainly do Balaam, he said, but I think that I have come up with a plan that will be mutually beneficial to the both of us.

"What if I can guarantee you and your own family, which consists of Mamie and the children, along with your grandfather, your freedom, based upon the number of slaves that you can actually return, be they either dead or alive! We could come up with a number of returns and whenever you reach that number, I will guarantee safe passage to the north, and I will personally draw up legally binding papers that will be all notarized, that will keep you all free forevermore. As I sat there dumbfounded looking at Master Jack, he waved his hands and then pointed one skyward, as he said, Balaam look at that bird, which was still in our view, in the distance, look how totally free it is.

Well Balaam, that bird could be you and your family, if you accept my proposal and do this job for me. You owe it to Mamie and the children, as well as your beloved grandfather, to at least think about my proposal. And, please take your time with your decision. If you do not think that you can do this, I will understand, and not be the least bit mad at you, or hold this against you. I know that this is a big thing for you to decide right now, so please do not rush into anything.

Always remember that I trust you with my life, and I would have not even asked you to do this, if I did not think that you were capable of accomplishing the job. You would be the representative from our plantation, and your work would be strictly in secret. The plantation owners don't want any of this knowledge or information to ever get out—that we have to recruit or hire individuals to return our lost property. Because it would mean that we do have a serious problem of control.

So to hide our shame, we will act secretly and hunt these escapees down without a lot of public knowledge or fanfare. So your part would be to aid or assist by using your superior tracking skills and senses, to aid these other men in finding the missing property. And for every person that you help to track down, you and your family will all be one step closer to actual freedom.

With that he turned the wagon around and headed back for home and warmth as we sat in total and complete silence. Like two strangers sharing a ride to nowhere would do, as the cold and crisp air now pushed against our backsides. When the wagon pulled back up to the big house, we both hopped out of the wagon, still not saying anything to one another.

And, I turned to walk for home as I tried to think about what my life was really about in terms of feeling. I mean, was I going to be able to hunt down fellow slaves, and not feel anything? How would I be able to even sleep at night, knowing that I was a part of something evil, which was pure evil at that, even if it was masquerading as a legitimate business enterprise.

How could I even look others straight in the eyes, and still feel like a decent and honest man? Gosh, what were Master Jack's real intentions, and could I honestly trust him to actually give us our freedom? What was freedom anyways?

All of my life, I had only known one kind of life, and that was that someone had always owned me and my family members. The elders had always said that this thing called freedom was something that one day we all would get. Freedom in death was probably the real freedom that they were really and truthfully talking about. But it was a notion that always amused us all, in strange ways. So did Master Jack actually mean "real freedom" and if so, why then did he make it cost so much?

What a high price I thought, to be a true free man, and would it be worth it, I wondered as my mind raced back and forth. How would Mamie and Abeulo both react, would they still both love me, or better would they ever speak to me again, once I told them of Master Jack's plan? Or would they laugh in my face for even entertaining the thought or better than that, for bringing such a crazy sounding notion before them?

After pausing at the entrance for minutes, which seemed like hours, I slowly walked inside of the carriage barn, taking a careful notation in my mind of how everything was arranged Mamie was quite the homemaker, and even if we had modest accommodations, she kept everything arranged and orderly, with the floor swept and things always in their places. A table always had as the centerpiece, a vase with fresh flowers with a bucket of cool water nearby, and she always had a hot meal ready for me and Abeulo, whenever we came into our living area.

She was a great cook, and she could pan fry, bake, boil, griddle, and roast and make it always look so easy, as she did it with smile, no less, like she was happy to be doing this. She kept the children clean, and neat. And she did all of this after her daily plantation chores, of helping her parents was done.

Mamie was seated at the table, softly crying as I walked in, and the sight of tears in her eyes, immediately changed my mood, as I shifted to address my wife's needs, and, to give her some comfort. " Mamie, I asked, what is wrong, with you, why are you crying?" " Balaam, she said, do not worry for these are not tears of sadness or hurt, but they are the tears of joy."

"I just found out a little while ago, that we are going to have another child, number three of three and I feel so blessed and quite lucky to have such a good man as you, in my life. The thought of having you in my life as my mate, has made me so very happy, I just teared up is all, so nothing is wrong, we are just gonna have another young one is all, and our family is growing."

I was kind of shocked in a good way, but relieved. And as she folded herself up into my arms, and right then and there, at that very exact moment in time—was when my mind was made up. I wanted a chance to improve my family's lot in this life, and if I had to sign a deal with the devil to accomplish this, then I most certainly would do so. And, then deal with the consequences that came later, no matter what they were.

The next morning, as we lay together on our straw bed, Mamie could sense that something was really bothering me, and she demanded that I tell her. She then started peppering me questions, like, "You didn't want another baby, you don't love me and Lita and Tine anymore, or you want to run away with someone else?" "No Mamie that is not it at all," I answered, as I gathered up the courage to tell her the plan that Master Jack had devised for me.

As I told her, she looked scared, and she instinctively reached out and hugged me tightly to her bosom, and she started rocking me ever so gently without ever saying a word. We sat in silence for a long time. But as little Lita began to awaken, and stir around, she whispered, "What are you going to do Balaam?"

"I do not know," I whispered back. "What do you think?" She just shook her head in a manner, like I don't know, and as Lita started rubbing her eyes, and really started to wake up, we both just sat there looking first at Lita, and then at the still sleeping Tine and finally at Mamie's stomach. As I then placed my hand over her stomach, she nuzzled me, and whispered, "Balaam, I am not going to lie, I am scared, but if you honestly think that Master Jack is telling the truth, then do what you feel is right."

"Always remember that it is for better or for worse, and would our lives be that much different if we were free? Our love would not change, the children would be free is all, so you decide, and I will back up any decision that you make one hundred percent." Feeling much better, but not knowing really why, I passionately kissed my wife, and with that I felt a huge relief.

About three weeks later I was summoned, up to the big house, by Master Jack. I was led into a room that was called a study, by this old slave named Buck, who glared at me the whole time, as he was showing me the way. "Don't set down," he snapped, as he whirled around to leave the room, "Massah Jackson, will be in directly and don't touch nothing, and when you leave, if anything becomes missing, I will introduce you to my whip and then tar your behind, so do you understand me?"

He was a real mean bastard of a man, but I just looked at him, and sucked my teeth at him all in one motion—to serve him notice that I was not studyin' him and his babblings, because I knew what he truly was. I knew his kind. He was the worst kind of house negra, the kind that inflicts cruelty and sourness upon other slaves because of his, or her, own lifetime of misery and despair. This kind also thought that they were privileged in some kind of morbid way. Just because of the position and the place in which they worked. It marveled me.

Slavery is slavery, so it is not about where you worked, because your labor wage was free for your owner. So instead of sticking together against a common threat to everyone's survival, this kind takes the lead, in keeping everything divided and confused. If you look at it, is kind of like a bunch of crabs in a basket type of mentality, always pulling each other down. Right then an adjoining door on my right, opened, and Master Jack entered in and ushered me with him, into a room that looked like a mini sitting parlor.

He asked me to sit in a fancy looking chair as he sat down himself, and he then inquired if I were thirsty and in need of some refreshment. I said no thank you, and it was then that I noticed the nice pictures that were on the walls, which displayed a French provincial kind of look. Okay Balaam, have you considered my proposal? I nodded, yes. So what do you think he asked, as our eyes locked directly onto one another's? I said that this was really a tough choice for me, but at the end of the day, the quest for freedom was always the same answer to all of the questions that kept coming up, over and over, inside of my head.

So with that, he gave to me a white feather pen which he had dipped into an inkwell. And he told me to scribble my mark, right there on a line that was next to an X. I signed the paper, and he took his ring off, and then dipped its face that displayed the family's crest into some wet and freshly burnt candle wax, pressed it onto the paper, upon which was left an official raised seal. With that done, he said that we had a legally binding deal, and at that exact moment was when my deal with the devil was struck. And he then asked me, "Do you want to read the agreement?" I nodded yes, and everything seemed in order, as I read the words and thought about their meaning.

Master Jack then stated that I would be told of how the arrangements had been made surrounding my getting of a copy of the agreement when the time was necessary. He had convinced the other owners, that he had found the right point man for this job, but he had not told them of our delicate arrangement, because "our business was our business." I was to never, ever say anything while I was in the company of these men and if I had to speak, to do so only in Spanish. I was to also follow their instructions implicitly at all times, unless I thought that my life was in danger.

I was to just track or hunt down the runaways and nothing else. I was not to participate or partake in any punishment or remedy against them, and I would get credit for all slaves that I tracked down whether they were from our plantation or not, as long as they were only being returned anywhere within the old Province of Carolina. The contract stated, "That you agree to track down, 250 runaway commodities, in order to secure you and your family's freedom." So that means that you can track down for example, either 50 per year for five years, or 5 per year for 50 years, but 250 is the agreed upon amount or number, and then and only then, at that point in time, could the contract be legally and lawful enforced.

"Do you have any questions, comments and or concerns," he asked? I shook my head no, and he then pulled out a fancy cigar that was grown somewhere on his family's plantation. He then lit it, took a few strong puffs, and then looked out of one of the windows. Balaam, this is a dangerous job, your safety is never guaranteed and once you leave this plantation, I cannot protect you from what lies beyond the gates.

So we need to come up with something creative that will aid you in accomplishing your goal, discreetly so that no one will ever get wind of our arrangement. But always remember that you will be entirely all on your own," he said again—a second time for emphasis, I always thought. We must get you formal horse riding lessons, and also some new clothes, a pair of boots, a buck knife, and everything that you need to be a traveler—like a sleeping blanket, a coffee pot and a metal plate with utensils for meals, and so on.

He then took me to a storage room, that was fully stocked with all new things, and he let me pick out some clothes, a long sleeved cotton shirt, a pair of thick cotton pants, along with a pair of Levi work pants with a matching vest and jacket, a long rain duster jacket, a pair of woolen socks, some gloves, and a pair of boots. I rolled everything except the boots, which I carried in one hand into a nice and big wool sleeping blanket.

The horse-riding lessons started within a few days, and they were prearranged at another plantation, and done in the usual highest of secrecy. I thought that it was strange to now be able to ride the horse, because it made me remember all of those days of me running behind the horse, and then riding on the back of one with Master Jack determining the route. But look at me now atop the horse all by myself controlling it's direction, and the part about getting expert training was simply amazing to me, "boy have I came a long ways," I thought over and over to myself. My training lasted a few weeks, until, Master Jack was satisfied that it was both a fact and a certainty that I had totally mastered the art of riding a horse.

And, how I showed him that I was truly ready was after he had finally given me all of his various riding tests that I had to pass for him, I then all on my own, made the horse lay down on one of its sides and then get up in one smooth motion, with me still in the saddle. The look on his face was one of sheer amazement. This was actually a bow and arrow shooting trick that I had on numerous occasions, seen mi Abeulo perform and he always made it look so easy and effortless.

For he would pull back on his arrow, ready to shoot and then make the horse lie down on one of its sides, with the arrow still cocked and ready. And after a few long moments, he would make the horse rise up, and stand straight and tall, and at that exact moment he would fire upon his target, and always find his mark. Most folks would be stupefied about the horse's ability, but I would always be stupefied by the accuracy of his shot.

So Master Jack had never ever seen this done before, and all he could do was to just shake his head from side to side. I was then told that in two day, I would begin my new job. I was told to tell no one of my new job and the word or cover story that was being circulated about, was that I was being loaned out for long stretches of weeks to a slave owner, who was a distant cousin to Master Jack, down in a place called Georgia.

I was to help him hunt and fish a new and rather large tract of land, that he had just purchased that was adjacent to a rather large lake that bordered parts of Georgia and South Carolina. I was told to take tomorrow off, and do nothing except enjoy my family like it was a holiday, and then the following day after that, a wagon would arrive to take me to a remote line shack in the hills that are at the base of the mountains, and from this point two days after that, I would ride further west, to meet up with my party. And, we would embark on our quest to capture and return the "lost property."

All of the plantation owners in the old Province of Carolina would post a list of their missing property, and we would hunt them down. I went home, to rest and to gather my things Mamie had fixed up a nice pot of tender greens with fat back, and flapjack biscuits and we all sat down as a family, to eat and enjoy one another's company. As we sat there, I contemplated how my life was about to seriously change.

For one, I had never ever since we were married, been apart from Mamie, for any extended period of time, and with a new baby on the way for a visit, what if she needed me? Mamie sensing my mood, reached over and kissed me lightly upon the forehead, and said "Do not worry my darling Balaam, I will be fine, we will be fine, my daddy and mamma are both gonna look in on us. And, your grandfather has already pledged that he will be staying with us, on all of those days that you will be gone."

One thing thought Balaam, are you going to tell him, or are you going to keep it a secret, like Master Jack had said? It was agreed then, so after dinner, I went down to the barn, where he was. And, even though he was old and all gray about his head, he still had that twinkle in his eyes and a firm grip with his hands.

"Abeulo," I said, "I have something to tell you, and even though it starts tomorrow at first light, I want you to know my real whereabouts." With that, I told him everything of Master Jack's plans and of my part, and why I had been so mysterious these last few weeks. He just sat there and shook his head from side to side, and he pounded his fist into the palm of his hand, because, he was shocked, and a bit angered by Master Jack for even putting me in this situation.

I also told him of my dilemma, and how I knew that if anyone ever recognized me, or my face, that everyone, even him, would be in danger. But if my actions could help us to all gain our freedom, then I was more than willing to try. He sat back in his chair, pondered a bit, and then got up, and went to an old bench that the top opened up on.

He took a jar from under some old rags, from inside the bench and twisted off its top, and then used a stick to stir it around the contents. He then took a rag and wiped off the stick, and on the rag was this white substance, that had this kind of sticky tar look to it. He then took a small bit of whiten ash from the fireplace, and combined it with the tar looking substance, and then he showed me how to wipe it around my eyes, so that I looked like a raccoon about the eyes with white rings around my eyes.

He then took an old pillowcase, and with a knife he fashioned two eyeholes, and then placed it upon my head. "One cannot tell who you are, when you have this over your head and if you cover your whole body from head to toes with this substance, then it will shield your identity from the Blancos. You should always remember to never mingle with them, or never eat with them, or never, ever trust them about anything—and never, ever sleep around them either."

"Your identity must remain a secret, as you do the devil's work. And in the summertime, if they are in need of your services, then we will figure something out then. But now, in the fall and winter months this pillow will not only shield your face, like a mask does, but it will also keep your face warm."

"Now also remember one more thing that these kinds of men are dangerous and savage, and murder is a way of life with them. They have no qualms about killing and I have seen with my very own eyes just how brutal they can truly be toward anyone that crosses their paths. For these men are some of the very same ones, that ride with the sheets over their heads."

"And, I still remember that evening just as dusk was falling in the sky, I heard this sound of thunder, that came tearing down the road as a group of hooded riders came at a full gallop, like they were after something or someone. I had first heard the sound from a long ways off—like a rolling ground thunder, so I got off the road, and gingerly worked my way into a sticker bush, and settled down to see what all of the commotion was about. In two shakes of a lamb's tail, their horses were whizzing by, as the riders whipped and drove them relentlessly."

"After they had passed by and the dust on the road had settled back down, I tracked them to a place that was nearby in the woods, and watched as they surrounded whatever that was which one of them was dragging with his horse—which turned out to be a man, who was still alive. They then took the end of the rope and threw it up and over a thick tree branch and another rider grabbed the loose end, and strung him up, by his feet, as he swung back and forth. They jerked the poor fool's pants and shirt off, exposing his nakedness."

"They then whipped him with a leather strap, across his back and chest and legs, like you do to an animal. And, then they dosed him all over his body with kerosene. And, despite his pleas for his life, that he had a family, and 'that he weren't a runaway, just an unlucky soul, who had been caught on the road right before the sun had started to go down, he was truly on his way home, from doing his master's biding, at another plantation,' they still set him on fire, and hung him all at the same time."

"They then used his lifeless body for target practice, just for spite, as they pumped many bullets into it. Now when they were finished after burning, and hanging and then shooting the man, they all gathered around the tree, and had a few laughs. They then just left, and they did not even cut his lifeless and smoldering body down from the tree limb."

"This is what all negra deserve and let this be a lesson to all of them, 'bout what happens when they do not follow the rules," one shouted. "Now Balaam, perhaps he was innocent, but the real lesson was that being a negra, and being in the wrong place at the wrong time, with bad people can cost you your life," he said. "So always be careful, and always keep your guard up at all times. There is never ever going to be a time, when you should feel at ease, so get used to this feeling, and act accordingly."

That next morning around first light, after I said my goodbyes, to Abeulo and the children Lita and Tine and hugged Mamie ever so tightly, followed by a warm kiss—I jumped up into the wagon next to Master Jack. And we set off on a new chapter in my life, as mean ole Buck with his nosey self, watched us slowly go out of the main gate. He is so nosey I thought to myself, and he makes it his business to be in the know about everything slave related. So that he could snitch, if need be, to bring folks down to his level of meanness and despair. He is such a miserable old soul, and one day he is going to get his, and I only hope and wish that I could be around, to see his expression when it is his time.

We rode to an out of the way line shack, that was fully covered by a lot of trees, deep into the woods that was many miles from The Plantation, towards the mountains in a hilly area. And, I took out all of my things from the back of the wagon that I had fetched to create this illusion, that perception was the reality. Master Jack looked a bit nervous, but he never let on just how scared he truly was on the inside of his mind. But his actions betrayed him, by his sudden clumsiness, as he suddenly began dropping everything in his grasp.

The line shack was actually quite nice, and it had been his father's secret get away from it all, on those days that he simply had wished to vanish for a few days. It was built over a small water pond, so there was always access to water, with a water pump and a medium-sized bucket on the inside so that one never had to go outside, in search of a drink.

There was a fireplace, and the shack was fully stocked with things to eat. And there were a couple of shiny pots and pans that were hanging from hooks next to the fireplace. There was a small folding table with two chairs, and there even was a rather small, but nice cot to sleep on. The place was even made so that you could even bring a horse or two inside, depending upon their sizes, so that nothing was left outside.

Master Jack lit a fire while I untied the horse and left it in the fence pen that was right next to, but a part of the house. He had a picnic basket that had a lot of various things inside of it, and we sat at the table and ate in silence, as he gathered his thoughts, and worked up his nerves to speak. Once we had dined, he lit a cigar, and he then pulled out a letter, that would provide my cover story to my fellow slave catchers.

He then pulled out a flask so he could have a taste of some kind of spirits, and he went over the plan, detail after detail. And he then made me dress up, so he could instruct me on how to wear my clothes, tie my tie, cuff my pants over my boots, and how to wear my hat—which was a funny European looking top hat just right, so that I could look the part that he had created. He even made me practice using a fork and knife with a metal plate, so that I would fit right in with the others, and not draw any suspicions, as to who I really was.

He then told me that in two days' time, my job would begin. Then he then pulled out a map of the area that was for me to always keep, and he made me learn the terrain and area. I was to meet up with everyone at a large rock on a hill that was carefully circled on the map, at around two in the afternoon. And, this was about six or seven miles from our current location.

He then pulled out a pocket watch that had a long chain on it, and he then showed me how to attach it to one of my vest's buttonholes, and how to casually slide it in and out of the vest's pocket. The watch would be the key in the illusion he stated. Because, what slave would have such an expensive looking watch? he boldly proclaimed. It had been his, but since his father had died, he took his father's expensive gold leaf pocket watch, and just gave me his. He even had, had it engraved with the name Emmanuel Garcia on the back of it, so as to trick anyone looking closely at it even more.

And it was as if he had thought of everything and had left nothing to chance. We finally went to sleep, and in the morning after a fine breakfast, we went over everything all over again, as he watched with a keen interest, my progress from the previous night's lesson. But he could tell that I had picked up everything that he had required that I learn, so he seemed at ease with everything, as he slumped back in a chair as he first smelled, cut the end, and smoked another cigar.

He decided to take his leave, so around midday he left me so that he could get back to the Plantation while the sun was still in the sky. But before he left, he gave me an envelope that contained one hundred dollars. This was a shock because I was not expecting anything at all, but I guess all noblemen did have some kind of monetary freedom that resided in their pockets.

I then decided to do my daily routine of exercising, so I did my routine of running and stretching, just to calm my nerves, and to help me focus more fully on my approaching task. The day went quickly, but I felt that it was important to practice dressing up and applying the white substance all over my body to perfect the technique. I went to sleep early to get my rest for my big day.

But I remember that I could not really sleep soundly because the whole thing seemed odd and crazy. Then when the first light appeared, I was up and felt this nervous kind of energy that had me feeling wired up and a bit anxious. I decided to do my exercises and as I went outside to begin, I remember seeing a red-tailed fox that just sat there. It watched me in a strange manner as I watched it being probably more afraid of me, than I was of it. And, I marveled at how free it seemed, and how locked in, I was starting to feel.

I then started my daily morning ritual of prayer, and then of limbering up my joints and muscles, and then I slowly started getting dressed. I first put the white powder all over my body and around my eyes, so that I looked like a raccoon about the eyes. And then, I put on my clothes and boots, and tie, and over coat. I put the re-stitched pillowcase over my head, and pulled the edges firmly down, and then tucked them inside of my over-coat.

This gave me a sinister look. And who would ever know who I even was, I thought, as I slowly opened the door to walk out-side and to meet the morning and its cold air. I did look respect-able I thought, as I nervously pulled my watch from the vest pocket to check the time. I mounted the horse and trotted to the meeting place, in a rather slow but gingerly manner. And, as I got closer to my destination, a knot grew in my throat. I saw standing by the rock, about a baker's dozen or so men and eve-ryone turned to look in my direction as I approached, and slowly eased up on them.

"Howdy," one man said, as he smiled at my getup. And an-other one said or really mumbled "Good idea 'cuz it is cold as the dickens out here and keeping the face warm is a must." What is your name fellow another one asked, who is you? Scared, I started speaking in Spanish in a low voice, which sounded strange and much different from my natural voice.

"Mi nombre es Emmanuel Garcia y soy de Madrid Espana. Puede alguien hablar Espanol? Mi Ingles es limtado. Yo soy un seguidor (In English - My name is Emmanuel Garcia and I am from Madrid, Spain. Can anyone speak Spanish? My English is limited. I am a tracker)." I pulled out the letter and handed it to the nearest Blanco, who looked at me kind of crazy like, and who then handed it right to another Blanco who slowly started to read the letter out loud for all to hear.

"To whom this may concern: This is the representative from the Strickland Plantation. His name is Emmanuel Garcia and he is from Spain, and he has a somewhat limited vocabulary. He knows some basic English, like yes, no, come, go, stop, and so on, but he is not comfortable with whole sentences yet. So, he doesn't talk much, but he is a great tracker, and therefore he will serve our purposes.

His job is only to track down the runaways, and nothing else, and I mean nothing, so never ask of him to do anything but track, or you will have to answer to me, is that perfectly clear? Now one thing, his face was horribly burnt and disfigured in a fire, which has caused him to become extremely shy, and this is why he chooses to wear that covering over his face. So, he will not have to expose his shame and humility, so please just leave him alone, stay out of his way, and let him do his business. He is our gift, and we are extremely lucky to have an individual of his talent assisting us on our secret Mission. Please afford him the courtesy that you would of any gentleman of nobility.

Sincerely yours, Jackson Bernard Strickland, Esq."

They all kind of looked around at one another, and a couple of them started laughing, and ridiculing and mocking me, as one man said, 'Spain, Spain, what is he doing here I wonder?' 'While another said he probably ain't never felt this kind of cold before, so it will be mighty interesting to see how he reacts to it.' Another one sucked his teeth and said, 'Nobility my ass, I could give a damn about nobility, who cares about affording him a courtesy, just who is he suppose to be?'

Then a fat one replied," hush up, for here he comes." "Who is he," I wondered as everyone turned left 45 degrees to face the fast approaching rider, with a dog running closely behind him.

"Is that him?" one asked in a serious sounding voice, as another nodded, and said "yep, that is him, Jebediah Scott, in the flesh, and he is one of the meanest ole cuss's in the whole state and the South for that matter."

He was hired to lead the group, and they say that he would rather kill you than look at you, and he never ever smiled or made small talk. They have said that he has never ever said a kind word a day in his life. This was they said, because his mammy died when he was really young, so he has always lived a hard and rugged life without a woman's touch, so he is a cold blooded cutthroat killer with a sinister nature, who hates everyone and everything in the whole world.

He must be getting a pretty penny, if he is even involved with this operation, so those darkies ain't got a snowball's chance in hell to get away. Because, he loves money, just as much as he loves killing, or being mean and nasty, and, he should never, ever be trusted at no time, if you know what is good for you. He is a great tracker in his own right, and he learned his tracking from an Injun tribe that he use to trade and conduct his fur business with.

So they say that he can hunt down and track down any and everything. He may look old, but do not let those old looks fool you. For he is a killer of men from way back, and he takes pleasure and pride in the fact that he has killed many, many men, women and even some children they say, as if killing is his badge of honor. As he rode up, he slowed down just enough, and grunted angrily, "Let's move time is 'a wasting, and I's cold, so let's go and get the job done. So who is the tracker?" he said, as everyone scrambled to first, mount their horses, and then keep up. I raised my hand like a school kid, and he yelled, "Can't you speak?" as he spat tobacco juice in disgust towards my general direction. He then slowed to a complete stop, and as we all gathered around him in a semi-circle.

He then yelled, "okay we will work in two groups, with the tracker fellow leading a small group, which will funnel the runaways toward the bigger group. We will ensnare them in our trap, and if they run, shoot them down right there, no sense in fooling around with them. Just make quick work of them, rope 'em, and just drag them back to the pickup wagon."

"Now, telling just who they are will be hard. But let each owner deal with what slaves are his, our jobs are just to bring them back, dead or alive, more dead than alive if it comes to that. And as soon as the pick-up wagon catches up to us, just throw the body in the back, and get back into the hunt."

Right then, the person who had read my letter out loud from Master Jack, handed it to Jebediah Scott, who read it. And then, all in one motion, he savagely crumpled it up into a ball and tossed it onto the ground, as he again spat more tobacco juice in its general direction seemingly this time, in both disgust, and in general contempt.

He then said meanly, "Okay just so that you all know, my deal is separate, from what you all will get. I want to just be able to return a body—warm or cold, so that I can get my return and percentage fees. So don't ever ask me about your money, because I don't know, nor do I care, so am I making myself clear?" he said as he slowly moved his hand over his gun holster, while he gritted his teeth. "So remember," he said, "don't let any darkies get away, always shoot them, and ask questions later, and if you wound one of them track them down to the gates of Hades if you have to, but bring me back a body."

With that, he pulled out a paper, which had the list of who had escaped from what plantation. He then separated us up into two groups, as he jawed a bit with certain men that he knew. And, as the wagon that he was talking about approached, he turned to me, and said, "Okay Spaniard, your job is to do the actual leg work, do you understand? Go on and get going with your group, and work to find them and when you do, send word back—what direction they are moving in, and most importantly what way is you going to turn them to us? So, we can be waiting and ready. Do you understand you stupid looking bastard?"

I nodded my head yes, and I then naturally assumed my new position in the lead, or on the point. So my group, which was five in total, set out in a fast gallop after our first target—which was two runaways who had escaped just two nights ago and headed due north by northwest. As I looked for clues along the way of their whereabouts, that very first time was actually very easy, because those two runaways were easy to track and catch, and they just gave up all together, without so much as a fuss, when our tracking party had caught up to them.

So they were treated pretty decently, and they were, after all, alive. We did not even have time to send word back, and it was really, all over before it began. Who knew? What could I say? These poor fools were cold, and so any source of heat was an attraction to them, like bees are to certain flowers in the springtime. So I just followed the clues, that all pointed towards any source of heat, and just like animals who follow their natures, these fools had gone and started a small fire to stay warm.

The smoke led us right to them, and instead of sending back word, we rejoined the main hunting party, back at the Big Rock with slaves in tow. Their hands were tied tightly at the end of a medium sized rope, as they ran to keep up, with us on the horses. So the main group had this look of amazement, as we came into view with our victims, 'on the rope' so to speak, and us eagerly, looking for our next assignment.

Jebediah Scott, excitedly yelled, "Now that is what I was talking about, getting the job done, in an efficient manner, without a bunch of wasted talk, but next time don't waste the time to come back to the big rock, stay there and always send one of you all, back, with the word of where the next meeting place, on the road will be. We must move as a unit and coordinate our efforts. You did do good work though—make no mistake about it. But listen, and understand the plan, and stick to it, no matter what. For the other team's goal will always be, to catch up to the five of you all, and close the jaws of the trap or snare." This then, became the general pattern of my new job, assembling at the big rock, getting the hunting report, and then capturing and returning the property or chattel, as Master Jack called it.

As I became more knowledgeable, there were always three kinds of runaways that we were after. The first kind is the kind that stays local, which always made no sense at all to me. These poor fools would escape, and then stay around locally, and even at times attempt to sneak back, to their plantations, every so often to steal food or a blanket. They would also give up immediately, seemingly glad or relieved to be caught, with maybe having to endure a beating—but at least they would be alive and eventually warm.

The second kind of runaway was the kind that would hide out miles and miles away, from their plantation. They wanted to wait until the weather would break, so they would change their location from day to day, or even every few days or so. But at least they understood that they needed to keep moving.

But to most of them, they did not think that by them leaving a fire still slightly burning or lukewarm, or by them not even covering their trails, that they would even be caught or sought after. But the cold does make you do strange things, when it is affecting you. So tracking them was really like tracking a wild animal that leaves obvious clues as to their whereabouts in the cold months of the year.

Then, once you were able to determine their general hideouts or locations, it was easy to know where they would be, or could eventually be going. So just like the wild pig, which marks its path, these hapless souls, just blundered about in a random fashion, while they were betraying themselves, marking their direction and route. These kind, were also prone to run, when we caught up to them, and many of this kind were shot or wounded, and even killed.

The third kind of runaway was the most difficult—or shall I say the hardest to track. Because, they always seemingly had a plan, and they really were trying to escape for good, right then and there. They were not taking any chances or fooling around, and so these were the kind, that would just up and disappear right off the face of the earth or so it seemed, always heading north. We would track them to a point, and then, they would vanish out of the thin air.

Even that old devil Scott himself was mystified. And, it seemed as if these kinds, of runaways had a definite method to their movements. We would ride around in circles for hours and then days upon end, but nothing it seemed to offer up any clues or hints as to their whereabouts, which we knew was north, but in what direction north was the question that we could never ever seem to answer.

We even tried tracking them at night, because it seemed as if, they only traveled at nighttime or after dark, but this was dangerous for the horses because of holes, branches, uneven ground, and such, but nothing seemed to work. "Where had these nigras gone?" Scott would scream, "they could not have just up and flown away,' so look around, again, and make sure that they are not hiding anywhere nearby."

But I knew that these kinds of runaways had boarded a ghost train, on a secret underground railroad, that carried them to freedom, and that they already were long gone, and far away from where we were. Now the whole time that I was becoming acclimated with the new job, I was becoming a ghostlike figure in my mind. Because even though at first, I thought that my current job did not bother me, but deep down inside of myself, I knew that it really did.

Then one day I discovered that, yes, I had become affected by the hunt, and although it did not bother me outwardly in the beginning, now things had taken a new turn in my mind. At first, I could not eat much or even really relax, and I was always extremely cautious whenever I went anywhere and especially back to the line shack. I would ride in circles sometimes for hours and, or retrace my own route over and over again, in fear that someone would discover my resting place, and then un-cover my dirty secret.

At times I even felt this wave of emotion that was centered around, being ashamed because here I was a slave, who was catching other slaves. And, I was returning them back into slav-ery, just so that I could one day secure my family's freedom. This whole thing felt wrong, because here was I, participating in a system that enslaved other human beings for profit.

Now, everyone had a different story concerning how they became entwined up in this mess, but I slowly recognized that in the end, everyone was a victim because of it. Slave master, slave, and even slave hunters all were on some kind of level, affected by this sad business situation and everyone seemed ruined because of this experience. And that was one of the real reasons why slavery just had to end.

So this job began to eat me up on the inside of my mind, making me like an emotional cripple, because I had to act like I did not care. But sure I cared, and I cared a lot more than I was willing to admit, I later found out. Besides, in my mind, I was like an actor in a play, because all that my job required was that I was to track them down and point the others in the right direction.

I did not re-chain anyone, or whip or beat anyone, nor did I ever shoot or rope anyone. I never lifted a hand, to do anything bad to anyone. So, I just concentrated upon doing my job, and tried not to think about what I was really doing or contributing to. So, as long as no one knew who I was, it was okay I gathered in my mind, and I also figured that my part in the catching would only put my family one step closer to our promised land.

But it is funny the way that life has a way of changing and testing and hardening a person. Life also can twist you up on the inside of your mind, and even though you think that you are doing okay, things have a funny way of slipping out, and start to affect you on different levels at first in small ways, and then finally, in big ways, shapes or forms.

So you then start to naturally begin to lose your self-respect and focus. I recognized that this was the way that they coped with the situation. So what would I use to cope? And, I had better do something fast, before I would go plum out of my mind, because of this whole sordid and nasty business.

I was even becoming listless and sullen, and I had no appetite most days. I had no real vices, and I needed something to focus my attentions upon, before I went insane or worse with all of this turmoil happening inside of my head. The new job itself was a huge success, because we were extremely efficient in our operation. After the first month, we had such a high return rate that our services were in high demand, and we had so much work that we had to add additional riders, just to keep up with the increase in demand from the plantation owners. We also were getting offers from states that were outside of the Old Province, and this increased our overall numbers. So by the end of the first year's winter, we had brought back 65 runaways.

So if my numbers were right, then in four years or less time, the lives of my family and me would be changing for the better. Spring and then summer both came, and I had really expected to end this costumed lie. I had expected that things would be going back to normal, until the next winter approached. But it was not that easy, or simple. Because, things started to happen all throughout the South, as it was called—and, it looked far uglier than ever imagined.

The Northerners, called Yankees, were pressing the Southern states and landowners to stop slavery all together. They said that slavery was wrong, but in reality, they wanted to stop slavery because in the North, these Yankees paid labor wages to their workers, but the Southern slave owners did not. This created an unfair advantage, the Northerners said, because there was an unequal division of the labor wage itself, which was in effect creating two separate but equal United States of America.

This advantage, the Yankees said was also tearing up the very fabric of the Union, so sooner or later it was eventually going to boil over and come spilling out upon everyone. So the whole issue over slavery now was changing, and these Yankees, it was being said, were even aiding the runaways, and, were thus making the runaway issue itself, not just a wintertime situation, but now in effect—a year-round pursuit.

Those damn Yankees were now making it really easy for me to get spotted, because in the summertime, there were more prying eyes, than in the winter, and my costume was for the winter and did not contain summer types of clothes. The mask could be worn year-round, but I would just have to continue to wear my same outfit no matter what season we were in, because protecting my identity was a must. Someone could spot me, and everything would be lost.

I now had to be even more careful, and really cover my trail because, if anyone ever discovered my rest stop, the line-shack, I could be doomed. I finally after a few weeks of soul searching, and personal reflection, decided to create a second hiding place that no one, not even Master Jack would know about, so that I had a fallback or plan B if my resting stop was ever discovered. So when I had free time, I searched both high and low, until I found a suitable place that fit my needs and wants.

After scouring the woods for a suitable location, I finally found, close by the secret school, a partially covered cave that was situated about halfway up a medium-sized hill, hidden in some thick trees and bushes. It also was wide enough for the horse, and if you did not know what you were looking at or for, you would not even spot it. I borrowed some farming tools, and then used them to carve out the cave's entrance and inside the cave itself, just to make it a little bigger and easier to access.

Then I cut down a bunch of scrub bushes and branches, tied them all together, and put the ends in an old burlap sack and bound the bag with some rope, and then used the loose end of the rope to pull everything toward the opening that created a natural dirt sweeper broom and hole plug.. This would be how I would defend against any unwanted company, whenever I was in the cave. I also brought some supplies to this new hideout, and when I lit a fire, the smoke would always go towards the back of the cave, and not be visible from in front of it.

I next fashioned a small bed of soft fern leaves and branches, upon which I placed a bed sheet over, and to my amazement it actually was quite comfortable to my back and body. I was then ready, if something was to ever happen, and this place was like my secret fallback position, because having my very own, that only I knew about, was a plus in my favor. So now feeling a bit better, I returned to the now year-round hunt, still confused— but now even more than ever determined to really get this dirty business over with, as quickly as I could. Because all of this, I feared was slowly driving me insane.

It was getting harder for me, to keep pushing this feeling of remorse that I was having, to the back of my mind. It was as if the filter in my brain that allowed me to do this, was slowly ceasing to work right, because of all of the stress I was under. So I was extremely concerned that I was going slowly mad because of this whole sordid affair.

The business with the tearing of the fabric of the Union was getting worse and worse, and things between the southern and northern states, seemed a bit tense and were starting to unravel. Master Jack was always in Raleigh, and he always looked troubled whenever I saw him. He also would look tired, as if his life was really no better.

I was tired and troubled too, but the one golden thing in my life was Mamie, who was my angel, who was sent down by Amen Ra, from the heavens to enrich my life and to make me become a better person. Mamie understood my pain, and she always would console me, without saying one word, or by not ever judging me. She would rain her kisses down upon my forehead and hold me so tight that sometimes I really felt as if I could not breathe.

But Master Jack had no angel from heaven to save him here on earth, and he always had a lot of things always on his mind, that he did not have anyone to really talk to about, but me. One evening, Master Jack came seeking me out, and he turned up at the line shack. Waiting for my return, he just sat there on one of the chairs in the near dark, with only a tiny lantern burning, and drinking some liquor.

His loud and heavy breathing, kind of startled me, as I walked in from the outside into the near darkness of the inside. And, he tried to stand up to greet me as I entered, but he drunkenly kind of fell backward, and into the folding table and then onto the dirt floor. I helped him up and placed him into a chair. And after he took another swig from his flask, he started rambling about how war was inevitable, and how the whole situation was going to drive him to the poor house.

Also, he said everything that his father had worked for could be subject to possible loss, and how this all did not seem fair and just. He may even have to join the state militia to protect and preserve what was built up over time because, all Southern gentlemen would be required to defend their property and possessions, and more importantly if the Southern states succeeded from the Union, then there would be no going back.

A war would wreck the Southern states, economies and stifle production, and if it could not be waged up North, then a southern battlefield, would doom them all, because their economic landscapes would be ruined. He then started talking about his wife, who did not understand him, at all, and how she was more concerned with her image, her ability to go shopping in Charleston and Savannah, and of being that gentile southern lady, with good looks, charm, and hospitality. Their relationship was going nowhere, just like a stick that is stuck in the mud, and she provided no mental relief, in these times of instability and uncertainty.

She also had a not so secret lover, on the outside of their marriage, her childhood boyfriend and really, they should have never ever gotten married in the first place. But it was an arranged marriage, that she did as a favor to her daddy, who was a good friend of his father, and her father only wanted a business connection from his empire, to the ever growing and enormously vast, Strickland empire. And, that combination of the two empires would have created an even bigger business entity.

He also stated that he had, never ever trusted her, and she had never trusted him either, because she had somehow always known about his certain tastes and preferences in women. And, she was quick to use this information against him, whenever the chance occurred that she could use it to her advantage. So as long as she could maintain her title and good looks, and she had all of the 'clout' that being married to him, Master Jack, offered, she could maintain the look of being an honorable Southern lady of distinction and grace.

It was funny too, because honor was everything to all Southerners, yet being dishonorable is really what occurred almost daily, all throughout the South. He then abruptly out of the blue, changed the subject and said," Balaam, you must leave the South, as soon as you can. I will change the stipulation of our Agreement, and I will reduce the number from 250 to 200 and you have almost already passed the halfway point."

"So, when you reach the number 200 you are free, my good friend, free like that bird on that day, that was up in the sky, do you remember that bird Balaam?" I shook my head yes, as he lowered his head upon the table and passed out. And, I just sat there stunned beyond measure, wishing and or hoping that he was telling the truth, and more importantly that he would be able to remember his drunken boasts when he came out of his drunken stupor.

I laid him gingerly down onto the cot, and loosened up his tie and shirt, and it was at that exact moment in time, that I kind of felt sorry for this Southern gentleman, that lay before me, dead to the world, in a liquor induced slumber. Because, he seemed like he was on the verge of losing everything that he held near and dear to him, or so he thought. And, there was nothing that he could do about it either.

His life was trying to maintain the Southern public face that everything was all good and was actually better than ever. And of course, never ending, even though the threat of war was a very real possibility as both the north and the south jockeyed for position and bargaining chips in the great houses of the Capital, which was in some place called the Federal District of Washington. He was one of only a handful of men, who knew the real ramifications of what was actually going on, and how things had taken a bad turn for the worse, some years before. So, he was reacting to a real and definite possibility, that scared him, and he seemed so helpless and vulnerable, as if he could sense the beginning of the end of his way of life. So he had started drinking to ease the pain of this burdensome quandary, but there were no easy answers or solutions to the problem, so this caused him to drink a bit more each and every day, until he was using the drinking just to cope with the each and every day to day. So, he slept for a long while, and finally around first light, he suddenly, lurched up from the cot, as if he had been pulled awake by some unseen force. His eyes were extremely bloodshot, as he looked around surveying the dimly lit room, for his travel bag, that was under the table. He opened it up, and he pulled out a half empty whiskey bottle, that he took a long and hard swallow from and then wiped his mouth, and said, 'that he felt hungry'. I had already started a fire, and had begun to make some vittles, that consisted of some bacon, and eggs, and some bread that I had first buttered and then toasted over the fire. We ate and then he lied back down on the cot, and went back to sleep, as if he had never even been awake, and I just sat there for a long time and watched his body's breathing go in and out, as his chest moved up and down in rhythm with one breath after another.

Around mid-morning or around 10:00 am, he finally woke up, and he made himself sit up in that other chair, as he yawned and yawned, until he was fully awake. He then started to continue his painful story, which seemed odd, because he was pretty drunk when he had passed out. "Balaam, sorry about falling to sleep last night on you, in the manner that I did, but I have had very little rest or sleep, because of this sordid mess. I was really tired, and actually still am, if I can tell the truth. So that was the first real sleep that I have had in months. I do not trust anyone in my home, and my mind seems to be always thinking about first one thing and then another, so I get very little sleep. But I know this and that is, that we southerners are all now going to have to change, I am afraid, because our way of life is being threatened, and debates are not going to make things better. We, southerners have lived 'the life of Riley' for far too long now to change, and for the most part, we know that enslaving other men, is morally wrong and inhumane, but the free labor part of the business has been far too lucrative for us to ever walk away from or ever forget."

"Most of us are Christian and God-fearing people, but we have ruined all of our workforces, by bringing them all to an animal level that was always beneath us and used religion, and science to justify our behaviors. The labor wage situation is changing all of the good times of prosperity, for all us southerners and it is only the jealousy of the northerners that is creating this friction. They choose to pay for their labor, and pay a wage, while we do not, and our labor is free. So it has become a problem, a big problem, with slavery being seen as the main issue of this complicated set of issues. The so called perfect union is about ready to come apart at its seams because of the slavery issue, but it really is not slavery that is causing all of this unrest and turmoil, it is really the free or non-costing labor that is behind the whole strife. There is no way out of this mess it seems, but if it is a fight that them Yankees truly want, then it shall be a fight that they will get. Some people are even talking about and exploring the possibility of southern states succeeding from this non-perfect union, and erecting barriers and gates to divide off our state borders."

"We will fight Balaam, yes we will, because we won't be told how to rule our own lives. I control my own destiny, and no one shall dictate how I will choose to seek a profit, no one, and I would rather die protecting what I have created than to just give up and do nothing, and accept what these northerners say is the correct way to now conduct business. In life, I have been always told that we should always strive to do better than our parents, and if your parents give you something, you should try to make it grow and increase. I sadly may not be able to accomplish this, because a war will destroy everything that my father created and worked so hard all of his life to sustain and grow. So I am trying hard to devise a way that my family's business enterprise, will continue to flourish and be bountiful and filled with plenty. The hard part is, how to quickly diversify, my current business assets and move into new areas of businesses which are profitable and, on the forefront, and needed by the general population, in this ever-changing America—before the war arrives. And, it will arrive because this conflict appears to be our fate and in the cards for us as a nation. I also did not forget what I had promised you," he stated, "and when the time is right, we will explore how we will release you from our enterprise." He then yawned and it then seemed as if he started to get sleepy again, and so he suddenly got up said good night, then went and laid back down onto the cot and in an instant fell into a deep slumber. I just sat there kind of stunned, trying to process everything that he had divulged to me. And to be honest, the very first thing that came into my mind, all jokes aside, was that these Blancos, as a people are really a strange bunch. They seem so bent on having their own ways that they would rather die, than even try to change, in any kind of way, and survive. They always talk about high ideals, and a more perfect society, and how noble they are, but in reality, they always say one thing and then do another. They are quick to say that they, as a nation, should not be judged, but yet they are quick to judge other nations. And in this country that was founded upon great words and ideas, it is amazing to see just how contradictory that this place called the 'United Snakes,' actually is.

So for the northern and southern states to not communicate with one another, is basically just crazy and very short sighted, and dangerous because once the bullets start flying there will be no turning back. These Blancos will be the death of us all, and I need to come up with a serious escape plan just in case things do really fall apart, and we need to take our leave, and head either up north or out west towards the area, that is known by the Blancos as simply the 'bad lands.' Because if these two groups do commence to fighting over economically based principles, the Negra may get caught in the middle, which could be bad news and hard times for Negra's, just like someone whom is caught between two bears that are fighting one another, which sounds kind of scary. So right then, I began to think of how I could learn more about the underground railroad, and how I could make a connection to it, that would enable us all to use it, and ride it's rails all of the way to freedom.

I looked into the light that was coming from the small lantern, and as the light itself got bigger and bigger as I concentrated upon it, and it alone, it then drowned out everything else in my plane of view, and I clearly remembered the very first time that I had come across it, and seen it with my very own eyes, as if I was experiencing it all over, once again, for that very first time. I was hunting with mi Abeulo, and he had wounded a rabbit, and it had suddenly disappeared, as if by some magic trick, from our view. It had gone down into some kind of carved out place, that had tracks that led into it, but it did not exit out of. "What kind of place is this," I asked him, "where tracks go in, but do not lead out?" He shushed me to be quiet, by using the "be quiet look," by sliding his finger from one side of his mouth across his closed lips, to the other side of his mouth. And after a quick surveying of the scene, we went down, into the sanctuary and secured the catch.

Inside, the place had a stone ringed fire pit, a bunch of hay, and it had another exiting point in the back of the area. The way that it was made, was that the covering had a roof of leaves and sticks that were tarred to the manmade canopy. This provided and excellent illusion to the naked eye, and if you looked right at it, and did not know that it was there, you would assume brush and foliage on the side of a hill, and nothing else. It would appear to be a part of the natural scenery. We quietly eased out, still without saying any words, and only after we were miles and miles away, did he finally answer my questions. 'Balaam', he said 'that place was a secret hiding place for runways'. He said that he had seen something like this before, and it was during the time that we first arrived, in this strange land that is filled with strange people. The seasons had changed, and the very first cold had arrived. He was out hunting and had given his guardian angel and the masters the slip, by staying on his prey that he was tracking, and not slowing down for a rest.

He had come up over a ridge, and had thought that he had smelled smoke, and had heard people talking, as a baby cried. Everything sounded muffled, and then got real quiet, so feeling somewhat curious like any cat, he instinctively doubled back and dropped to one knee, went into his quiet hunter mode, and after a few minutes, the sounds came back to life. There under a manmade lean too, were runaways inside, and their hiding spot was ingenious in its effectiveness and in the simplicity of its design. He slowly crept away and took up a location where he could spy on the location, using ground cover, as his shield. Then, in less than an hour, around dusk, the lean slowly opened up and a man and a woman, with a very young baby, that was tied to her back, all came out, heading north by northwest. He tracked them for a mile or so, before he turned back to head towards home, before it got too dark, and so he could re-connect with his hunting party. He had also wanted to get a better look up close, under the lean to at how it was made or designed. The area was carved out and there too was a stone ringed fire pit, and the cover was used to shield the smoke and make the fire disappear, even at nighttime. Someone had gone to a lot of trouble to design this hiding place, he stated, and it really served its purpose, he had marveled.

So this, Balaam, was just another version of these same kinds of sanctuaries and said that I should always be aware of where they were. Because these sanctuaries, he felt were a part of something that was like a fable, or myth on our plantation, which was called the "underground railroad." He first had heard about it from two older slaves that he had given some of the extra days catch, to, and although they did not have anything physical to give in return, what they did have was a gift of knowledge. This gift of knowledge was centered in and around the name of this certain thing, and this thing was called the "underground railroad," and how if one could connect to it, they could ride its rails all the way to freedom. That this so-called Underground Railroad had a map that was encoded in the stars of the nighttime sky, and this star map was the route towards this eventual freedom. They were too old to ride upon its rails, but they had known someone from our plantation, who had connected to the right people, and he had just up and disappeared one night and was never ever seen again, in these parts.

The masters had gone out in search of him, and they did search both high and low, but he had simply disappeared, like a thief in the night. Abuelo was intrigued by this talk, but he had not seen any evidence of proof, until that first night, and now he had second proof with me, so there must be something to those old head's story, and the liquor was just not doing the talking, it had just loosened their lips. So now years later, it was time to start looking for any connection to these rails that you ride towards freedom, because our very lives might depend upon it. The next thing that you knew, time itself, had flown and almost a year and a half had passed, since Master Jack's drunken revelation. The situation had gotten worse and everyone was on edge and scared. The whole southern confederacy as it was being called, by some people, was crumbling under the northern pressure and something had to change. The plight of slaves in the southern states had become downright hellish, and brutality was the norm and not the exception.

The slave hunting enterprise was really picking up, as more and more slaves were trying to escape to places up north called Ohio, Pennsylvania, New York, Boston, and a place called Nova Scotia, and a place called Ontario, which were both in a county called Canada. This was disturbing to me because—yes it did aid me in my quest for our family's freedom, but it also led to death, and or mutilation for the slaves that we caught. My team of killers, who all now had adopted my style of protecting my face, and now they also wore masks to protect their identities, and they were simply vicious, and swift to shoot first and check things out later. They had gotten more violent, and they were determined because of the money, to kill, no matter the age or sex. They now never brought back runaways alive, and to me, it was just plain old murder, and state sanctioned murder at that, with both the law and their 'God' on their sides. They seemed so dark sided and full of evil. I daily started to question myself, again, like was I also evil, and really was I also just some kind of evil hooded figure that tormented and then brutalized runaways, just for the sake of a dollar for them, and my family's freedom for me? These killers seemed to be strangely addicted to both the thrill and the kill of the hunt. We already had a scary and frightening aura about us, as we now always appeared right around dusk with masks on, charging hard on our horses, and showing no mercy for anyone or anything that got in our way, and especially not "niggrahs." We did our jobs with ruthless efficiency, and I cannot begin to tell you and make you understand the unspeakable and brutal horrors that I have seen committed against runaways. This has been done in the most horrible and uncaring and unfeeling and sadistic manner that made me unable to face my fellow slaves, and even look then in the eyes, and act as if nothing was going on or wrong, and then to go on with my day.

The situation was ugly and getting uglier for me by the hour of each and every day. I truly felt as if I was walking all day on, never ending burning coals, feeling all hot on the outside of my body, while filled all up with pain and anguish on the inside of my mind. Everything in my thoughts seemed so clear in the beginning, but now my thoughts seemed all clouded and muddled, like a dirty stream's murky waters hides its bottom from view or eyesight. So how did I ever get caught up in this craziness? I must be a fool, to have even gotten involved in such foolishness, and even have been a bigger fool to think that I could succeed in obtaining my overall goal, of one day liberating my family from this madness that is known as slavery. But no matter what, I had to remain focused, and calm, so that I could be the hero for our family, despite this twisted and hellish existence.

But the only good thing was that by my count, I was getting closer and closer to my new target number, which was now 200 and on that day when I had finally gotten within ten of this figure, my life was turned upside down and inside out, by a disheartening turn of events. My new older brothers were both living out their lives, but they had never ever gotten over seeing their dead daddy swinging in the wind, while hanging from the tree that day. They had both become hardened and mean ole cusses, and like Abuelo had said, that fate always has a strange and or funny way of repeating itself, as Mark and Paul both became a bunch of trouble to themselves and more importantly to everyone else. Once John, the oldest of Rufus' three sons, was sent away forever, there was just not anyone in their lives that could make them listen, or whom they would heed advice from, and they had just gotten worse and worse. They would work because they feared the lash, but beyond that, nothing else was getting done, and they both had no discipline, or any desire to better themselves in any way.

Now slavery was not any easy thing, and people, when telling stories about it, will probably make it out to be easier that what it truly was. But believe me when I say that it was "exhausting work." Niggrahs were treated worse than animals, and it was vicious on men and women alike, but folks still had a desire to make a way out of no way, but sadly not my two older brothers. My older brothers both had families, or pieces of families, children by different women, unmarried yet married, adulterous sinners, who did not care for anything except each other, and to drink and tell tall tales about their pappy Rufus and their oldest brother John. They were just the two opposite sides of trouble, and everyone always gave them a wide berth, or steered way clear of them, whenever they appeared and their nicknames on the plantation were, 'No Good' and 'No Count.' They were really perplexing indeed, because there was goodness inside of them, but it had become lost somewhere along the way. They could pick a fight with you, to rob you, and then the next day appear at your door asking to borrow something that they needed in a very sincere and humble manner. They stole mostly everything or anything that they wanted or thought that they needed, and if you got in a fight with one, the other, if he was close bye, was bound to join in, like they had some strange bond or oath that bounded them together, like twins. They rarely traveled alone, or without each other, and if anything turned up missing or broken, they usually were the first suspects.

Now one of the Strickland plantation's hands, a fellow named Morrison, lived with his family in a rundown line shack, which was on the outer edges of the property, that he was using his salary to fix up and purchase. So because of his job title, which was that of a junior overseer, he was able to use the wagon to go into town each and every week, to buy items that his family needed to survive on and to fix up the shack with. Now he had a daughter who was 19, who would often stay behind, to tend to the shack, while her folks went into town, but she had a dark and dirty little secret that she was keeping from everyone. She had a weakness, for the niggrah flavor, and many times she would invite certain males up from the slave quarters, when her folks had gone into town to help her 'tend to her chores,' and as reward for such service, she would treat them to a certain sweetness, that was found between her legs, her 'heaven on earth.' So as she became more and more experienced, she became more and more adventurous, and she required older acquaintances.

On one such day, she required Paul's services, and not knowing of his troublesome ways, she just assumed that he and he alone would be coming up, for a service visit. When Paul showed up, Mark was with him, and after they had hastily helped her to do her chores, she falsely assumed, that only Paul, would be bedding her down, that mid-morning or early afternoon. Well as soon as Paul was finished handling his business, Mark hopped right in, and when she protested, he forcefully took her 'heaven on earth,' by beating her about the head and upper body until she stopped her protesting. After Mark had had his fill, they then ransacked the shack, and only when they heard a wagon approaching, did they leave—with certain items in their possession, leaving her whimpering and moaning and laying all butterball naked and sprawled spread eagle on the floor. The Morrison's quickly, of course cried rape and robbery, and they demanded to know from her, who was the guilty man or men. She fingered Mark and Paul to cover up her naughty deeds, and they were both either stupid or simply too lazy to run, and they were quickly caught, and then severely beaten across their backsides with a pig hide switch, and then locked in a salt shack for six months. They were also sentenced to hard labor, and when they were out of the lock down, they were going to be sent away to some place called Florida, at one of Master Jack's distant cousin's plantation. The plantation was adjacent to a swamp, that was called O-key-fun-no-key, and the place was rumored to be 'hell on earth.' Now about three months before they were to be released and then sent away, them, boys somehow up and escaped, and not only stole supplies, they also mysteriously got a hold of some guns, while vowing to never to be taken alive.

Now I had seen trouble before, but mind you never ever like this, and I had no idea that all of this was even taking place. This calamity would not simply blow away, and it seemed like all of the white folks were out for blood. A white woman's virtues all soiled by niggrahs, and all niggrahs ain't no good, hang 'em, lynch 'em, and we need to teach these niggrahs a lesson, were just some of the things that they were saying. I had been out on my weekly patrol and did not know any of what happened, when I was summoned to return to the Plantation immediately, post haste, as fast as possible. So to continue my illusion, of my whereabouts, I had to set out for the line shack, and then change back to my real identity. Once I changed clothes, I set out on foot, but was eventually met by old man Caldwell, who picked me up in the wagon, and he harshly ordered me to get into the back, as he kept his hand on his gun the whole time. What had happened I had wondered? Did someone die? Why is this Blanco ready to shoot me? What did I do to him? Why did he seem so angry? Why was I pulled off patrol?

Something must be really up, because he seems like he is ready to explode from sheer anger at someone or something I thought. When we finally arrived at the Plantation, the whole place was a ball of confusion and turmoil. There were no slaves in sight, not even the house slaves, I thought, so something must be really up. Groups of white men on horseback with dogs, thundered down the path towards the road, all giving menacing looks as they rode past the wagon, angrily shouting something about 'catching those rapists.' When we pulled in front of the big house, there was Master Jack standing there, giving out orders and he was actually sober, which was shocking, because for the first time in months, I was not seeing him in some kind of a drunken state. He had even taken a shave, but he seemed on edge and that is when I realized that he had a gun strapped to his waist, as did all of the Blancos, I began to notice. "Balaam, go home, and I will speak to you directly," he barked, no warmth in either his voice or eyes, "Because this situation needs my immediate attention." He then directed groups of waiting men to search in one direction or another, and to 'take dogs and lanterns, but do not come back without them boys.' I was bewildered and dumb struck, wondering to myself, just what was so blame important that had happened to create such a ruckus.

When I approached the little barn, where we lived, Mamie was at the gate, and upon seeing me she ran straight to me, and fell into my arms. She started bawling and it seemed like it was almost a full bucket of tears, and it took a while before she calmed down, to tell me what had happened, to create this gawd awful mess. Upon hearing of this sad tale, I took her inside the little barn where my entire family was all holed up; looking like the grim reaper was inside the room with us all. It was really quiet, like the morning after Christmas, and everyone looked concerned and up tight. There was also something else in the room that overtook me, as soon as I stepped inside of the space, and it was fear.

Yes, the smell of fear was in the air, and it clung to everyone like the smell that a skunk sprays you with, when it acts defensively to protect itself. She did not know the whole story, but she repeated the part of the sad story that she knew and by and by the whole story came out as everyone told about the parts that they knew. Mamie's daddy made the most sense, when he said, "Balaam, these white folks are really riled up, like a summer storm. Them boys done went out and got they selves into a whole pack of trouble, that this time cannot be overlooked or dismissed, or even fixed. Boy these white folks act like all niggrahs did this, and they act like they want to kill us all, for their actions. The slaves on the plantation are all mad at us, for bringing the white folks down upon their heads, as if they think that we can honestly control Mark and Paul's actions. So it appears that everyone is mad at us, and judging us, because they see us as part of them boys family, and no matter what happens—they will always judge us differently. My family and I, he continued have never ever been bad or in any trouble, so why should we all be judged so harshly because of these two crazy ass idiots?"

Finally when everyone had had their say, all that I could do was to lower my head and sadly look toward my mother's location, as she just sat there in silence with tears streaming down her face. Master Jack finally summoned me, late in the evening, up to the Big House, and as I strolled up to it, there was a strange soberness about the whole Plantation. Master Jack still looked upset, as he himself let me into the house, and the first thing that I noticed was that he still was wearing a side arm. He took me right to the library, and he ushered me to a seat. And as he plopped down in his chair, he opened up a drawer and pulled out a cigar that he lit, and he just stared at me for a long time, before he finally spoke. "Balaam let me first say that, I know that all of this does not actually concern you, but it does, because this involves your so-called brothers. Also that this could have not happened at a worse time, and let me be blunt in saying that, I really do not need any of this right now, and I need to know where you stand concerning this issue? Can I, once again, count on you Balaam to bring your brothers back, and do it quickly, before everyone gets further riled up, or really before your brothers, do something even more stupid."

Raping a white woman was bad enough, even though it appears that it really did not start out as a rape. But to escape confinement and then also to steal guns and rifles, well folks get scared and start thinking about the infamous and well known insurrections, and about the Nat Turners from 1831 in Southampton County, Virginia, the Demark Veseys from 1822 in Charleston South Carolina, and the Gabriel Prossers from 1800 in Richmond Virginia, that reside on each and every plantation, in the South—that are just waiting for a spark to start the fire that creates the boil up, and then the revolt. Do you know how many slave revolts have occurred in North America? Well starting in 1712, in New York City, to the 1842 slave revolt in the

Cherokee Nation, there have been 12, and not including four others that were not on our shores, 11 of which were suppressed.

So you see Balaam, your brothers have made people's fears come to life, and another truth is that they do not EVER want any other slaves to even find out about this, and think that they too could escape, steal weapons, and evade detection. There are also a lot of rumors that are floating about that are also not helping the current situation, such as 'that your brothers have vowed to make this a slavery issue, or that they have secretly already visited other plantations, trying to recruit fellow disillusioned slaves, or that some slaves on our plantation have even flatly stated that they are thinking about joining your brothers, to create a following. Well I do not know what is true or what is false, concerning these rumors, but folks are nervous, and unrest is on the rise, and we need a quick resolution for this messy and unfortunate occurrence. They need to be caught—and fast, and there is not a finer tracker than you in the whole state, but the question is 'where do you stand?' Will you help me to catch them before they can inflict any more damage and or even kill someone?" His eyes glared and bulged out of his head like a fish's, and he seemed like someone who was slowly going mad in his mind from some unseen pressure or force.

What would I do or what should I do? Also if I do nothing, how would the Blancos and the slaves all react to my family? With that thought a cold feeling passed from my mind, then down throughout my entire body, and as I winced, I knew what my answer was, and what I must do. I looked at Master Jack firmly in his eyes, and then stated that I would go out, find them, and then bring them back. But this would be my very last such 'deal,' and when this was over, that it was time for me and my family to both take our leave of this place and the Plantation, and move somewhere, anywhere up North. I also had fulfilled my tracking duty numbers, and by my count, my two brothers put me over the new number that he, Master Jack had quoted that day and night in the shack. I also had the letter, which was our original legally binding contract of law that released us, from the covenant of slavery, and I was merely exercising my right to pursue a better life for me, and 'mines.' Master Jack, who had stood up, kind of like gasped in amazement and his hardened eyes grew soft and kind of gleamed. He had been so taken with all of the events swirling about his head that he had forgotten about the letter's contents.

As he sat back down in shock, he mumbled something about his God, " oh my God", and then something about how time had really flown, and how by some cruel twist of fate, my last job would be tied to my very own kinfolk. "What a way to lose the closest thing to a true and real friend that I have ever had," he sadly uttered, "and even though it involves your no count brothers, it still does not make it any easier to bear. Everything in my life is constantly changing, and things were so much simpler when we were littler Balaam," he said in a flat tone, sounding very much like someone who was lost in the woods and given up or who'd surrendered to being lost, with no hope of research. Master Jack's countenance had gone from being a raging madman, to that of a scared little boy whose leg was pinned underneath a dead horse, about to face uncertain consequences, all within a matter of minutes. He looked so helpless and saddened, as if he did not possess a single friend in the entire world.

But I'd had enough of the slave hunting business, and this game was sickening, and I wanted and needed, and deserved a better life for me and 'mines.' So I took my leave of Master Jack, leaving him sitting there in his favorite chair, staring into nothingness. And, I let myself out of the room, and then out of the house—and I did not even look back, because I was done with all of this, and once this last hunt was over, we would all be free. I also would be going solo, by myself, on this slave hunt and no matter what it took, they would be coming back, be that dead or alive, but I was determined to bring them back, and then retire, so to speak, from this crazy job. Now I figured that my loco brothers had about a three days head start on me, and a day and a half's head start on the hunting party. But I had one advantage, which was I was determined that they be located before a bigger price must be paid, and they must be stopped before our family was made to suffer from their reckless behaviors. Besides I did not want my brother's behaviors to ruin my goal of freeing the family—and if they were not caught, then all of the hard work in my quest for freedom could be lost.

So, as I walked back into the barn, I could see the grim look on everyone's faces. I explained to everyone what Master Jack's meeting with me was about, and how he wanted me to help track down the boys. I then told everyone about my plan and how our survival in this strange land depended upon catching them and then, to follow my instincts to have us escape into the night. I would work out the specifics and get back to everyone on how and when we would accomplish this feat, but we had to have a positive attitude to accomplish our goal. I then started to concentrate on my next task, which was how to catch my brothers.

I then started thinking about our family's history and how my grandfather had said that we were the actual descendants of the Root clan of the Bandar tribe, from Benguela which is in the kingdom of Kongo, which were the loyal servants of the 'El Fantasma Caminante.' Our oral and written history tells us, that for over 280 years and more, we have protected the 'Fantasma.' This Fantasma's legend goes back well over 280 years, and how in the year 1566 pirates had seized and ransacked a ship, killing everyone on board except the son of a nobleman. They then set it on fire, and scuttled the ship, causing it to sink, and they thought that their work was done. But the son escaped and made it to our Island home, which lies off the coast of, and is a part of Benguela, which is on the continent of Alkebu-Lan. On the island, the son was nursed back to health by our descendants, and upon his return to good health, he swore eternal vigilance on these pirates, and that one day, he or his descendants would get their revenge against them. The son learned from our tribe, the warrior ways, and some years later when these same pirates came to the island to evade arrest, and plunder the island for the things that they needed, he began his fight against injustice and it's many forms, by defending the island and turning back the tide, to become the Fantasma Caminante, the Fantasma that cannot die, that moves like the wind. Our family was at his side during the battle, and at the battle's end, we were entrusted with the oath of eternal allegiance, because of the way in which we had protected him, in his time of need.

So down through time, each successive son and or in some cases daughters, took their turns as being El Fantasma Caminante. Over time, we became inseparable, and we assisted him in various ways all throughout the centuries, and if Portuguese slavers had not intercepted mi Abeulo's family in their boat which was coming back from a trading roundup and fishing trip, on the mainland, Abeulo would have been given his turn to be the protector of El Fantasma Caminante. Abeulo and his mother and one of his brothers were in the boat, and the brother died defending them, and thus Abeulo and his mother were sentenced to a life of servitude in Hispanola. They left behind his father and, his oldest brother who was the protector of the 'ghost that walks,' plus 2 younger brothers and three sisters, but although they were cut off from everything that they knew and loved, mi Abeulo never ever forgot about his duty, and why he was trained. That is the real reason why he had trained me so hard, in a ritualistic manner, repeating what he had been taught, of our secret family business, because he knew that our family's duty was an eternal bond.

His eyes would twinkle and shine, when he spoke of our family, and of 'the ghost that walks,' and this was so important to him, that at times, this is what helped him to survive all of these years, his at times hellish fate. I then realized, at that particular moment in time just who I would become, which would be the slave version of the New World's Fantasma Caminante, a real life phantom menace from the shadows of the night, and lead my people to freedom, with my first true test being to track down my very own brothers. I instructed my beloved Mamie to be ready to leave when I came back, and we would get out now, before Master Jack changed his mind, and there will be no questions asked—and please have everything ready to go, on the quiet of course. I then saw my Abuelo, who gave me some strips of something, that were all wrapped up in a handkerchief, and he told me to only chew on these one at a time, when it was the proper time, and I would know when that time was. I then waited until sundown, and as the sun slowly crept out of sight, I slowly eased myself out of sight, and off the Plantation.

As my eyes slowly adjusted to the darkness, the night began to come alive and I made it to my secret hideaway and applied the white clay substance all over my body. This would be to give me the appearance of a ghostlike figure that would be scary, and menacing, and hopefully it would scare off any interlopers as I tracked down my brothers. As soon as I applied the white powder to my entire body, I felt invincible and confident, and I wondered who or what would be foolish enough to even get in my way, as I looked like 'death come a calling.' I suddenly came back to my senses, and began to really quicken my strut, as I forged through a set of heavy and dense trees. My senses seemed alive, and for the very first time in my life, everything seemed to start to make sense.

I suddenly smelled the scent of a fire to my left, a ways away, but my sense of smell was keen and sharper than most folks I reckoned. It was like the white clay had helped me to reach down deep inside of myself and pull out something within myself. But what I was feeling was the tradition through training that my family had developed through time. Nothing now seemed too great a challenge, no obstacle too strong, because my vision and hearing and even my sense of smell, were all now enhanced or heightened. And yet as I ran along, my very feet felt as if they were not even touching the ground, thus leaving no trail, as if I had never even been there, like a true ghost that walks. As I got nearer to the fire, I could hear it cracking and popping, as the Blanco's sat around the flickering flames.

I normally would have veered away and around such a setting, but the clay seemed to have given me another advantage or power which was, that because my body was covered with it from head to toes, my body scent was completely covered up, thus enabling me to stand upwind from anything and not be spotted, or more importantly to not be smelled out. I crept almost within spitting distance of the shadowy figures, and it was as if I was invisible or something. I could hear them talking about catching those neggrahs and getting the bounty money to live high on the hog with. They were about either four or five settled down eating and talking loud. And, if my brothers were around, they would spot these fools right off, and move away. They had a dog with them that was asleep, but suddenly awoke and started to move in my direction.

I stood perfectly still and watched, as the dog seemed confused by its own senses and eyes. It saw me, but the clay must have given me the appearance of a Blanco to it, with no smell, so it just turned back around and slowly walked back to the fire. The men around the fire hardly even noticed what had happened, but to me, this was a revelation. Not appearing to be a negra or a Blanco, would help me to evade detection, move amongst nature and be a part of the land. I eventually backed off and started looking for a pattern of clues that would lead me to my older brothers. It took me about one and less than a half of another day to find their trail, and then come up with a decision about what must be done. I knew that they were not going to travel that far, so I decided to go to the line shack, to rest and come up with a suitable strategy.

My heart said' go to them and peacefully coax them back to the plantation', but what my head said was an altogether different suggestion. I was all 'tore up' inside my mind, like a battle that was raging inside my mind, and I was caught up smack in the middle. What must I do? What could I do? I knew that they would not come back with me, and that they would resist my suggestion. If they were as determined as the Blanco's seemed to indicate, then it could be a struggle, to make them even listen. They also could be a rose thorn in our family's quest for freedom, because their behavior could really ruin my long-range goal of securing our family's freedom.

Their selfish behaviors could bring us all down, and I was not going to let our family down. So what should be my response, I wondered? I then decided to get some rest, because I really had not gotten any real sleep since all of the commotion kicked off, like a summer storm that suddenly sneaks up on you on a bright and blue clear day. So I lied down and began to formulate a course of action in my mind, and at some point, before the darkness that is called sleep, I very slowly realized what I had to do, with a strong resolve. I would go to sleep, and not think about it, and just rest as long as I needed, to be as fresh as possible. I slept for the rest of that same day, and deep into the night. It was as if I was dead to the world, locked into an eternal rest, unable to revive myself. When I finally started to wake up, it was a first a struggle, but once I really was fully wake, I felt alive and alert and confident. I stretched and then began to coat my entire body from head to toe, with the white clay substance. I felt like the white clay gave me an edge over everything and everyone, and I coated it on thick. I also used the coal from the fire, to make black circles around my eyes, to even give me a more menacing look.

As everything dried, I opened up the covering in the floor, and decided that I needed arrows with medium length shafts, study enough to pierce most thick hides, and also three long shaft arrows, for greater distances. I would also bring a long rope to be used to bind things together, and a blanket, and a pair of gloves in case I hand to use my hands in a rough way. I also needed a couple of sharp knives, to be used to cut wood or bushes, or human flesh if need be. After the clay had fully dried, I donned my attire, and jumped up on the horse and then set out on my quest, with the morning sun still many hours away from appearing. I got within the area where the boys were hiding out, hid the horse in a grove of trees, and sure enough they were still there, holed up towards the top of a hill, right were the rise broke off sharply behind some large boulders. They were in a semi cave type of impression that bent into the rocks and provided excellent shelter from the elements.

They would light their fire just beneath the smallest of these rocks, because it was not easily detected. They would only be visible when they stood up on the woody and hillier side. And if I worked my way around the bluff on the backside, and found a spot through the dense wooded thicket, I then could get a clear shot—even though it was a little longer—and dispatch my older brothers to the hereafter. I felt nothing, as if the sleep had washed away all of my fears, thoughts, concerns, and more importantly my doubts away. I knew what I must do, and more importantly why I had to do this. I took my time, positioned myself in the thicket of bushes, used one of my knives to fashion a clear path for my arrows flight pattern, and then leaned back and just waited for my shot, as the sun started to slowly rise in the eastern sky. My brothers were talking low, and barely moving about, and as the daylight finally started to appear, they begin to stir about. I popped one of the chews in my mouth, and readied my bow pulling on the string, testing its tightness. In about 5 minutes or so, Mark stood up and started to yawn and stretch, and began to move towards the fire that was situated just below their location.

I positioned the bow, judged the distance, steadied my legs, and mounted the first long shaft arrow which had grooves cut in a circle around the entire shaft, pulled hard on the string, took in a long and deep breath and as I slowly released the breath, I released the first messenger of death. Quickly I reached for and mounted the second long arrow and pulled hard on the string, all in one smooth motion of body movement, as I waited for my second opportunity. The first arrow whistled in the air and found it's intended target, true and strong, striking him just above his eye, in the eyebrow area, on the right side of his face, causing his lifeless body to tumble down upon the rocks. I felt nothing.

Paul heard the sound of Mark's body falling down to the ground upon the rocks, and stood up to investigate, to see what had happened to his brother. I waited for him to see his brother's lifeless condition, and then about a split-second right before he turned around towards my direction, with a glazed look of wild eye horror in his eyes, I released the second arrow. It sounded like it was whistling, as it whizzed through the air, and he had this funny look upon his face as it impaled him directly in the top and middle of his forehead, instantly dispatching him to the next life, and I still felt nothing, as if my guilt had flown away like a bird. Maybe it was the chews I wondered? I made my way to their encampment, and decided that I needed to fashion a litter, so that I could take their bodies back to the plantation to end this storm that they had created. I lined the two bodies upside by side, like prey and retrieved my arrows. I carved a litter out of three stout and thin tree limbs, used a small piece of the rope to bind everything together and went back to where the bodies lie to conclude my business.

But just as I got back, a sound startled me into a defensive posture, as it moved upwards towards my location. It was the Blancos with the dog, from the previous night before, heading directly towards my position, and as they got closer and closer, they started to sound like they were directly below me at the bottom of the hill. I knew that things were about to get sticky, like a beehive that is loaded with honey. The one leading was talking that he had spied them boy's location late last night, and he had hunkered down, so that they could not get away in the wee hours of the morning. He had witnessed the arrow shots, and he was amazed at the accuracy of the shooter. It had to be Injuns, he stated, because no other race could have fired arrows with such skill. He could not see who the shooter was, because the person or persons was obscured in the thick trees. He had thought that he had seen something moving around the rocks, so he had waited until he saw nothing movin,' and he was scared as hell, so when he finally had the nerve to approach the rocks, from below and go up to see where the bodies were laying he gingerly walked up over a rise in the hill, then around a large boulder, and he could see that both of them boys were goners. But strangely they had been lined up side-by-side, right next to one another, and the guns were still there, as well as a lot of things that they had stolen on their rampage. He had gone back to get them, and he now felt much better about his chances to get his piece of the reward money, because strength is always in numbers, or so he thought. I coiled my body up, and quickly readied myself. My mind whirled as it changed over to an on-the-battlefield mode of mentality as I simultaneously analyzed the situation and developed an attack strategy.

How many I wondered? Keep your ears turned up, and tuned in, for the sound of the dog, I told myself, for it will be moving faster than any man as it makes its attack run on my position. I readied myself, and just as they got to the half way part of the hill, on a somewhat rocky part, I leapt out, into plain sight, as if I had suddenly appeared there from out of thin air, my bow drawn, with an arrow mounted with the string pulled back hard, and with another between my teeth, just looking at them ever so calmly. Now here is the strange part, it then was as if everything slowed way down, but I was moving faster than my normal speed as if I was able to control time, in some kind of odd way—and slow them down, and yet speed myself up. Maybe it was the chews?

What I thought was four or five men, was really six, and they seemed quite startled by both my presence and my ghostlike white appearance. I could see the expressions of surprise and horror on their faces, as they slowly yelled or mumbled something, they then slowly started reaching to draw their guns, I assumed towards me. The one who was leading the group, and who had been doing all of the talking, slowly turned and started to run back down the hill, as the second and third men both froze like a river in the dead of winter, while the man with the dog slowly broke to the right as if to out flank me, to get behind my position. The last two men stopped, and both dropped to the ground, to secure their positions. I released the first arrow, I put my hand to my mouth and pulled the second arrow from between my teeth, re-fitted and mounted, and rapidly fired it, as I pulled the third arrow from the quill.

I re-fitted and fired the third arrow, and things kind of like sped back up in a funny sort of way, but then slowed way back down again. The first arrow impaled the running chicken, right into the left side of his buttocks. Arrows two and three both found their marks, hitting the two frozen men, one in the throat, and the other arrow landed in the middle of the victim's chest. I heard a sound, from below, it sounded like it was a gun shot, and then I heard something else, something that curiously whizzed above my head, as my ears re-focused on a running and scrapping sound that approached my position from behind me and to my right. I could now feel myself dropping down to one knee, at the same time pulling arrows from my quill, and releasing three more messengers of death towards where the sound of the gunshot had originated from, which was from the same location where the men had dropped down to the ground seeking cover. The fourth arrow stuck deep into the back of one man's leg, around the calf area, while arrow five stuck into the other man's shoulder, effectively stopping him from shooting his gun any longer. Arrow six stuck into the very same man's boot, forcefully impaling it and his foot both, to the ground, as he still was groaning from the arrow five's impact upon his shoulder area. I wheeled 180 degrees around to my right, and instinctively pulled both knives from my belt, and waited for the dog and the man's murderous onslaught. The man was just about to emerge from around a boulder, but the dog was already almost upon me. So, I readied myself, and because I had never ever taken my ears off the trashing sound of its feet making contact with the ground, I knew exactly where it was the whole time, as it rapidly approached my position.

I could see it's extremely sharp looking teeth were clenched, and they looked ready to sink into my skin, but I just calmly and without thinking or using much effort, threw the knife, which struck the dog right in the gum line of its sharp looking teeth. The dog crashed into the earth headfirst without so much as even a whimper—another victim of my assault, just as the man was about to emerge from around the boulder. When he came into clear view with his gun drawn, I threw the other knife, which sunk into the upper middle section of his body, as he crashed to the ground in a heap, with a loud thud sound. I turned back around to see two men now further down the hill struggling hard to get away, shooting their guns wildly and blindly over their shoulders behind them at no apparent target. They seemed to be shooting them to just appear to be shooting, as if they were trying to scare me with the shooting sound. But they had no real target or objective and really were just wasting good bullets.

As I surveyed the battlefield, I could see that the first man had stumbled, and dashed himself upon the rocks, once the arrow had struck into his buttocks, which caused him to fall awkwardly. And he was alive, just a coward covering himself up with his arms over his head and not moving. As if by being quiet, I might just think that he was dead, and simply go away. Arrows two and three's victims were both dead, as was the man and his dog. I let the remaining three escapes the scene in their struggling manner, because all three seemed scared and unwilling to really join the fight at close quarters. Only the man and the dog had truly died glorious deaths, because they had displayed some courage and had sought to bring the fight to me, and it was at that moment in time, when I truly had realized what one of my slave hunting associates had meant one night, when he talked about "the battlefield and how it has only one real and true test, which is the survival of the fittest."

I quickly went and retrieved my knives, as I pulled the dead bodies of the dog and the man to my original position and then moved quickly down the hill to retrieve those bodies and my arrows, because the sound of gunfire may have brought curious onlookers. I lined up the bodies of the men and that of the dog, like I had done with my brothers making them too look like prey, all side to side, and next to one another. I took my brothers' bodies and lashed them to the litter, put the blanket over their lifeless corpses, put the guns on top of the blanket, donned my gloves, and then dragged them to where the horse was tied up, and then went back to wipe out my trail. Once I had decided that my trail was covered, I used Abeulo's trick of putting covers that were made from old rags onto each of the horses four feet to mask it's hoof marks, jumped up on the horse, and then dragged everything back to my secret hiding place to lay low for a while and to rest. For someone or something had just dispatched 3 Blancos to the so-called pearly gates of Hades, and there was going to be hell on earth to pay for such a ghastly deed, but still I felt nothing.

But los Blancos were looking for Injun raiders, who ambushed these southern gentlemen. The three that had lived, all told the same but different versions of the same story, and all three of them stated that they did not actually see who or what had jumped out in front of them because the sun was in their eyes. They just had all seen one person, they all flatly stated, who appeared to be white, who fired such a deadly and accurate volley of arrows so fast that it seemed unreal. How could it have been only one person, and it seemed to have to have been at least 2 or 3 people. How could one person kill three men and a prized hunting dog, wound three other men, and then disappear with the bodies of the wanted criminals? It was as if they themselves were being hunted, like they themselves were the prey of this phantom menace. Two stated that they never even saw the bodies of the two Negra, and so they did not even have any evidence to confirm that they were really and truly both dead.

Only Boles, who was also himself wounded in the attack, was a witness to their deaths, and he claimed that he saw the both of them boys dead, and that their bodies were lined up, just like the dead three men and the dog were. But he was knocked unconscious when his head hit the rocks when he had fallen down from taking a arrow to his behind. He just remembered staggering up and going down the hill and getting the hell out of there as best as he could, under his current circumstances of being impaled with an arrow, in his derriere and all. So he honestly was not looking back to see what was behind him, because he had lost his courage, and was truthfully only fearing for his very life, and nothing else mattered. A posse of about 20 men went back to the scene, and who or what had done this was not known. All that they could tell was that the dead bodies were all lined up next to one another, in a row, all side by side and the bodies of the two slaves that were named Mark and Paul were missing. This also naturally led to another question, that they also could not find any answer for, which was why were the bodies of the dead all lined up in that manner?

Did it mean something? Something like a horse had appeared to have drug something away, but the trail had ended and gone cold, and was lost forever. The Blanco's were now more nervous and frightened, because what if Paul and Mark were still alive, and out there somewhere? Could the two of them have done all of this to somehow escape, some wondered? But no slave or slaves could have done this, because such a skill and accuracy requires rapidly quick thinking and exceptional eye and hand coordination, others stated. Now everyone knows, that negra do not think or react quickly to nothing, except the lash or a meal, so there is just no way that them two boys could have done all of this without some kind of help, was the commonly held opinion. So Injuns took the blame and the Blancos became even more riled up.

The Blancos were plumb scared, and to think that a killer or killers were out there on the loose was even harder on their nerves. The deaths frightened the whole of Cumberland County and its neighboring counties and I decided to get back to the plantation as quickly as possible. I had hid my brother's bodies around the area of the little shack, in a bunch of sticker bushes. I went back to the shack and washed the clay off of my body, and only after the sun had gone down, did I even venture outside to scout the land on guard duty. I waited until the deep of night two days after the battle, to move the bodies. I decided to appear to be a Blanco, when I was dropping off the bodies. So I donned the costume appearance of the Spaniard who was my other self, and using the horse, I dragged their lifeless bodies out of the sticker bush and back to the Strickland Plantation.

I wanted to leave them hanging on the big tree that is in front of the big house, but there were simply too many people moving around for me to pull that off, so I improvised and decided to leave them down in front of the slave quarters. I first stripped them of their meager clothes and left them hanging on a tree, so that in the morning they would be hanging there by their feet, in all of their nakedness, for all to see. Master Jack—as was the entire plantation—was awakened to blood chilling screams in the early light of that next morning, as two dead and naked-as-jay-bird men were found hanging upside down by their feet, from the biggest tree down at the slave quarters, lightly swinging in the morning breeze. Mark and Paul were both dead and stiff as boards and they appeared to have been dead for a few days. No one had seen a thing, was the commonly voiced story, but in the slave community, a story started to circulate that there had been a witness.

Ole man Buck, had been not doing very well since all of this ruckus had began, because he was scared of losing his house servant position, that defined who and what he was. He could not sleep, because he was not used to the rough treatment of confinement to only the slave quarters and "nowhere else" commandment that all slaves had been receiving ever since Paul and Mark had committed their eternal sins. So his sleeping pattern was thrown off, and then throw in the facts that he was drinking heavier than usual, and that now he had to sneak off to smoke the leftover cigar butts that he took from Master Jack's study, it all made him be up at all hours of the night, so that no one would see him smoking. So he had gone outside to relieve his bladder and to sneak a smoke. He had crept down in some bushes to handle his business and just when he was about to start draining the liquid from his body, is when he claims that he saw something that really scared the b'jesus out of him.

It looked very much like a white man, because of the way in which he was dressed and handled himself, with a hood over his head he first rode up dragging something, calmly looked around then unhooked the rope off from the horn of his saddle, threw it over the largest and sturdiest tree branch—grabbed the loose end and then wrapped it back around the horn, then used his horse to string them Boys up by their feet until they were swinging in the wind. This figure looked twice in his direction and even rode to very near where he was in the bushes, and when it was finally leaving, it even turned around and shaped his hand in the fashion of a gun, and then pointed it directly at his location while clicking his thumb downward two or three times, as if to say that he knew that Buck or someone was there secretly watching. Ole Man Buck said that "he was so scared by this gesture that he peed on himself right then and there," and he now has taken up with the bottle even harder than ever before.

But who is going to believe the babbling of a mean ole house slave who always stays drunk? So this story stayed only within our community, because we all knew that if the Blanco's had someway gained this knowledge no matter be it either true or false, we would all be at risk, as they sought to verify its validity. I laid low for a few hours, and then went back to my hunting job, still dressed the part of Emmanuel Garcia. They had not even known that I was gone, so I just blended back into the hunt, and later that evening Old Man Scott told everyone to take the next couple of days off, that he had been summoned up to the State Capital, and that we should meet back at our meeting place in about a week. As we were about to break up, a fast-moving rider caught up to us, to give us the news of the deaths of my brothers, as he rode onward like an express rider to relay the good news, to the surrounding counties and districts. My fellow slave hunters roared in approval, and two of them even shot off their guns, as we all went our separate ways.

I waited at the shack for about one day and rested and killed some game for the trip back home. As soon as my folks saw me, we all started crying and lamenting about my brother's deaths but on the inside of my mind, I still really felt nothing. Master Jack had forbidden anyone to even cut them boys down. Then after three days had passed, he had an overseer to set their bodies on fire, until there was not much left of them, and then and only then, were we allowed, to give their remains, a proper send off. The next day, I was summoned to go see Master Jack up at the Big House, in his study. He seemed extremely nervous and on edge, and he paused for a moment at the door, as our eyes locked onto each other's. He stared at me for a long time, as I stared right back at him, unflinching and strong.

He finally started mumbling about something, which he then repeated a second time, but with more volume in his voice, "I know Balaam that you, have done all of this," as he slumped down in his and his father's favorite chair. He then reached for the bottle that was next to a shot glass and poured a full-to-the rim glass to drink. After downing the whole shot glass in one quick swallow, he stated again, "You are the only one who could have done this Balaam, and you know that I know it was you, and only you. Do you know that you are one of my closest friends, and that I love you like you were one of my own brothers? I will never ever turn you in to the authorities, but you know that the only person, who could have fired those arrows with that skill and accuracy, was you or your grandfather, and we both know that he is too old, and besides he was being watched at all times. It is just not possible that he just could physically have been there and here at the same time. So it was you, and only you Balaam, because I was there that day when you shot the arrow to save my life, and it was and still is an amazing feat of skill, but more importantly it was a longer distance, than the shots that killed your brothers!

Now when I told you to bring them back, I did not say to kill them, so why did you decide to end their lives? But then damn you, you went and killed three men and a dog, and wounded another three? It looks to me like you hunted down and killed five men and a dog, with the coldness and ruthlessness of an assassin. One against eight and a dog and you did it as easy as taking sweet bread from a two-year old baby. What have you become? It is my fault, he continued, because I am the one that exposed you to such darkness, when I asked you to do my evil bidding for me, my oldest friend. In hindsight I should have never given you the slave hunting job Balaam, because it has changed you. I guess being around such evil, is such a hard thing for the mind to comprehend, no matter how truly good a person is. Because being around evil all of the time, will cause the dark side in one's nature or being to arise, and snuff out the light side. Has the dark side awakened in you? And if it has, are you at least trying to fight it, because you seem so un-emotional and coldly calculating, like a machine, a killing machine that apparently has no match or peer.

You have somehow changed yourself into a weapon of death, and I shudder to think about the consequences, for once one tastes the taste of killing, where will it truly end? So our agreement is now dissolved, you have fulfilled your quota, and I am forbidding you to never, ever again ride with the hunting party. Do you hear me? Never ever ride with them again—for any reason, no matter what, he repeated a second time! I am giving you and your family their freedom, but this would only be Mamie and the children, and your grandfather, and all of the others will have to stay. I will draw up the papers, to make you all be free people and I will even throw in the reward money that was placed upon your unfortunate brother's heads. Take the money and leave this place and never ever come back or look back. Not that you are not welcome here my friend, but I want to help you to start over so that you can escape the dark forces that are at work here. Please Balaam, try and stay in the light, and with that he got up from his chair and walked over and gave me a hug that lasted for a long time. When he did finally let me go, he walked to the window, and just stared out of it, and when he turned around to face me, his face was wet, and his eyes looked so very sad. He looked into my eyes once more, and for the first time, I realized that in reality, he was now truly scared of me and of what I had become, with his help. But deep down inside of his mind, he was also scared that our grand little experiment would be found out, and that he would also be implicated as an accessory to the crime of teaching a slave to read and write, and then giving him the power to change his life.

So he really was trying to get rid of me, and of our dirty little secret, in a quiet manner to wipe the slate clean so to speak, before the genie was released out of the bottle, and could not be put back in. For if the Blancos ever knew of our sinful and unholy alliance we all would be good as dead to them, and his own life would be worthless, and everything that he owned would be forfeited as a penalty because of his sin. We stood there in silence for a long time, until I finally mumbled out that I was extremely grateful for everything that he had ever done for me, and my family. That he was unlike any other slave owner in the known world, because of the things that he had given to me, like reading and writing, and the freedom to travel, and experience new things. That because of him, I had gained a better understanding of the world in which we lived as he told me of other places and spaces that were far, far across the great watery divide—that some called the Middle Passage. For these places whose names were Paris, London, Alexandria, Madrid, and so on all sounded like and seemed to be mysterious and enchanting.

So it was he and he alone who had made me had this quest and thirst for knowledge, all of which in the end helped to create me, by allowing me to grow in the mind. He was now closing our chapter, by allowing me to become a free man and by also letting me take my family along to boot. I was eternally grateful to him, that we would be taking our leave directly. He ushered me out of the room by a wave of his hand, and as the door closed, I wondered if everything else to come, would be so easy? As I was making my way home in the dark, I then started to try to figure out how to begin to come up with a plan that we could all use, to take us all to freedom. I also then remembered what Abeulo had once said which was, "in any journey the first step was always the hardest one." So I then just had to come up with a plan and figure out a way to bring everything together, in one smooth motion.

So after mulling this over and over in my mind for days, and of course after consulting both mi Abeulo and my beloved Mamie, I finally came up with a strategy that I could follow that seemed to be sound. First off, I decided that I would ask Master Jack for a few things like a horse, that I felt that I would need for such a monumental task that lie ahead, but not tell him of my deviation from his decree. Because I had decided that all of my family would be free, from mi Madre, to my younger brothers and sister, and even my deceased older brothers' children if they also wanted to come, that is but we would all be taking our leave of this insane place. So my problem would be how to move a fairly large group of people, through hostile territory, in very trying times.

Because the Blancos had sensed that things were changing for them, they trusted no one, and viewed everything with suspicious eyes. So there would be no way on God's green earth that 20 or more people would just be able to move towards the north or the west, and not be stopped and searched many times over again. If caught, we would then be arrested and then returned back to the Strickland plantation, which was the only world that we knew up until that point. So, the so-called Underground Railroad would be the thing that I would use to sneak all of my folks to freedom. I would then study and accumulate a lot of valuable information that I would in turn use to try to formulate a plan to discover what this Underground Railroad was really all about.

I would scout the trails around the plantation, and go out far and wide, to see if I could find any evidence of this railroad. I knew that it was real because I had experienced it myself, so it had to be based upon something that was hidden right in front of our eyes. I then purely by accident one day was down in the quarters giving away some of the days catch to some of the less fortunate than myself, and got to speaking to an old head ancient one, who was born as a slave in this country, and he was actually much older than my own Abeulo. He had been put out to pasture, so to speak and he was just biding the time that he had left on the planet, experiencing the last years of a long and rough life that was filled with a lot of memories and practical life knowledge. Because he had survived when others had not, and more importantly also because he had both seen and heard a lot of things.

In a low voice, as he constantly turned his head from side to side to see if anyone was listening to us, he pulled me off to the side and told me that he believed that this riddle called the underground railroad was really a set of trails that the First Americans had used in this land, for over a thousand of years. Because the First Ones were the original inhabitants of these lands, and thus they had evolved a set of natural roads or pathways or routes all throughout land, that they used to travel on to get to places. These trails existed all over this great land, and the Blancos being the interlopers did not really know the lay of the land, so they were always discovering things that were not lost or hidden, but not these trails. Theses trails were of common knowledge to the First Ones, and were the backdrop for the Underground Railroad, so I had to find a trail and see where it took me.

Finding an original trail was kind of easy, because I just went back to where me and Abuelo had found the first sanctuary, as a starting point and followed the clues, because I was fortunate to know what I was looking for. The trails I learned over time, were a complex set of natural trails or routes, safe houses, hiding dens, sanctuaries, caves, or even holes in the ground. Some of these trails went north, by northeast, that ended up in places called Ontario, and Nova Scotia, or some of these trails that went west by northwest, and ended up in places that bordered on a place called the Badlands, or due west past a large set of mountain ranges, too far away fertile lands, that have an abundance of game and have sunshine year round and warm weather. The routes that pointed due north were being watched and staked out, by people who were similar to those from my old job, and the western routes were less known, but folks were still out hunting for their origins and locations, so we would use the routes that pointed directly to the Ohio River Valley territories and then on through to the Badlands.

So the Ohio territories would be where Mamie and Abuelo, and El Diablo, and the kids and I would first go to, and set up a homestead, and seek a new beginning. I'd put El Diablo on guard duty, and then have my family sit tight and await my and the rest of the clan's arrival aboard the railroad of freedom. We would also establish a safe place within these so-called Bad Lands, that we could go to if things got sticky for us in the Ohio River Valley. But the real question that kept revolving around in my head was when would be the best time to try such a bold and daring plan? I decided to just be patient and realized that everything would unveil itself in the fullness of time. I would just study and do the proper planning, and I actually began my quest, by silently tracking a band of runaways, that consisted of three males and five females with four young ones. They moved about only at nighttime, always around or after midnight, the wee hours of the morning. They rested in the daylight hours, and they always seemed to have a male on guard duty.

I trailed them off and on for about three days, noting that it was like they were being led along to various stops, along a path that went steadily northward. On the third day, I realized that another male, or so I thought, was instructing them in where their next stops would be, leading them to route markers, that were cleverly hidden into the clues held in the natural formations on the path, like notches that were cut into a tree, or rocks that were stacked up and pointing in a certain direction. This person, who was really a guide so to speak, would also provide or leave them with food and water, and would always leave out about an hour or less before them and scout ahead to ensure that the way was clear. After the third day, I decided to track only the guide, and this is when I made the startling discovery, that this man was actually a woman, who had steely eyes, and a firm jawbone. She was short in stature and very wiry, and I even saw her dip some snuff once, and she carried a gun. She was always looking around, and she had this keen sense of both hearing and smell. She actually almost saw me one time, when I had gotten too close to her, and I always felt as if she could sense that I, or something was watching her. She was rugged and determined, and she sounded stronger than most men that I knew, and her actions seemed like an old habit, or routine.

Who is this woman, I asked myself over and over again, and why or how is she doing this, by herself, without any help I wondered? As I trailed her, I watched her every movement and I even learned a lot of tricks, from her that would become useful to me in the days and years to come. For instance, she would always make the runaways walk towards a stream or river and then instead of crossing it, she would make the runaways walk backwards, carefully retracing their individual footsteps, so that it appeared that they had crossed into the water. They would then carefully use branches to wipe away their new course, and then choose another carefully chosen path, to create the illusion that they had gone into the water, which caused any trackers a lot of grief, as they searched up and down the water's edge, for a trail of where the tracks came out of the water.

This tactic bought the runaways a lot of extra time, and time is the one thing that all runaways needed. Another trick was to use branches of leaves that were tied to the runaways' waists, by ropes, that drug on the ground, to wipe away each person's in-dividual trail, and then walk in a circle to make any tracker really confused and or tired. So the point was it seemed, was to create a situation of frustration for the hunters, and use their tracking instincts against them, which was one of the greatest lessons that I learned in this very short time, from this mystery woman. Only years later, did I find out just who she really was, and her name, which I will never ever forget, was "The Black Moses." After tracking her for days, I finally turned back and made it back to my area of the Carolina's. It had just started to rain a cool summers' rain which is a nourishing and gentle kind of rain, as I trudged back onto the plantation.

I had killed some game on my quest, so it looked like I was on my usual routine. I took the meat, two skunks, a rabbit and 5 squirrels to the big house, divided the meat, and then headed on down to the slave quarters to show my face. I had been gone for days, and the mood of the quarters was downcast with an almost eerie quietness, and I wondered what had happened now. Well unbeknownst to me, four of Mamie's kinfolk had tried to escape and had been caught, and subsequently hanged till death, and of course strung up as a constant reminder to what happens to folks that try to escape. The look in Mamie's face told me everything that I, her husband needed to know which was, "it was really time to leave this place, as soon as possible." Mamie had endured much—as we all had, in our own ways of course, and she had always tried to remain strong.

She had bore us young ones, and never ever complained about anything. She had accepted my comings and goings, never once even sounding troubled, and even if she was scared or frightened, she never ever let on. She has always my savoir, my confidant, my soul mate, my wife, and a really good, good friend. We have never argued and even rarely disagreed. And so, when her face showed to me that she had had enough, then, I knew that she was silently signaling to me that it was time for us to move on.

She also had another secret that she finally told me, as we lay down to go to sleep, which was that we had another young'un on the way, and that she both wanted and needed this child to be born as a freedman or freedwoman. And that could be in any free place or lands, just as long as it was far away from here, from this place, and this hellish and godforsaken life. Days later, my plan started to come together, and it was simple and daring, and—It involved a different course of action. I would first need Master Jack to create the illusion that I, and my family had indeed all been sold to another Plantation. I would be taken away with Master Jack in a wagon, and then a couple of days later, Abeulo,
Mamie, and the children, along with Diablo, with all of our things would be all taken away by Master Jack and a strange masked man, who spoke only Spanish.

Master Jack would of course draw up the papers that gave us our freedom and we would all travel as far as we could, until we hopefully reached freedom. Only after we had gotten far away from the South, and crossed into the Ohio or Pennsylvania territories, would I reveal myself to everyone, and then Master Jack would bid us farewell, and he would then return to the South. We would then set up a homestead and seek a new beginning in this new place and then unbeknownst but to only three people including myself; I would go back in secret and rescue the rest of my peoples. Master Jack was eager to accommodate me, and he even gave me three hundred dollars to help our relocation costs. He also had our papers notarized and authenticated, and being true to his word, he even threw in the wagon.

He agreed to my plan, and never once did he ask any questions, seemingly content to just relieve his burden, which was his guilty conscious mind. This burden was secretly graying his hair, and withering his skin, all of which intensified his body's march towards decay and the final eternal rest. So anything to get rid of his monumental problem, or blunder on his part, would be always encouraged and dispatched without haste and speed. So he was more than willing to drive the wagon on the final day. He had even let Saturday become like a Sunday, so that everyone could say their goodbyes, and so that we could have a gathering of all of the slaves, to eat, drink, and be merry. It would be like a Christmas day and a wedding day all rolled into one, with no work and a lot of good eating, singing, with loads of laughter and horseplay for the children of all ages. We all said our goodbyes, and our story that we were instructed to tell, was that we were being moved to some new property that Master Jack had acquired along with a certain Spanish nobleman, who had been horribly disfigured in a fire.

I would be leased to this gentleman's newest business venture, a hide making business that would require certain hunting skills that I possessed. My family would be thrown in to strengthen my resolve—in a business sense and thus erase any home sickness that I might acquire, which could both damage or bring harm to the output of this newly formed joint business venture. Now most slaves do not understand big words or their meanings, but they do know when folks are about to move on, and never be seen again, so the mood was happy, but yet sad. Things were changing and cruelty and death lurked around every corner. And when extended family members leave, by whatever means, folks get plain ole confused and dumbfounded. So the Strickland plantation, our home for all of these years was changing, most folks said for the worse, and one of the good things about this horrible existence, was our being taken away. Who would be the plantations hunter now? Where would the free game for the taking and the words of encouragement come from now? Who would step up and be a real man? The kind of real man that forged for his peoples and who provided solid leadership and guidance.

So folks truly were sad because everyone knew that things never ever were going to be the same ever again. And the old saying of the ancients was true, 'that you do and will miss your water once the well has run dry.' The plan worked to perfection and everyone saw what everyone was supposed to see. I left with Master Jack, in a wagon that was pulling a horse, and we went straight to the line shack, and rested. The next morning, which was a windy blustery kind of day, we hitched up my tracking horse along with Master Jack's horse to the back of the wagon, and went back to the Strickland Plantation, but this time I was in the costume of the Spanish nobleman. We gathered up our awaiting things, along with Mamie and the children, Abeulo, El

Diablo, and the girls real live toy the cat, that lived in the barn with us that was named 'Everybody's Cat," and put everything in the back of the wagon.

And, without any acknowledgement or farewells, and without anyone on the whole Plantation not even saying one word, we were gone with the wind. Not one of us said anything, and it was an eerie and awkward kind of silence, as we rode for hours, mile after mile, at a quick pace traveling due north. We rode all of that day and deep into the night, before we stopped to rest the horses. We then rode all of that next day and well into the next day after that, until we decided to stop again, and all get some rest. We all then slept for some hours, before we resumed our journey, this time west by northwest, and we did not slow down until we were sure that we were in the Commonwealth of Pennsylvania and then finally in the Ohio territories. Then and only then, did I reveal myself to Mamie and the children, who were shocked by my deception and guile because both Abeulo and El Diablo, already knew who I was.

Mamie only then began to understand my behavior, over those last few years before our freedom, and she threw herself at me, and began hugging me up something fierce, as I could feel the tears of joy as they streamed down her face onto mine. She then whispered over and over into my ear, "Oh Balaam do you know how much I love and cherish you, and just how much I have always loved you my darling husband?" But to me, it was okay, because for the first time ever in her lifetime, her tears were those of a free woman. But sadly her tears were also for me, and the sorrow that she felt for me, her husband, because she had also now realized that it was I who had dispatched my own brothers into the afterlife, so that we all could be free. She also had wondered what her husband must have gone through in his mind, to ensure that our being free truly happened and how he had never ever said even one word. And, that was probably the reason why he had just always hugged her like there was no tomorrow, whenever he came back from wherever he had been. All of this had made their bond only stronger, and she knew that it was she, who was truly the blessed one for having such a loving and strong and wonderful man in her life, who was a part of her destiny. The same man who had always provided her with security, love and respect, and now this man had provided their family with the sweetest gift of all, a word that had this sweet sound to it, and that word was called "freedom." So no matter what her husband had done, they would have to live with it, and heal together because of it, and grow together and more closely, despite it.

Master Jack had gone the long way, because he said that it was safer than going through Kentucky to Ohio because the slave catchers were out in force around the Ohio River area. We then proceeded first straight to Lucas County, Ohio, which is where Master Jack established our family's legal status with the sheriff and the County Clerk's office by first paying a good behavior bond, and then having our freedom papers notarized by the town's leading legal establishment, which had a lawyer working there that Master Jack had known from their law school days, and then finally registering our whole family so that finally, the whole legal matter of our status, in the free state of Ohio was eternally laid to rest. We were actually free! But, freedom ain't always free!

Then the whole family rather sadly and in total silence bid our farewell to Master Jack, as we all gave him a handshake and

then a hug. He hugged me last, harder and tighter than everyone else and he just turned around and hopped up on his horse
and was gone, never looking back not even one time, riding
south by southeast, back down to the South. As we all watched
him finally fade from our view, we all looked around, and it was
finally starting to hit us, that we were truly free, and on our own,
for the very first time ever, in all of our lives. We then kept moving, going east and we stopped next in Sandusky, Ohio, as we
decided if we would be crossing Lake Erie to true and total freedom that was in the Canadian Provinces. But we decided that
staying in the United Snakes, right now would be what was best
for our family, and so we kept moving, onward going southeast
and we then proceeded directly to a place that is called Xenia,
Ohio. We chose this place because the name Xenia was Greek
for hospitality, and that was one of the first things that our family surely needed in this strange land.

When we got to Xenia, I gave to Mamie all of the money that
Master Jack had given to me, and let her handle that part of our
family business, and so she decided to set up a homestead, in
this town, that was comprised of a certain amount of runaways
and escapees from the business enterprise that was called slavery. The folks in those parts or shall I say town, were unlike
most folks that we had met, or run across, because they were
and still are both generous and kind, and are willing to pitch in
as a collective group to help newcomers make a decent start. So
anytime anyone shows up and appears to want to plant real
roots in the town and are not simply pushing through and looking for something better, they respond as a committed group,
and assist with the raising of the roof. The work of raising this
roof was hard, but the reward was so sweet because, everyone

contributed in their own way in this roof raising process, until it was done.

From the great tasting food that the women folk came up with to show their support and appreciation, to the labor that the men folk supplied, everything came together, until the project was finished or pretty near finished. When the work was done, your only debt was that you had to participate in the next raising of the roof, to ensure them that the lesson of required mandatory cooperation and participation was advanced onward. Because this was the only way in which their town would truly be built and become a place for people who were striving to make a way out of no way, and who were seeking a new beginning. Because Xenia truly was an "us" kind of place, a together kind of place, a kind of place were trust was earned through hard work and not just given because of sharing a similar plight in life. So sticking together and learning to support one another was a must, in this town, and really there is no better feeling to have a solid roof over your head, that belongs to you and yours, that everyone helped you to build.

Now while all of this house building was going on, I was plotting and planning in my mind, the next rescue phase of my plan, which was to free my other family members. It seemed as if it would require at least five to ten main steps, as a basis or foundation, of this plan because to be able to sneak 20 to 30 folks at least four hundred and fifty miles to freedom depending upon the escape route that we would be using, would not be an easy task, so I decided to look at it from a different angle. I had to stop thinking of the trip from the somewhat overwhelming notion, of how hard this was going to truly be. I had to push that out of my mind, because it becomes easy to think of the enormity of a task or goal and fall mentally into the mindset of the possibility of failure.

Because if you go into something, thinking and knowing about the possibility of loss or failure, then the battle is already half lost, before you even begin. Because the human mind is a clever trickster, because of the so-called higher reasoning that all us human beings possess so we can and do talk ourselves in and out of doing things based upon our mind's ability to rationalize the notion of failing. So you might not try as hard, or not believe in yourself and your abilities all at the wrong time, which all could lead to gloom and doom, in a real manner. So I resist the notion of failure, because in my life, failure has never been an option that I chose to seek, nor ever wanted to experience.

Besides, through my warrior training, I have learned that my mind is the sharpest tool in my tool box, and also that my mind is both my greatest friend and my greatest enemy, which is why controlling it, at all times, has always been a part of my training routine. So I just needed to control my mind, and to expand my viewpoint, in a wider manner and see the completed total picture of what I was trying to get accomplished on the field of battle, and more importantly to always think in a positive framework, no matter what the situation may actually be or not be. So, what if I reversed my goal, and looked at this whole process in a backward manner. And, while thinking in a reverse or in a kind of backwards mode of thought, I asked myself, "What if I was starting here in Xenia, and I was sneaking down to the Carolinas, how would I accomplish that goal?"

And then, once I had finally gotten back to the Strickland plantation, I would use my newly acquired skills of cunning and guile, and boldly just take my family members and go backwards or retrace my steps as I returned to Ohio River Valley, using my route down as my escape route back to freedom. Because the trip was like a long and winding road that had many bumps and pitfalls and traps all along its route, both going and coming. Thus, proper planning and discipline were necessary elements, in the overall plan and creating a series of steps, would help me to see the overall picture, and hopefully remove any blind spots, that could hinder my performance. I also needed to be able to see at all times the small things as well as the big things and never lose sight of the both of them. Because, my rescue phase of the plan had to have a combination of big and small things that worked in concert with one another, like the inside metal pieces of a pocket watch does to make the watch work right.

So the first few steps of my rescue part of the plan would be, step one to always trust no one, at all times and to remember that vigilance is foremost an eternal necessity. Step two would be to set up locations, all along the path down to the Carolina's, in the North and the South, and stock these hidden sanctuaries with the needed essentials, like food and water and blankets and wood. I would create a series of my own stations, and make my passengers travel light and not permit them to carry any food, because food creates its own tracking trail, and people need food daily, which could get them caught, as they took time out, to roam around trying to secure a meal. A lot of the Blanco slave hunters would simply camp out, and wait by obvious food sources, and sure enough, a few poor lazy souls would always get caught, because of their bellies' need for nourishment from food. The food then was like a trap, so to avoid all of that foolishness, and to move much more quickly, I would have that angle already taken care of.

Step three is to have weapons stored of bows and arrows and lances and bushido's, along with a gun or rifle or two, that would be hidden in different locations, from the station stops along this same path—maybe even on a path that ran parallel to the stations to ensure that we always had access to something to protect ourselves with, which would enhance our overall security on the field of battle. So I would get started right away on the weapons part, and go to the local blacksmith in Xenia, to put in an order to start getting the weapons that required iron, like lances, and bushido's, made right away. I would also use mi Abeulo's expertise in weapons making and have him to help me to start making as many bows and arrows as we could, so that we would always be ready for the family's eventual day of emancipation.

I would also purchase rifles and guns from as many places in the Ohio River Valley as I could, to even the odds, and increase our chances of success. Step four, would be to calculate the number of station stops that we would need, and so I needed to get the total distance of the trip and then divide it by the number of miles that we would do per night, until we crossed the Mason Dixon line, and that should determine at least the minimum number of actual Southern Station stops. Once we got to the Commonwealth of Pennsylvania we would be somewhat safer, but not by much more, but better than in the South, and so step five is, that we could have wagons to meet us, so that the trip to the lands of the Ohio River Valley would be easier, and quicker than on foot.

So that means that we have to figure out a way to have the wagons ready when we cross past the Mason Dixon line, from the South to the North. That means that either we set up

something with some of the locals, to hire or rent out their services, paying them for a roundtrip journey, to the Ohio River
Valley and back or we simply do it ourselves, trusting no one.
So I needed to go on a research Mission, to figure out how much
it would be to hire a couple of wagons and to see if it was truly
even worth it? Or, we could use El Diablo, and send him back
to Xenia, when we were so many days away from the Mason
Dixon line. He would then be the signal for us to meet up at a
pre-determined location. We would then make our way to Xenia, and the plan would be completed.

Step six would then be to go back to the Strickland plantation, as soon as possible to get the folks ready for their ride on
my version of the Underground Railroad. Only certain people
must be let in on this rescue part of the plan, and secrecy was a
must at all times, because step one—trust no one and remain
vigilant—was to be in effect at all times. So they themselves
must be kept in the dark, and only when it was time to board
the train, would they be told in small pieces of the plan, of what
was actually happening, but never of our route, because if they
did not know where they were going how could they tell if they
were ever caught, of just where it was that they were trying to
get to, as the final destination?

Then once onboard the train, they would be told only by a
set of clues, revealed each and every night where their next
night's destination would be, until we reached actual freedom.
So I would have first to go down and get them initially prepared
to walk away from their lives, leaving everything behind and
taking none of their things and to also check the actual mileage
and to scout for stations among the field armory locations, and
for the actual routes that I would be using in the rescue part of

the plan. My days with the slave catchers would come in handy, because I among other things already knew the lay of the land in the Southern and Central Virginia part, as well as all over the Carolinas. We had also just ridden with Master Jack into freedom, so I knew the route that he had used which was a main path that the Blancos used to travel north or west, but there were countless other trails, and footpaths, and hills and such that I needed to study, and understand, and then commit to my memory, before the rescue part of the plan was finally put into motion.

Step seven would be to not rush, and to take my time because when you rush, you have a tendency to get careless, and when you get careless that is when mistakes can and do happen. And any mistake in the field of battle can cost you, or the people around you their lives. So no matter how long this would take, it would just have to take that long, and the goal was to have the plan succeed without a hitch, and really it was not about seeing how quickly that this goal could be completed. So slowing down just a bit, and making sure of all things, at all times, should always be adhered to, and never be taken lightly or for granted.

Step eight would be to use the Latin alphabet to mark the route for my passengers, to recheck and denote appropriate time periods for adopting the particular numbers of letters. There are 26 letters in English alphabet and 24 in Latin, 23 if you do not count 'w' as double "u" letters in the Latin alphabet, just like in the English alphabet, except that there are no letters "j" or "u". So starting in the Ohio River Valley and working backwards, I would begin with the last letter of the alphabet and go backwards until I get to the secret cave that I had created, which would be marked by the first letter of the Latin alphabet. I would carve the letters into trees or into rocks to mark the routes and these letters would be what the passengers would look for to find the sanctuaries or stations. Now using the Latin alphabet letters would work I figured, because most of the Blancos were illiterate and could barely speak or read or write English themselves, so most of them would have no idea of what these symbols even meant in the very first place, let alone the significance of what they actually stood for.

Now, in the course of my research on this Underground Railroad, I found out that some conductors used a peg legged figure to mark their paths, or even a series of stacked up rocks that denoted that something was happening. For instance, three rocks stacked upon one another could mean danger, while two rocks stacked upon one another could mean that the path was all clear. So I would use different tricks to communicate with my passengers, so that we could always, at least try to stay in communication with each other, despite the fact that we could not constantly talk to one another. Step nine, would be that I would mirror the behavior of the one that was called "The Black Moses," and use her style of conducting as a guide for my behavior. She seemingly had the conducting part down, and, she made it look so easy and smooth, but in reality, I knew that she had learned this behavior through her many trips and through a series of trials and errors. I would copy her actions and learn on the run and stay focused on my chores and objectives as a conductor. I would use her tricks to outwit and outlast and frustrate any slave catchers, and the goal would be for us to simply vanish into thin air and leave no traceable path of detection for anyone to discern.

The final step, step ten, would be to always include Mamie and mi Abeulo in every decision that I make concerning the rescue mission and to use them as a constant resource in everything. Because six eyes, and six ears, and three brains, are always better than two eyes, and two ears, and one brain. Besides the both of them are highly intelligent in their own right, and they may have seen something that I may not have seen, or feel in a certain way about something, that I may not, all of which could only serve to enhance our desired overall goal which was to free as many of our family that we left behind in North Carolina as possible. So I would always consult with them, to get their opinion or perspective and the three of us together would craft a well thought out and well devised plan of action that worked like we had envisioned that it would.

I then decided to scout out the surrounding area, and see what this free state of Ohio, was really like. I learned that the Ohio River Valley was the first American West and frontier area and it was created in the year 1787 when the Congress of these United Snakes passed the Northwest ordinance, which was nothing more than a plan of government for the Territory. This ordinance prohibited slavery and encouraged free blacks and escapees, to seek freedom within the Northwest Territory. I also learned that in the state of Ohio, itself, that there were a lot of rivers like the Maumee and the Miami and lakes, like Lake Erie and that the mighty Ohio River separates Ohio from the slave states of Virginia and Kentucky. The river was used by the First Americans, as a trading and transportation route and in the Ohio River Valley area, the Osage, Omaha, Ponca, and Kaw were the original inhabitants of the River Valley area until the Iroquois ran them out and made them migrate westward.

I learned that slavery was illegal in Ohio since the first Ohio Constitution of 1803, but that there were many people who still made money and profited from it, because of the Federal Fugitive Slave Laws of 1793 and 1850, which permitted slave owners to reclaim their runaways, even if these ex-slaves had moved to a free state. These federal slave laws were also designed to impose a penalty in the year 1793 of $500 and then later in the year 1850 of $1000 against any person who hindered the arrest of, harbored or concealed a fugitive slave. I learned that beginning in the year 1804, like many other States, Ohio passed laws called the 'Black Codes,' that placed special burdens on blacks, and that consisted of Blacks having had to prove that they were free before they could settle in the state or to get a job, they had to post a bond to guarantee their good behavior and the ability to support themselves, and lastly, every black individual or family had to register in the local County Clerk's Office.

I learned that there were a lot of underground stations that were crisscrossed all over the state, and some folks said that there were well over two thousand miles or more of Underground Railroad trails that existed in Ohio. These trails were just the ones that the First Americans had used for well over 300 years before the Blancos had arrived, and one of the more used ones was the Bullskin Trace, that went from the Ohio River to Lake Erie, and this trail actually passed close by to the north of Xenia, which to me, was really good to both know and understand, as I learned the lay of this new land. I learned that there were also over 23 points of entry into the Ohio branch of the Underground Railroad, that were established along the Ohio river, so that if you came across the River in the right spot, you could instantly be riding the rails towards freedom.

I also learned that there were also at least eight cities all along Lake Erie that served as the starting points towards real freedom and a new beginning that lay across the Lake in Canada. Conneaut, Lorain, Toledo, Huron, Sandusky, Cleveland, Painesville, and Ashtabula all served as the last and final stops in the United Snakes, and once these passengers boarded the boats, the province of Ontario and freedom was directly across the Lake staring at them in their faces. I also learned about a group of Blancos called Quakers, who were unlike any people that I had run across, because they were determined to face down slavery and all of its evils. These Quakers, like Levi Coffin, the King family, the Haviland family, the Butterworth family the Howard family and the Eckhart family, were some of the ones who had dared to give the underground railroad in Ohio it's start, and they secretly kept it both alive and running smoothly, and it always seemed like they were at all times, willing and able to help all runaways. Some of these very same Quaker people were also teachers at the Black settlements that were established very near but to the east of Windsor, that is in the providence of Ontario, Canada that lies directly across Lake Erie from Detroit, Michigan.

The Dawn, the Buxton/Elgin and the Refugees Holmes settlements, all have flourished, and are extremely successful at providing a new beginning for the lost souls, and these Quakers have proved themselves to be a vital resource, to the development, growth and education of these places. There were also around maybe 30 freedmen or really escapee settlements that were established in the state of Ohio itself, and they had colorful names like; Africa, Guinea, New Guinea, Pee Pee, Longtown, Brown, Wilberforce and so on, and the earliest of these dated back to the year 1818. Now a lot of these places are gone now and are but tender memories, but some are still struggling onward, and it is amazing to think of how people's lives have been changed in a real manner, because of these places on the road to| a new life. So after my thoroughly having checked out our new surroundings, I then decided to carefully begin the next phase of my plan. Because, time was steadily flying and before you knew it, three months had already passed, and this trip would be to alert my family as to what was to come.

I figured that this quick trip would take about two weeks or so round trip, and that this was going to be the longest extended period of time that I would be away from my ever-growing family. Mamie, my rock, already knew what I had to do, and she also knew that this whole business was both risky and dangerous. But she also knew what the benefits would be, and she liked the way that freedom tasted and what it felt like on her skin. So after a quiet but nice evening enjoying her company, I set out with El Diablo and the horse, towards the South. My first real stop, about one week and a half later was at the line shack, where I rested and ate some bacon and beans, with some biscuits. I waited for night to descend, to give me some additional protection, and to heighten my senses. Nighttime comes slowly, and the bugs all start doing their sounds, very quietly at first, but as the nighttime starts to assert itself, the bugs get progressively louder and constant, until they become the most dominant sound at night, after dark.

Around midnight I reckon, I set out for the Strickland plantation, and before I knew it, I was creeping around the slave quarters. Now everything seemed like it was the same, or so it appeared, at first glance, but I immediately noticed the hidden guards. They were placed in various strategic locations, all around the Plantation and they appeared to be serious and not in a playing mood. This was strictly a scouting mission, surveying the lay of the land and tracking the enemy locations, and studying their habits, and looking for weaknesses. All total, each and every night, there were ten men that were guarding everything important on the property, and some were even making rounds with a pair of dogs, every two hours or so, like clockwork. They had a small fire going, to create the illusion of openness, and yet something was happening that was causing this cat and mouse game.

I left and then came back the next night, and I stayed in the shadows and watched everything unfold once again, and then I started to realize that something else was going on, and I wondered if it was just at the Strickland plantation, or were other plantations also on guard. So I visited neighboring plantations, and it was then that I discovered what was truly going on. This other plantation also had a guard set up, but the owner did not have the financial resources of Master Jack, and therefore the one guard was not able to stop a group of masked riders, who just swooped up, and forcefully took a number of slaves, for a forced relocation to another plantation. I followed these riders, as they stole these poor souls, in the middle of the night, and took them to another owner, who probably needed them as replacements, so that he could get around paying the slave head tax. So this stealing slaves, was just another new variation, on the problem that now plagued all slave owners, and so Master Jack was only protecting his business interests.

No one was going to forcefully take anything from him, and even though it seemed as if it was now the preferred manner of doing business for some owners, he was not taking any chances. I followed these crazy men for about two nights, lying low during the daytime, watching them sleep and take it easy, waiting for the night time to arrive, as they went from plantation to plantation and took what they wanted from one owner and gave to the next, for money of course. Finally, after a week of hiding in the shadows, I decided that it was time to visit the slave quarters to see my family. There was a quarter of a moon that was shining in the nighttime sky, as we—El Diablo and myself—crept up onto the property, and easily eluded the perimeter guards. But upon arriving down in the quarters, my heart dropped down to the souls of my feet, because boy had things really drastically changed in the last three or four months.

First off, the doorway to each shack, was now chained and locked at night, and everyone was required to be in by no later than an hour after sunset or be locked out and then subject to a severe beating. So those days of sleeping outside under the stars was now over, and that made the conditions inside each shack both cramped and tight. The shacks now must have felt to some, like slave ships, because of the cramped and extremely tight sleeping accommodations, that maybe were not that tight, but tight enough to make everyone uncomfortable and wound up. I had already scouted the shacks, so I knew in what shacks my people were, so I told El Diablo to wait and to watch my back, while I climbed up on the roof, and then easily cut my way through the straw thatch into the inside. Naturally folks were a bit startled and frightened, and all kinds of commotion was started by my appearance, as I lowered myself down by rope, but as soon as they saw that it was me, they quickly quieted down, and wanted to show me all kinds of love and affection.

This shack contained Mamie's peoples, and after speaking first with my in-laws, who wanted to know how Mamie Elizabeth and the girls were all doing, I then gave to them the elements of the escape plan. I then took my time and spoke to all of her cousins and the rest of the assembled people. When I had finished speaking to every single person, I then bid them farewell, and climbed back up and out, onto the roof, and as I looked back down, I could see their upturned faces, all looking like a sea of colors and hue's. They watched me ascend upwards like an angel, that was going towards the heavens and I will never ever forget the look on their faces, all scared and sad looking, as they waved goodbye to me. But I assured them that I would be coming back for them, and to try not to worry, that help was on the way. I then easily crossed onto another roof, and then another, until I had made my way to the shack that contained my family, and I then again dropped down for a visit.

This roof was even easier to cut through than the first one, because this one had holes in it, and my family was elated to see me lowering myself down on the rope, and the first one to hug me was mi Madre. The first thing that I noticed about her was that she looked as if, she had aged nearly 10 years in four and a half months, for the grey streaks in her hair really now stood out, as if they had multiplied, and her hands now seemed like weathered leather, and they were oddly now stained black in color. Her comfortable cooking job in the big house was now gone, because Master Jack no longer trusted me, so he also no longer trusted her. Her new job now was to work in the area that the dye was used for both leather and cotton goods, and thus the black dye that was sometimes used, had permanently stained her hands. She said nothing for a while, and all that she did was to softly cry and cry some more with her arms all wrapped around my neck. My brothers and sisters were all doing fine, as well as my older brothers' families, so that was a huge relief for me. But ever since we had left, things were now very different—and to everyone, the days seemed harder and more grueling. The Blancos were much rougher and tougher, with all slaves—and the good times were gone, and over and folks were not any longer caught up with that crazy notion, that even though this was slavery, that everything was okay, or not okay, but far better than on a lot of plantations. Master Jack had always been seen as both fair and lenient, and almost like a Negra himself in certain respects, and really sympathetic to our plight, and like a big brother to me.

But now ever since we had left, it was said that he never visited the quarters in any capacity, and he never ever went beyond the yard of the Big House. He was now a changed man, they all had said, and really if the truth could really be told, he now was just a normal Blanco these days, with normal Blanco fears and mistrust of Negras. So now, he would just look, always from a distance and then abruptly leave or disappear, if the overseers were delivering a lot of extra lashes of the whip.... He seemed more sullen and withdrawn these days, they all said, and he appeared to them to have a serious drinking problem. I then noticed that there were sixteen faces in the room, and sixteen was a rather large number and actually there would be more than that when I added in Mamie's peoples, and as soon as Master Jack had realized that they were gone, he would be sending the hounds from Hades to bring them back. Because even though Master Jack, my true Blanco brother would never ever admit it, my family was his most prized possession. For we were his hardest and most diligent workers and we never needed to be scolded or chastised or treated with any harsh language. We always did what we were supposed to, and whatever we did we displayed a pride in our work. We all had different jobs around his plantation, and we were at the tops of all of the job lists, even the young ones. We bought him a lot of value and respect, from other plantation owners, and for him to lose his best, would crush his spirit completely, and push him over the edge.

So he would be like a raving and raging mad man, once he discovered that they were gone, and really no distance of ours would be safe from his wrath. So our only option may be for us, all to go to the Province of Ontario, until things cooled down, in these United Snakes. So we would have to move fast, so that these twenty something lives would forever be changed. So I went over my escape plan with my family, and decided to create a chain of command, so that my orders would not be questioned, and they would be carried out without hesitation. We also would need to create a private army that could aid me in the protection part of the trip, and so I needed to figure out who was the surest shot, and who had the steadiest hands, and who possessed the true spirit of the warrior. I told my family that I was close by and that I would be back within the next few days for another visit from the heavens. They also had to be extremely careful not to speak on any of this, because if the Blanco's ever got wind of this, then everyone would be at risk. As I climbed back up and out of the shack, I could see mi Madre's face, smiling with a fierce pride, because her oldest born son was fulfilling his destiny, and taking our family to freedom.

El Diablo and myself, snuck back to our hiding place and once we got there, I started to formulate in my mind just who would be the commanders for our trip. I decided that my brother John's oldest son, Gabriel, age fourteen, was a natural candidate, because he was the most skillful hunter, of all of the children and he had actually caught Abeulo's eye for his skill and cunning while hunting. So he was in the commander's group just because of his advanced skill set. He was a little subdued, and somewhat of a quiet child, but his skills at shooting a bow and arrow were quite exceptional for someone who had only been given a very small taste of Abeulo's lessons.

Next was my brother Paul's daughter, Kara Grace, age ten, who we all called K.G. and Kay for short—who was my next choice to join the commander group. I choose K.G., because she was the supreme warrior of the children, in our family. She was a fighter, who never backed down and they say that she was the most evil and yet the sweetest child on the whole plantation. She always would wrestle with all of the boys, and she was considered a known dirty fighter, because she would do whatever it took to come out on top, so if she had to scratch, claw, cut, pull hair, gouge eyes or even bite her opponent, she would do it. She always ran with the older boys, on the plantation, and it was rumored that she at all times, carried a knife hidden on her person, but she was one of the prettiest looking children that you ever wanted to meet, because she had this beautiful long and flowing hair, that at times seemed like it danced in the wind. She was tough, could run fast, and she had this ability to quickly think on her feet, and therefore was another prefect commander group candidate for our trip.

Last but not least was my brother Mark's second oldest son Aaron, age eight, who had always been secretly fascinated with guns and he had a steady hand, a great eye for any target, and he had this ability to judge distances with uncanny certainty. So this ability made him another obvious choice for our commander group, and Abeulo, had taken a liking to both him and his cousin Gabriel, and he had actually began to formulize their process of warrior enlightenment, when all of the trouble with my older brothers had kicked off, and sped up our quest for freedom.

So on my next secret descent from heaven, I took the three of them off to the side, away from everybody, to a quiet corner of the shack, and the very first thing that I did was to use my thumb to put the white substance on their faces, and under their eyes and across their foreheads. I then took my bushido and drew blood from the palms of the four of our hands, to consolidate our pact, in blood. I then very quietly, so that just only the four of us could hear, began to chant and made them repeat after me 'As in the way of the ones who have come before us, we pledge to remember the old ways, and bring both honor and respect to our family, we the guardians of the Fastasma Caminante, and we will never ever rest until our family is safe, and far away from bondage.' With that I gave them all the implements of war, which were bows and arrows and daggers, and I required that they practice as much as possible in the upcoming weeks, so that they would be ready for what lied ahead. I also reminded them that this was very serious and was not a game in any kind of way, and if they did not think that they were up for the task, then that would be okay, but once they decided to go forward, then there would be no turning back.

They all nodded yes, and with that we began to go over the plan of escape that I had designed. I would also equip them with a full arsenal when we began our trip, and they would have access to all of the implements of war, and they should be ready to use them, if the need ever arose. They must also follow my instructions implicitly, and never deviate from what I instructed them to do. We would also be bold in both our design and purpose, and we would use this escape plan to accomplish our objective, which was for us all, from the youngest to the oldest to be totally free. We then started practicing shooting the arrows at a target that was inside the shack and close up, but what I really wanted them all to do, was to just get use to what the bow and arrows felt like in their hands. They must secretly sneak away, and practice on their own, and they must do this as much as possible, over and over again because not only does practice make perfect, but time itself, would be moving quickly and before they knew it, it would be time for us to leave, and it was important that they be ready, willing, and able when this time came.

I also told them about a math term that was called a triangle, which is a basic shape of geometry, and how you have different kinds of triangles, like equilateral or isosceles and or scalene, all which are measured in degrees. Now in an equilateral triangle, there are three points that are always an equal distance or length from one another. So I wanted them to align themselves in this equilateral triangle configuration, with equal spacing between the three of them, and practice shooting at a fixed target or point, which is called the centroid or center point, that was inside of their triangle. This equilateral configuration would also allow them to watch one another's back sides and flanks, and defensively it just makes more sense. But they must also be able to switch into the various different types of triangles with a moment's notice, because their safety relies upon their ability to stay in some kind of triangle configuration, and I did not expect them to grasp this geometry right away, but over time, it would start to make sense.

They must also learn to push one another, and demand that one another grow mentally stronger, because strength is what this family needed in the tough times that lie ahead for us all. I also told them that they must be prepared to kill if necessary, and that we must be determined by any means necessary to accomplish our objective, even if it meant that they had to give their own lives in the service of our family. As I was about to leave I hugged each and everyone in the family, and that is when I told them all, that when the time came for them to leave, that they must take only what they could comfortably carry on their backs and nothing else, especially food or water, because I had already taken care of that angle. They must also coordinate with Mamie's peoples, so that we could have a accurate head count of who was making the trip, and everyone, in these two families, who wanted to leave was welcome to join us, but no one else. I would be back in no later than 12 moons, and that they must say nothing, because one wrong word or sentence could ruin our escape plan, and that I was not playing with them about this either. and I was indeed deadly serious about this whole thing.

So I guess the look on my face showed them all, that I was not messing around, because everyone kind of became quiet and looked somewhat scared. So with that—using the rope, I climbed back towards heaven and El Diablo and I returned back to the Ohio River Valley, and things seemed to be finally all coming together. Once I got back, after hugging up Mamie and the children, I sat down with Abeulo, and we talked strategy for hours, because I needed his insight and wisdom, for the task that lie ahead. We decided together, that if we were going to take over twenty people from the plantation, that Master Jack would surely be sending more than the usual amount of slave catchers, and that we must be ready to change our plans accordingly. So we must devise an alternative action plan, and always be ready to implement it at a moments' notice. This alternative action plan must also contain an element of surprise, and this surprise should contain a trap that we would spring on the slave catchers, who would be unaware and caught completely off guard. Because they would be trying to catch us, but it is we, who would be really trying to catch them, and if we did it right, we would create a certain amount of confusion, amongst them that would give our people more precious time to escape even further away and towards freedom.

So we would split the group into two, and then lead them in such a way that the two groups' paths crossed at a certain point, and at the point where the paths crossed, is where we would spring the trap. We would use the commander group to first shoot their guns and then fire arrows inside of an equilateral triangle at a fixed point, which would be the slave catchers themselves. I would be the bait to lure them in, and I would use our friend named Destiny to finish them off. If everything worked, we would crush their pursuit, and drive them back and give our people more valuable time, which in any escape is the most important element. If we did this right, we could keep our losses to a bare minimum, and the family would be safe. So the first thing that we would need is to get at least four to eight guns, or rifles, and then we would need to figure out where we would spring our little surprise on our pursuers. We also would need to go through Kentucky or Virginia because that was the fastest way to Ohio and not through Pennsylvania, which was a safer but longer route, to get to Ohio. So we would create an arsenal and hide it under ground, and close to our trap and then send the three commanders ahead to set up their equilateral triangular field of fire, and when everything was ready, we would use the family to guide them into the jaws of our trap.

Twelve moons came and went quickly, but everything was in order when it was time for my return trip to the plantation. We had every time set up and every detail had been worked out, and re-worked out, so that I was confident that we had done everything that was within our control. We had gotten the guns, we had figured out where our trap would be set up, we had rented wagons that would be used once we got across the Ohio River, because we had decided to take the family all the way into Canada for their safety. Because Master Jack had too much money, power, and influence, and so there would be blood in the water for him, and this whole thing would be personal for him and he would not never stop pursuing us in these United Snakes, so we must go somewhere beyond his reach. All of the sanctuaries or station stops were stocked up and supplied with everything that we would need from food and water, and blankets, and firewood. We had devised an escape route that was totally new and we even had a backup plan if the original plan failed, which was to follow the 'North star' and head due North to Pennsylvania, and the only thing that was left was for Abeulo to give me his final blessing.

So about three days before I was to leave, he took me to the side and said that he wanted to give to me one more secret advantage that he had told no one else before. He unwrapped our friend named Destiny from a blanket, and he then told me, that when the trap was about to be sprung, that I should awaken the spirit of the bushido (blade), and when fully awakened, this sword had no match or equal. He said that one night many many moons and thus years ago which was on the day of mi Abuela's death, he was feeling very lonely, so he went out by himself to grieve and mourn her passing. He usually would no never partake in the drinking of any spirits of liquor but for some reason this year and on this night, he seemed extremely vulnerable and he started drinking from a bottle while sitting next to a fire that he had made inside a circle of rocks. He also had pulled out Destiny and swung it about in the air, as he drank more and more. Well at some point all drunken and distraught he flung the sword into the fire, as the jade handle pointed skyward. He then remembers throwing the nearly half-filled bottle into the fire in a drunken rage, causing the flames to shoot higher into the air.

Well he then remembered that maybe he should not have done this, so at some point he grabbed the handle that was also hot, and it felt like it was burning into the palm of his hand. Well as he quickly pulled the sword directly toward himself that was the last thing that he remembered as he fell backwards and passed out into a drunken slumber. Now in the morning, as he slowly woke up, he was still holding the handle, and that is when he noticed that certain rocks from the fire were cut cleanly into two, or in half. As he looked, he could see that the drag pattern of the blade on the ground matched the direction from the fire, that he had dragged the hot sword. Then he noticed that the palm of his hand had marks that were permanently seared or burned into his flesh, and these matched the skulls that were craved or etched all around and into the handle. So somehow when the sword was heated up, it becomes sharper and to have cut through solid rocks, was an awe-inspiring feat. He then gathered his things and went back to the plantation, but days later he decided to conduct an experiment, and yes it was true that when heated this sword was like nothing else that he had ever seen or even heard about. It glowed, and it actually sounded like it was humming or singing when he swung it in the air, like it had a voice of its own that was awakened by the heat of the flames. It also could and more importantly would, cut through any and all things, from wood to even most metals, and maybe this was the deadly secret of why everyone through time always seemed so intent upon truly possessing it, because it was the weapon of all weapons.

So that is the real reason why the battle was fought on the high plain that day, in the land of mi Abeula, he had surmised and why for centuries countless wars had always been fought over it, because this sword was matchless and had no peers, and thus it was truly the ultimate prize. And whoever owned and wielded it had a powerful weapon that was unlike anything on the entire planet, and this was the sinister secret that everyone else in the Yamato clan seemed to both know and understand. Yes it was extremely sharp when the spirit of the bushido (blade) was asleep, but when fully awakened, this blade was dangerous, and downright scary because nothing in the known world could withstand its cut. Yes it was extremely sharp when the spirit of the bushido (blade) was asleep, but when fully awakened, this blade was dangerous, and downright scary because nothing in the known world could withstand its cut. So that is why Abeulo had always made me practice with it over and over again and learn how to precisely hold it. And, why he had always instructed me to be extremely careful when it was in my hands, because he did not want me cutting myself with it, which was easy to do because it was naturally so very sharp. So with that, he gave me our friend named Destiny, and he also gave to me two bottles of liquor that also had other stuff added to the bottles. He told me to create a fire and to stick the sword into the fire, or to build a fire around the sword and then light the fire and when I was ready to throw the glass bottle into the fire, in a way so that the bottle would break, and release the fluids inside of it, and this action would make the fire even hotter. This increased heat should awaken the spirit of the blade and once fully awakened it would protect the family and me, which is why he had always called it our friend whose name was Destiny.

So with that I was ready to begin our rescue mission in the land down under the Mason-Dixon Line, to save my family members from an uncertain and hellish fate. So I then returned down to the Carolinas, with El Diablo and everything seemed in place, and I now had to start everything in motion. I sent Diablo around, to let everyone know that I was around, and after a few days, I crept back to the slave quarters, but I stayed in the shadows until everything slowed way down and got sleepy for the night. I descended once again from the heavens on a rope but unlike before, there was somberness about my family, when they saw that it was me, and strangely mi Madre was missing. Master Jack's new cook had taken ill about six weeks ago, and us being creatures of habit, we always fall back to the things that we know and trust. So he had moved her back to the big house, and for whatever reason, he had now required her to stay in the house at night. The family rarely had seen her and when they did it was just in passing, and I have always wondered, did he move her because he knew that something was going on? She had gotten word to us that if she could not figure out a way to sneak away and past all of the numerous guards that were guarding the Big House, we then were to go on without her and to not worry because she would be alright. Master Jackson was good to her, and she forbade us to even try to liberate her, because trying to save her could get everyone else caught and doom the plan. So we were in no certain terms even to attempt, to do anything about her situation, and always keep her in our hearts and minds. We would be together again one day; we should just stay hopeful and she would be thinking about us each and every day. I was crushed by this news, and a part of me wanted to ignore her orders and still try to liberate her, even if I had to dispatch every Blanco in sight, but she was mi Madre, and at all times I have always done what she wanted me to do. So with a heavy heart and mind, I turned my attention to my task at hand, and tried to concentrate on just sticking to the plan.

So everything was set and in two days. On a Saturday night, I cut through the two shacks and all total 26 people minus mi Madre had decided to make this quest for real freedom. We first gave everyone moccasin shoes to wear and then we divided the group into two, with eleven people in one group and fifteen in the other, even though we did not actually do the split because we actually had made good time. Because with Sunday being the slave's traditional day off, the group was not missed, and we made it all over thirty miles in just the first two days alone, using the carefully hidden sanctuaries to our advantage for safety and security. I made everyone gather around and explained our strategy, our goals and what the rules would be.

There would be no fires permitted, no mindless and aimless talking would be allowed, and folks should need to get used to whisper talking and using hand signals. The commanders would have absolute say and anything that they said must be followed at all times. Selfishness would not be tolerated, and no one would be left behind. The path ahead of us would be bumpy and would contain many twists and turns, but together as a group and by staying both scared and cautious, we would all make it to freedom.

The slave hunters would also be coming for us for sure, so we were to never ever think this was going to be like a Sunday morning stroll. I then used a lot of the tricks that I had seen the Black Moses use like rags covering their feet, and a rope around everyone's waist that dragged sticks and bushes, that were used to brush the ground by each and every person, which wiped out their foot prints and so there was no obvious path or trail to follow, and I made sure of this fact. We used el Diablo to guard our rear flank, and as we traveled north by northwest, we made it to the hills of the mountains by the third day. I figured by that on Monday by mid-morning, the alarm would have been sounded and by Monday evening, the overseers would be looking for us in full force. But with no obvious clues, the Blanco's would have to call in the true slave catchers, and that posse would not be assembled until Tuesday or Wednesday at the latest. These slave catchers would then proceed to the area of the Great Dismal Swamp, which is located in the Northeastern part of the state, and stretched from Edenton, North Carolina to Norfolk, Virginia to search for us there, because going North, by Northeast, this was a great area to hide and evade anyone and to forge for food. It was rumored to be a known destination, where all escaping slaves from the South always hide as they passed through the Carolinas while following the North Star. They would have no idea that, yes we would be going North, but North by Northwest toward the Blue Ridge Mountains and beyond, to the Ohio River and we would try to evade any and every one until we got past Guilford which was in Guilford County, which was rumored to be a major stop on the Underground Railroad in the western part of the state, that was started by the great Levi Coffin and his cousin Vestal Coffin. But we would not use the Railroad stop because there was just too many of us, which would be dangerous for the conductors and everyone in general, and so we would therefore stay on our own and continue on our course or path. We continued onward, never looking behind us, like the Angel in the good book, commanded Lott to do always pressing forward in the dead of night, as fast as we could, as the three commanders scouted in front of us, as el Diablo watched our backs and behinds.

There was this certain determination and awareness that everyone in our family possessed, and to be honest, it was really impressive to see because there was no complaining or crying and there was this rugged silence that clung to us at all times. Once we got up into the mountain areas, we slowed down a bit, but not by much, and our goal was to always do at least twenty to twenty-five miles each and every night. We stayed off the known beaten paths and before you knew it, in about eight days we were actually near the Old Dominion, and we were making great time, for such a large group. Once we were in the Old Dominion, we did the split, into two separate groups that were traveling the same way, just in two spread out and parallel tracks, putting the three commanders in the middle between the two groups, because that way, they could get to both groups, quicker, if any security issues arose. I also encouraged the three commanders to continue their daily practice routines, because, there may come a day that this practice may come in handy, especially if we are being followed and have to spring the trap. I told el Diablo to scout ahead as I hung back, looking for any signs of the slave catching patrols.

There appeared to be a lot of daylight activity and movement, by the Blancos as I scouted the main roads, and beaten paths. And sure enough by day 13 of our odyssey, called the quest for freedom, I saw firsthand that they were looking for someone, and so I naturally concluded that they were looking for us, and that it was being to get interesting. So, on the creep, I hightailed it out of there and decided to start setting the trap up, because in less than two days' time, they should be closer upon us. We would pick the right location, where the two trails crossed based upon the terrain, the location, and then select one trail that could provide cover against the slave hunters' return fire. We would first off leave a trail that suddenly appears, for both groups that a blind man could follow, and after having our family members help us to carry as many arrows as they possibly could, on my signal we would fire as many arrows as we could and after the arrows were gone, we would then use our guns to target the ones who still had the will to fight, and I would swoop down like one of Allah's angels, on judgment day, to create a panic amongst them. We would also want the slave hunters, to stay bunched up together as much as possible, so we would create a ring of fire, to try to keep them inside of the circle. Hopefully the slave hunters would be caught completely off guard, and it was the commanders jobs, and duty to wound and or maim as many men and horses as possible, but to kill no one on purpose, because I did not want to expose them at such a young age to the feel of the human kill. I would be the only one to take a human life, if the situation required that to happen, but if the situation demanded a different course of action, then so be it. The family would never stop moving and when the battle began, they should start hiding their tracks again, start running or run walking as fast as possible. We would lay back and wait for the jaws of the trap, to spring shut and savagely catch these Blancos in its steel jaws.

So we found the perfect kill point, a piece of land that had a lot of surrounding cover, that opened into a rather wide clearing in the middle where the clearing was on flat land, but everything else kind of sloped ever so slightly upwards. We first dug out a triangle and then on the inside of the triangle we dug out a circle, and on the outside of the circle we dug a hole, and inside the circle we dug a fire pit that was ringed with large stones. Inside of the grooves of the triangle and the circle we added tar and oil, along with other materials that would get and stay hot, once we ignited the tar. We put foliage over everything and then we devised a covering that would be used to disguise El Diablo's hole to give him the element of surprise just in case we needed him as our wild card. The three commanders were each given two guns and ammunition, along with 25 arrows a piece, and they were told that if they could to somehow, if at all possible, to make every shot count, but to not shoot until they heard the bird call signal. Horses and dogs were just as important as men, and they were to keep shooting until they once again heard the bird call signal a second time. They were not to worry about me, and I would lure them in with the fire, and then as they got closer in, I would throw the bag of stinky leaves into the base of the fire, and these leaves when burned created a thick smoke that kind of just lingered in the air and hung around, in the same kind of way that fog does by all water sources.

I would also dress the part and look like a dead person, about the face and hands. I would use the white powder as a foundation all over my body. I would then use black charcoal to draw the outline of a skull with gum less bony teeth on my face and bony hands. It was also right about then that I decided that the commanders would also look the very same about the face and hands, as myself, and maybe this body painting could be used to our advantage and create fear within the ranks of our enemy. I would use the old Franciscan robe that I found a skeleton wearing one day when I was out on a slave hunt way up the woods in a partial cave and it had this hood that could shield my appearance until the last minute or so, before they were almost upon me. I would then reveal myself, and hopefully they would be so rattled, that when the arrows started flying, they would be totally panicked and caught completely off guard, and be more worried about their personal safety and not trying to retrieve some slaves to their upset and rich plantation owner. We made the paths of the two groups cross one another right in the choke point or kill area, and the four of us, including el Diablo, just settled down in our positions and waited for the oncoming riders, and hopefully the fire would lure them in to us. About two hours before daybreak, we could hear the sounds of horses moving toward our position at a fast pace, as we got ready with anticipation.

I put our friend named Destiny and the bag of stinky leaves both in the fire, put not one but two mushroom chew sticks in my mouth with one hand, and then readied the bottle of the flammable liquid in my other hand, and sat down cross legged in front of the fire with the hood on the robe pulled down low over my eyes. But what we were not ready for was that it was not 11 or 12 riders, but somewhere between 25 and 30, I thought, but at the end of the battle is when I found out that there had been 32 riders in total. Master Jack was very wealthy, and I did not anticipate how he would not spare any expenses when it came to getting my family back. The scouts who consisted of 3 riders came up first, but the fire and the smoke slowed them down, until the main body arrived, and lo and behold their leader was none other than mean old Jebediah Scott, himself. The very same Jebediah Scott who was my leader during my slave hunting days, and of course he was barking out orders. The main body of riders were a motley band of rebels, mercenaries, so called gentlemen, hanger's on and all in between, and they all looked confident and very mad.

The trackers went right to the spot that the paths crossed, but the smoke kind of obscured me from their vision. One of them jumped down off his mount and surveyed the ground looking at the obvious signs, as the two dogs with them must have smelled Diablo's scent, started growling in a low and uneasy manner which made the men uneasy and scared as they gripped their guns tighter, while waiting for the main body to approach. The main body rapidly eased up, and eventually they all came to a stop, with everyone within the confines of the circle and triangle marks, that were carved into the ground. That is when they spotted me sitting there, on the other side of the fire, and this kind of startled them. But just then as life will always have it, life takes another and different and unexpected turn, and something happens which changes everything, and in our case, it was Kara releasing her arrow early in her nervousness, which did two things.

One, it gave away her general position and two it made us lose our element of total surprise. So with that, all hell broke loose, and the battle had begun. Gabriel and Aaron both immediately joined the fight making it rain arrows as the riders turned towards Kara's position and started to return fire. She ducked but was hit, and as she yelled out in obvious pain, this anger arose within me, and suddenly I felt as if I was reacting and not thinking. I threw the bottle into the flame in a violent manner, which caused the bottle to break and made the flames shoot extremely high into the dark early morning sky, as our friend named Destiny glistened in the flames. This caused the riders to become startled and confused, as they sought cover as a general panic set in and began to take hold, but there was mean old Scott barking out orders to take a bead on the only position that they could make out, which was Kara's. Five riders broke away from the main body and started moving toward her position as they fired their weapons that pinned her down. Everything started to slow down, and I felt as if I was moving in a faster speed than everyone else. I fired six arrows, which struck four riders and two horses that were advancing upon Kara's location, and the last rider who was still advancing was taken out by Aaron's cover fire with a long rifle that had found it's mark directly to the back of his head and actually, if the truth can be told, it was a great and yet beautiful shot.

Mean Old Scott barked out more orders to use the scout dogs next to advance, but I summoned el Diablo to guard Kara, and he leapt out of the hole, as if he came up from nowhere, or really up from somewhere below, like Hades. And, he immediately dispatched the nearest rider to him by grabbing him by his throat with his teeth, and as he spit them out from his throat onto the ground and he then spun around to cut off the dogs by putting himself between them and Kara. He then quickly and ruthlessly dispatched both of them in the same motion, as he ran to Kara and leaned his body upon hers as he snarled and showed his mighty and bloody teeth. And, as she buoyed by his presence got back into the fight and she started to fire her arrows with uncanny precision and grace, because they were playing for keeps, and so was she. About 10 men dismounted, using their horses as cover from the onslaught of the arrows but the arrows were coming from all over. I then fired a special flaming tar-wrapped arrow into the ground and into the circular groove that we had carefully made, which caused a fire to erupt and spread to both the circle and triangle. And, this either burned some men and their horses, or spooked the other ones.

The situation was like total chaos, riders on horses trying to evade arrows, lots of arrows that were flying through the air, gun shots floating all about in the air, men and horses in agony—carnage and death all around. The smell of burnt flesh, with smoke and fire all floating about in the air, while sounds of screaming, a lot of yelling, and the sounds of gun fire—all combined to make the noise seem unbearable, as it sounded like pure and total chaos. I finished shooting my allotment of arrows and suddenly, I am pulling our friend named Destiny from the fire, and I could feel this curious burning sensation in the palm of my hand, as if I had become joined to the blade like it had become my master, making me to do its sinister bidding. I then am running forward into the fire, almost crazy like with Destiny gleaming and actually glowing, as I eagerly cut a path through everything that was in my way, as Destiny sounded as if it was humming or kind of like singing. And I still felt a strange nothingness. Horses, and men all were dispatched with minimum ease, and I could feel this stinging sensation on one arm, my left arm and another on the right-hand side of my neck. But still I moved onward, using Destiny like a doctor uses a knife during surgery, with that same skill and precision. Some riders were smart, and they started retreating, and really just plain old running for their very lives, while others tried to valiantly defend themselves, but they became consumed in the wake of our deadly onslaught. Some, once they saw me, dropped everything and just started running as if they had seen a true ghost—a ghost that walked, moved, ran, and killed with a cold and ruthless efficiency—as I sliced my way directly towards Jebediah Scott himself.

He was the undisputed head or brain of this outfit, and so taking him out would really spook the rest of the body which consisted of the other riders. His eyes got bigger and bigger as I drew closer and closer, and he tried to shield himself, the closer I got, by positioning his horse between me and him. He even drew his sword, the same sword that he had used one evening to kill an old slave on one unforgettable night for no apparent reason. I cut through the neck of the horse in one motion, as the horse's head with its tongue out, fell to the ground with a thud, and then I whirled around and placed the Destiny blade right against his neck causing him to slightly bleed, and looked straight into his eyes. He looked terrified, and he started crying and babbling something about not wanting to die. He did not appear to be so tough now I thought, as time stood still like a frozen lake does in winter, and I suddenly decided to show mercy to this now smallish looking person. I pulled Destiny back away from his neck, looked really hard into his eyes and then gave him the slit across the neck sign, as I then turned away with my back to him. The coward then suddenly attempted to man-up and run at me and try to plunge his sword into my exposed back.

But I could hear him coming and had already anticipated his course of action, so I was ready for him, and as I wielded around to face him, I swung Destiny downwards in a circular motion, cutting off his hand, which was still holding his sword, right below the wrist at the forearm—causing him to squeal out loud like a pig, as he dropped to his knees in sheer agony while everything and everyone all stopped. And, I just glared at him and returned to walking away. He was lucky, because I had just spared his miserable life, and now that the battle for freedom was over, I started to slow down and go back to normal speed, as I started to realize what had just happened. For death and despair were both all around me, and nothing in my path had been spared or had escaped—and I truly mean nothing. Some men and horses were struggling in agony, while most of them had been dispatched and lay lifeless on the field of battle that was littered with body parts. A head that was cut off at the neck, a horse's head that was also cut off at the neck—arms, feet, and even a nose had been severed off—and all those who were not dead, wanted to be. The survivors whom we allowed to escape had all run like the dickens to escape, but sadly some of them had made the mistake of running head long into El Diablo— who was still guarding Kara's position—which was the wrong thing to do, at the wrong time and place. For he made short work of them, and he seemed to be smiling, with like a grin on face, as he effortlessly dispatched them into the next life. The three commanders had all done their parts and they all had even dispatched something into the next life, be that either man or horse or dog, but they all had one kind of kill in common with one another—which was man.

But the real truth was, what I had not wanted to happen did, and each one had tasted what it was like to kill another living and breathing human being. And we all know that once the genie is out of the bottle, it's hard to get it back inside of it. I walked to Kara's position fearing the worse, but her wound was not life threatening, so we then we lined up all things dead so that when we were finished, we could quickly gather up our belongings and move out to rendezvous with the family. I could only imagine what they were all thinking, because they all had been exposed to a killing machine, that had no equal, except of course Abuelo, who was our teacher, so they seemed extremely interested and intently watched my every move, as I stacked the bodies of horses, men and dogs all up like prey, in a line as usual. When I was finished, we quietly crept away as we melted away into the woods. That is when I then checked out my wounds and I had been shot in the left arm, in the forearm area, but the bullet had passed clean through and through. And, on the right-hand side of my neck, a bullet had creased or grazed me, leaving a long and straight burn mark. It was also funny that I did not feel the bullets or any pain from the wounds. I now also had this curious burn pattern or mark in the palm of my hand that matched the skull pattern on the handle of our friend named Destiny. As a little child, I had always wondered what mi Abeulo had done to his hand to acquire this unique burn mark. So, now

I actually knew what had caused this pattern or mark which only occurs when Destiny is awakened from its sinister slumber by the ritual of fire, and so I would now be just like him, for the rest of my life.

All in all though I was okay, so I wrapped up my arm, using tobacco leaves to treat the wounds, and I as I looked around, I will never forget the look on the faces of the commanders, which was kind of heartbreaking. For they had seen the real effects of Abuelo's training up close, and they had watched me personally take human lives, without a single trace of remorse. I also started to realize that although I had battle scars of my own, I was covered in my victim's blood splatters. So I could only hope and pray that today's small victory would not ruin our young warriors' minds, for I had helped to transform these innocent young and naïve children into battle tested young warriors whose lives would never ever be the same again. We traveled for a while, moving to catch up to our family, all the time saying nothing, and when we finally stopped at a stream to tend to Kara's wound, I think that it was Gabriel, who first said that he and Aaron and Kara, both hoped that one day they could be fully trained in the ways of Abeulo and learn how to wield the sword, our friend named Destiny. It now could not be helped Balaam, he said, because there was just no going back to what they were or used to be, and with that he leaned forward and hugged me tightly, as the other two also joined in for a real live group hug. We tended to Kara's wound and got back on course and pretty soon, we had caught up to the group. When we finally joined back up with the family, these three children were changed, children of the field of battle, and they were right because none of us were ever going back to what we were or used to be.

Within six and a half more weeks, of being extremely careful and constantly checking our rear door—it was strangely quiet or those folks in the slave catching business seemed scared of something that was out there and did not want to meet what it was—we crossed the mighty Ohio River, and with that, the family was for the first time truly free. The group as a whole all seemed too plum tuckered out from the trip to be excited or really they did not know what the River itself signified, but they were happy, especially Mamie parents when they saw Mamie and the kids, along with Abeulo with the three wagons. Mamie was so happy to see us, and she ran directly at me and then jumped up in the air and into my arms and just held onto me for a long, long time. She had cooked up a passel of food, for truly hungry mouths, and folks eagerly gathered around the back of one of the wagons, to accept her offering with much joy, and it was then when passing out the food did she seemed surprised and had tears in her eyes, when she realized just how many children had made the freedom trip, because the children had outnumbered the adults almost four to one, and that mi Madre was missing.

The commanders immediately went to Abeulo, as they kneeled down in both respect and honor, and took a knee of allegiance to his presence. He seemed amused by their actions, but when they took him off to the side and gave him a mission recap, he was truly humbled when they thanked him for giving them the training that helped to save everyone's lives. They also wished to immediately resume their warrior training with him as soon as we got everyone safely into Canada, and they wanted to begin over again from the beginning and learn all of the stages, as I had done. For I was who they now wanted to be like or become, me a cold bloodied and ruthless killer of any and all things, that got in my way or crossed my path. When he said yes, that was the first time that I had seen those three children smile, since the Plantation, as they jumped up and rushed upon Abeulo and gave him a group hug, as everyone laughed. We boarded the wagons, and then proceeded to Sandusky, and there we secured travel for the group over the Lake called Erie, to the Provence of Ontario in Canada. We went directly to the Buxton/Elgin settlement, and everyone was immediately welcomed and made to feel at home, as the children from the Buxton/Elgin settlement welcomed our children like all children do, by asking them to come and go play with them. They all kind of looked around at the adults, silently asking the question whether they could they go, as Mamie laughed and then asked them out loud as if she was a mind reader, "Well do you want to?" I will never ever forget the look on their faces as they seemed to love the way that freedom tasted, smelled, and was practiced in this land up North, as a bunch of them went to go and play laughing and giggling, with their new found friends and playmates.

Epilogue

Balaam and Saladin are suddenly confronted by a whole pack of happy and hungry children, who respectfully bounce into the room. As a unified group or chorus the children in one voice tell them that lunch is ready and to come on and eat while it is still warm. Saladin wipes off his hands and looks directly at Balaam as Balaam looks at the children and tells them that they are coming, and with that they turn, and all run out of the room at a gallop's pace. Saladin in his mature sounding voice states that the painting is about halfway complete, and that once lunch is over, he is sure they will finish their task. He then smiles and says, "wow Pop-Pop you have had an interesting life and I can't wait to hear the rest of your story". Balaam gets up and puts his arm around his grandson as they walk out of the room to go eat lunch and he thinks to himself, "hum if you think that is interesting just wait till you hear the rest of my sorted tale..."

L. ALLEN FARMER

ABOUT THE AUTHOR

This is the debut novel of L. Allen Farmer, the first of three in the Ex-Slave Catcher series. He is currently working on several children's books as well as, a book of short essays.

Mr. Farmer, a native of northern California, resides in the Washington, DC metro area. He is a graduate of Howard University.

Disclaimer: This novel in no way reflects any attitudes, ideas, or feelings about any culture, religious group or nations by the author. It is a story, a creative work written to inspire thought and dialogue.

www.ingramcontent.com/pod-product-compliance
Lightning Source LLC
Chambersburg PA
CBHW070744180626
46818CB00007B/2983